EVERYBODY KNOWS

ALSO BY KAREN DODD

Deadly Switch

Scare Away the Dark

Everybody Knows

EVERYBODY KNOWS

KAREN DODD

First published in 2021

Copyright © Karen Dodd, 2021

ISBN 9781775122166 (paperback)

ISBN 9781775122173 (e-book)

To Laura, "Hans" and Steve,

hand in hand, float with the otters.

EVERYBODY KNOWS

"You don't lose your soul all at once. You lose it a little bit at a time, incrementally. Tiny imperceptible steps. Before you know it you're doing things you never thought you would do."

–Jordan Belfort

Chapter One

May 4, 2019

Gozo, Malta

The early-morning sun streamed in through the leaded-glass windows of the weathered farmhouse. Ariana Calleja rose from the child's bed and walked over to a dressing table under the wooden sill. She pulled a sweatshirt from a drawer and held it to her tear-stained face, inhaling the scent. It smelled of the sea. With temperatures well into twenty degrees Celsius, under different circumstances she might already have been at the beach making castles in the sand, listening to the whoops and cries of the little boy with the dark mop of hair and chocolate eyes.

"*Omm*, come and see what I've made," he'd shout over the squawks of the gulls that sailed back and forth across the lapis sky. They would hover, waiting for the time Ariana would unpack a picnic, and five-year-old Max would oh-so trustingly hold up pieces of bread for the birds to swoop down and snatch in their orange-spotted beaks.

"Be careful, darling, or you'll lose a finger," she would call to him. "Put it on the sand and they'll come for it."

Each Friday, Ariana caught the ferry to Gozo, or as the old-timers would say, *Għawdex*. She would stand on the deck as the boat pulled into Mġarr Harbour and feel the stress of her sixty-hour week melt away. As she breathed the fresh, salty air, it was as if she'd shirked off the ties that bound her to another life. One of never-ending legal cases that, even if she won, barely seemed to make a dent in the mainland's impervious underbelly of corruption.

A haven for tourists, the archipelago's beauty concealed a secret that locals knew but outsiders seldom saw. Instead, they erected a polite façade, like you might do when bringing an old college chum home for the weekend, not wanting them to see how dysfunctional your family really was.

Yet here she stood, alone in Max's room, surrounded by his things, as if oceans away from that life. The smell of him mingled with the sea and sand and sun. She wiped her eyes and looked down at the garden below. There was his blue plastic wading pool that he'd sit in and play for hours. He was a happy, carefree little boy. And though homeschooled for reasons of security, he was bright and social. For that, she had Francesca to thank. A friend since boarding school, she lived on Gozo with Max during the week whilst Ariana was working on the mainland, and then went back to her apartment in Valletta on the weekends. Francesca had witnessed the increasing vitriol and death threats Ariana had received following her bold statements to the media. Accusing senior government officials and heads of Malta's most prestigious corporations of corruption, didn't bode well for her safety. It was something she'd learned to live with. But when Max had become old enough to see what was being said about her on television, she'd agonized about whether to send him away until this investigation and prosecution—the biggest case of her legal career—was resolved. But how would she tell Francesca what she'd just done?

When dinnertime rolled around, Ariana wasn't hungry, but she knew she should eat something. As she often did, Francesca had left her a casserole that just needed heating in the oven. Although it filled the kitchen with the delicious fragrance of rosemary and other smells she couldn't identify, she hardly touched it.

She took her plate to the sink, poured herself a glass of red wine, picked up the bottle and took it out to the garden. The coarse crabgrass—the only type that grows on Gozo—tickled the underside of her toes. Everywhere she looked was evidence of Francesca's green thumb. Since Ariana had bought the house almost five years ago, her friend had turned it into an oasis of color and scents that aroused the senses. No doubt she'd used herbs freshly picked from the garden in the casserole she'd just pushed around her plate. Such a shame. Ariana sighed at the thought of her friend. By the following night, she would have to call her and tell her not to come. And why.

But before that, she needed to steel herself for an even more important call. The longer conversation would have to take place in person. In fact, she'd already booked her flight to Calabria. That part had been easy. But what she'd been putting off for five years might be worse than the threats of any criminal she'd faced down in court.

She poured herself another glass of wine and braced herself to make the call.

· · ·

"*Ovviamente!* Of course, I'm not too busy," Nicoló Moretti said. "How could you even ask such a thing, Ariana? I always have time for you. How long can you stay?"

"Only a couple of days, I'm afraid. I have to be back by midweek, but if you have Monday evening free—"

"Si, si! I'll take you to the new *ristorante* that's opened up ahead of the season. It's vegetarian, but you'll love it. What time should I make reservations for?"

"No, I'll cook," she said. "I'll have time to go to the market while you're at work. Shall we say eight o'clock at my place?"

"No, no. You'll be tired. *Per favore*, let me take you out."

There was a pause in which she said nothing. While Nico sounded delighted she was coming, they both knew her schedule rarely allowed for such spontaneity, let alone an offer to cook him dinner.

"Is everything all right?" he asked.

"Yes. It's just that . . . I need to speak with you about something important. Alone."

"All right, can you tell me—"

"Nico, I've got to go. I'll see you Monday at eight."

And she was gone.

Sunday was busy for Ariana. She had to tackle the mountain of laundry before starting her packing for Tropea. The fridge needed cleaning out for the week no one would be there—something she'd still not told Francesca about. She went back into Max's room to put his clean clothes away, and once again, wondered if she'd done the right thing. She tried not to dwell on the decision she'd made five years ago that she could never take back. The one that would soon change everything. What loomed ahead, pushed and strained at her heart like the buffeting wind of an incoming storm. In less than twenty-four hours, she prayed to God that somehow, Nico Moretti wouldn't hate her more than she hated herself.

May 6
Calabria, Italy

It was early morning, and the tiny seaside town in which Special Prosecutor Nicoló Moretti had been born and raised hadn't yet fully awakened. This was the time of day he loved most, where the streets were still but nature was just starting to come to life. Situated on a reef in the toe of the boot known as the Calabria region, travel brochures referred to Tropea as "*La Costa degli Dei*"—the Coast of the Gods. With its fortress-like cliff, towering fifty meters above sea level, every angle boasted spectacular views of the azure water of the Tyrrhenian Sea.

Nico's hair—what was left of it, anyway—was still damp from the shower, and the taste of the first espresso of the day lingered on his tongue. Eschewing the modernity of electric machines, he still made his own the traditional way, using a metal moka pot on top of the gas stove. It was simple, the way he liked his personal life.

With his leather satchel slung over his shoulder and the scarf around his neck rippling in the breeze, he walked the same route every day. He could have shortened the time it took to get from his apartment on Via Santa Domenica to his government office—there was a labyrinth of lanes and back alleys that led to the main square known as the Piazza Ercole

—but then he'd miss the sights and sounds that calmed him before he tackled the onslaught of work that awaited. It was his opportunity to savor his surroundings and remember why he'd chosen to spend more time at his Tropea office rather than the one in Rome.

The cobblestones were slick with water from the nightly hosing by the Piaggio Apes, the little three-wheeled utility trucks that cleaned the streets at night. Produce and flower vendors murmured among themselves as they set up their carts for the day. He made a mental note to pick up a bouquet for Ariana and some wine. As was typical for this time of year, the outdoor merchants were quiet, their only business coming from the locals who wouldn't emerge for another hour or more. When they did, they would be unhurried, stopping to visit with each other, and possibly share a coffee and *cornetti* in one of the cafés that surrounded the square. But as the end of the month approached, the laid-back ambiance in the historic town would give way to a familiar scene of chaos.

In a few weeks, the shop and restaurant owners would unlock their metal shutters and spruce up their premises to prepare for the tourists that would soon infuse the town with energy. It was a short season in which to make money, and they would have to make every day count. Then, as the hot days of summer sputtered to a close, the entire town would brace for the annual jazz and blues festival in September, when everyone from the small towns and villages that dotted the hills surrounding Tropea came down to let their hair down and enjoy the music. But then, all too soon, by October, the shopkeepers would once again draw their shutters and settle in for the wet winter months ahead.

As the muted conversations of the traders fell away behind him and the light of dawn emerged, Nico considered his conversation with Ariana the night before. He'd slept poorly. Her terse tone and reluctance to go out for dinner weighed on his mind. Though they'd spoken by phone once or twice over the past few months, their last conversation hadn't gone well and he'd hung up on her following a heated argument. Ariana was always right. For her, there were no shades of gray. He resolved to try harder; he didn't like the wedge that had come between them.

They'd met in law school in 2013. After years of being thoroughly miserable managing his father's cheese business from the age of twenty-five, Nico applied to every law school in Italy, and several abroad. At twenty-eight, he was finally accepted as a mature student at the Bocconi University in Milan. Similarly, Ariana applied in the last year of her undergraduate degree in political science and, much to her parents' chagrin, was immediately accepted. They'd hoped she'd settle into a nice government job in Malta, get married and raise a family.

Though there was a six-year age difference, he and Ariana became a couple. But a year after graduating, when Ariana took a junior position with the prosecutor's office in her native Malta and he was traveling back and forth between Rome and Tropea, their romance fizzled, but they remained friends. Occasionally, when she came to visit him, she'd let her guard down after too much wine, and they'd made love. Nico felt the same electricity he had in their college days, but he suspected for Ariana, sex was just a release from the tension of her job.

In spite of that, he would have been happy to carry on a long-distance romance, but in true Ariana fashion, she'd stated that she only had room for one relationship: that of representing the citizens of Malta against the corruption they'd become inured to. As in Italy, organized crime in Malta, though not spoken of openly, still had a broad and pervasive reach and Ariana was a passionate soldier in the fight against its influence, always had been. Many of the shops Nico walked past daily were a reminder of the tentacles that still gripped his own country, where anti-Mafia stickers littered windows declaring their owners' refusal to pay protection money. However, the reality was that shopkeepers knew their leases were only a wink and a nod away from a crooked city official. Many were on the Mafia's payroll and wouldn't hesitate to shut down a business for some ridiculous offense.

Six years on from their graduation, Ariana had become a legal superstar. That was the spark that ignited the argument the last time they spoke at any length. She'd announced that she'd been asked to take the job of chief anti-corruption prosecutor.

"I hope you said no," Nico had replied.

"Why would I? I've already accepted."

"For God's sake, Ariana, what would possess you? Do you want to end up like your predecessor? Shot to death in a restaurant in front of your friends and family?"

"How dare you! I, at least, have the courage of my convictions."

Normally slow to anger, Nico recalled the hot bristle of rage that started at the base of his neck and crept across his scalp. "And what is that supposed to mean?"

But he'd known all too well what Ariana was referring to. He'd just lost a huge money-laundering case that had been two years in the making—the first loss of his career. As it involved both their jurisdictions, he and Ariana had collaborated on it, only for him to lose when it went to trial.

"That's unfair," he'd said. "You know the defendant's connection to the 'Ndrangheta. And I didn't have a prayer in front of that judge. What more would you have liked me to do?"

"Big deal, you lost a case. Rather than feeling sorry for yourself, you could have applied to have the judge removed and demanded a retrial, but you didn't," she'd shouted.

Her venomous tone had taken him aback.

"Where do you think I'd be now if I gave up every time I lost a case or I was ridiculed?" she'd said. "I kept at it and now I have the opportunity to play a major role in blowing this thing wide open. To bring an end to the corruption that is a cancer on your country and mine."

"For what, Ariana? So you can find another eviscerated animal on the front seat of your car? So you receive another death threat? Don't you understand, this is bigger than us. It's been happening for years—"

"Like losing your soul, Nico. It doesn't happen overnight. You lose it one day—one case—at a time."

He'd had enough. Shaking with rage and disbelief, he'd hung up on her. How dare she speak to him like that?

Time passed, and Nico was the one to break the ice—it seemed he was always the one to make the first move —but eventually, they spoke again. There were no apologies; without discussion, they'd agreed to disagree.

Chapter Two

The evening started out well enough. Nico arrived at
Ariana's apartment a few minutes early, a bouquet of
yellow roses and a bottle of her favorite Sant'Anna di Isola
Capo Rizzuto Doc in hand. He kissed her on both cheeks, but
as he pulled away he was shocked to see how much weight
she'd lost and the dark circles under her usually sparkling
eyes.

"It's lovely to see you," he said, not wanting to start an
argument.

She smiled, accepting the flowers and taking them to the
kitchen. "And you," she said, reaching for a vase. "You look
well." She watched him over the flowers, as he searched
through a drawer for a corkscrew, then reached into the
cupboard for two glasses. "Though you have a little less hair
than when I last saw you."

The heat crept up Nico's neck, and self-consciously, he
touched his head. He didn't know one other balding Italian
man. Well, certainly not one in his late-thirties.

"I like it," she said with a grin. "Why don't you shave it
off and be done with it? It gives you a certain savoir faire.

Especially with the scarf and the round glasses you insist you don't need. You look like a younger version of Stanley Tucci."

"Stanley Tucci is handsome. He can pull it off."

"So are you. Don't sell yourself short."

While Nico knew he wasn't ugly, he'd never considered himself attractive. That perception had been further reinforced by his father, who'd referred to Nico as "*un tipo magro*—a little scrawny."

He put her wineglass beside her on the kitchen counter and retreated to a nearby bar stool to watch as she effortlessly pulled ingredients from paper bags and prepared dinner. Another time, he might have kissed her lightly on the back of the neck. But this evening, a certain tension hung in the air and he found himself second-guessing his actions.

Nico sipped his wine, although he noticed Ariana barely touched hers, while they caught up on each other's respective cases. He was both cognizant of not drinking too much wine and not broaching anything about Ariana's new position that might set off an argument. He wanted to enjoy their short time together.

After she'd tossed the salad and put a simple, but sumptuous meal of spaghetti alla carbonara on the table, Nico pulled out her chair and then sat at the table so they were kitty-corner to each other. He caught a whiff of her perfume. Yves St. Laurent Manifesto.

"*Saluté*," he said, raising his glass. "You said you had something important you wanted to speak to me about." The sooner they got that out of the way, the sooner he could relax. Perhaps after dinner, he'd be able talk her into going out for *pan di spagna di dipignano*, her favorite dessert, and a limoncello or two.

"Yes." She laid down her fork and took several sips of

wine. The glass shook in her hand, and she looked down at the table. When she looked up, she had tears in her eyes.

Nico put down his own fork and wiped his mouth with his napkin. "Ariana, what is it?" The way she was looking, it could only mean bad news. "Are you all right?" he asked, although he dreaded the answer.

She shook her head from side to side, and swallowed hard.

He reached for her hand and leaned toward her, his face almost touching hers. "What is it? *Bella,* you can tell me anything." Had something happened with her job? Nico would be lying if he said he wouldn't be relieved in some way if Ariana could no longer take up the anticorruption position.

She gulped down half a glass of water and took a deep breath. "You're aware of the threats I've been receiving."

"Yes, of course. Have they become worse?" He was determined to be supportive this time and not say *I told you so.*

"Yes, but now they aren't only aimed at me." She reached for her water again and downed the rest.

"Are your staff being threatened as well?" That would hardly be a surprise. Though he'd be loath to admit it to Ariana, his office had received more threats than ever since he'd lost that huge case.

She pulled her hand away and tears streamed down her face. In all the years he'd known her, he'd only ever seen her cry once: when she'd received the news that her parents had died. And even then, as their only child, she'd stoically gone about making all the necessary arrangements. That was Ariana's way; just get on with it. But to see her like this, he didn't know what to do.

He rose from his chair and gently pulled her into his arms.

She was as light as a feather. "Come and sit over here." After guiding her to the sofa, he returned to the table, refilled her water glass and sat down beside her.

"*Bella*, what's happened? Tell me."

Her face crumpled. "I'm afraid you will hate me forever."

"I could never hate you." But dread, cold, like an other-worldly creature's skeletal hand, gripped his chest. She'd been so distant or combative each time they'd spoken of late and against his better judgement, he hadn't pressed for details about what was bothering her. "Ariana, you must tell me."

"I have a son," she whispered.

The hand tightened like a vice grip, as if it was squeezing the air from his lungs. "I don't understand." He drew away from her and sat rigid, the arm of the sofa cutting into his back.

"He's five years old. His name is Max."

He stood up too quickly. Dizzy and numb, he struggled to slow down his breathing. What was she saying? This woman he'd known for years was telling him something he couldn't comprehend.

How was it possible for her to have had a child for five years without him knowing? Then it hit him. That's why she'd held him at arm's length off and on over the past few years. She'd been conflicted about being unfaithful to the father of her child. It wasn't that he expected her to be celibate now that they were no longer dating, but given how close they'd once been, this was a hell of a shock.

"But you . . . we—" He stopped. "Are you married to him? Is that why—?"

She leaped up. "No! It wasn't like that."

"Really, Ariana?" She reached for him, but he shrank from her touch. "What exactly was it like?"

"Nico, it's complicated. I kept meaning to tell you," she

said, at last looking up. "But there never seemed to be the right time. You were so busy, and each case I worked on got more and more demanding."

"That's ridiculous! I was never too busy for you." All the times they had sat over candlelit dinners for hours on end, and she could never find the time to tell him something as significant as this?

He felt the warmth creep into his face. He didn't know if it was anger at being lied to by omission, or if he was embarrassed that he'd held out hope that eventually they'd be a couple again. What an idiot he was; she must have known he was still in love with her. And all the while she'd been involved with whoever was the father of her child.

"He's yours, Nico. Max is your son."

Just like that, her words smashed into him like a runaway train.

"You had a baby—*my* baby, who I never got see grow into a toddler." He railed with a force so rancorous it frightened him. "What kind of person does this?" he screamed at her.

He grabbed his jacket and stormed out the door.

"Nico, *please*, we must talk about this!" She reached for his sleeve, but he pushed her out of his way, causing her to stumble backwards. "Nico!"

He ran down the stairs and out onto the street, heading straight to the bar he'd planned to take Ariana to for dessert and liqueurs, and proceeded to get so drunk he had no idea how he got home.

Nico woke up on his bed four hours later, facedown with all his clothes on. His mouth was the consistency of cotton wool and tasted worse. Trying to push back the pain of a pounding headache, he prayed he'd just had a bad dream. But it wasn't a dream; this woman who he thought he knew had gutted him with one declaration—he had a son that she had kept from him for five years. No matter how hard he tried, he couldn't wrap his head around it.

He stumbled to the bathroom and turned on the shower. After fishing in the medicine cabinet, he downed two headache pills with a glass of water, then peeled off his clothes and stepped under the hot water. He lost track of how long he spent there, sobbing, until the water ran cold, and he slid down the tiles into a heap on the floor.

Wrung out, he'd climbed back into bed, and sometime before dawn he awoke feeling marginally better. He reached for his mobile on the bedside table to check the time. There was a text from Ariana.

Coffee at Cannone, 11 a.m. Please, Nico, we must talk.

With a sigh, he turned the phone over and dragged himself out of bed. Literally overnight, his life had been turned upside down, and Ariana wanted to have coffee. She'd insisted they have dinner at her apartment last night, but this morning she was willing to discuss a matter so intensely personal at the café across the street from his office? No doubt, Nico mused, because if things got out of hand, the owner and their friend, Sebastian, would be there to referee. It wouldn't be the first time he'd had to do it, but Nico suspected it would be the last.

He dressed quickly and let himself out of the apartment. He took the shortcut through the back alleys so as not to run into anyone he knew. All the while, he did the math in his head. What was the longest he'd gone without seeing Ariana in person? There certainly had been times when their mutual schedules hadn't allowed them to get together, but how was it possible she'd been able to conceal her pregnancy? And more importantly, *why?* What was it about him that she wouldn't have wanted him to be a father to his own child? Even if she hadn't wanted to marry him, they could have worked things out. But that brought about another disconcerting thought; perhaps she hadn't been sure that he was the boy's father. What if Ariana had got it wrong?

When he reached his office building, he pulled out his phone and texted her.

I can spare ten minutes. Don't be late.

He yanked open the heavy wooden doors of his office building and ran up the stairs. Gina, his assistant, looked startled as he virtually exploded in the door.

"Get me Olivia Piccioni, please."

"The family lawyer?"

"Yes. And if she's not in, leave a message. Tell her it's urgent."

He slammed the door behind him. Before he met Ariana, he needed to be apprised of his parental rights.

Chapter Three

May 7

An hour later, Olivia Piccioni still hadn't called back. Unable to focus on anything of significance, Nico propped his feet on his desk and opened the newspaper. Flipping past the sports and leisure sections, he went straight to page six. The page where the country's legal cases, won or lost, were retried by the public.

A Tiger Declawed? blared the heading under the byline of investigative journalists Ervio De Rosa and Vincenzo Testa—Italy's version of Woodward and Bernstein. Usually, the journalists wrote their respective pieces under their own bylines, each delivering scathing rebukes on the latest corruption they had uncovered in their unique areas of expertise. Today's feature though, written under a joint byline, was their most recent exposé of Calabria's rampant money laundering and corrupt government officials. Nico's bailiwick. As be began to read, he groaned.

Gazzetta del Sud
May 7, 2019
*Contributors: Vincenzo Testa and Ervio
De Rosa*

A Tiger Declawed? Can Calabria's Special Prosecutor Rid Italy of Corruption?

How confident can the citizens of Calabria be with Special Prosecutor Moretti at the helm of the challenge to Italy— reported to be the most corrupt country in the eurozone—to clean up its act? A man, it appears, who will walk away from one of the largest money-laundering cases of his career, as he might dismiss a pesky fly.

Instead of releasing the stranglehold organized crime has on the infamous region of Calabria, politicians and others sworn to uphold justice appear to have tightened the noose. There is no better example than the recent supreme court case that was thrown out by Judge Claudio Bianchi, who is himself, the embodiment of corruption. Since he's been on the bench, the state of Italian politics has taken a turn for the worse. And Special Prosecutor Nicoló Moretti has been complicit in letting it happen.

Not only have elitist politicians turned a blind eye to a plethora of corrupt judges, but they steal from Calabria's citizens in the form of taxes, then use their money to pay off the likes of Bianchi, who is well-known to have Mafia connections. What other country would allow someone like this to sit on any court of justice, much less the kangaroo court we call the Corte Suprema di Cassazione?

To make matters worse, we taxpayers fund prosecutors

like Nicolò Moretti, who in a shameful display of ineptitude, backed down from applying to have the judge removed and retrying the case. For those who might say, "Well, he's won every case but this," the question that should be on the minds of everyone is how significant were those wins? While the average Calabrian may not see daily reminders of organized crime, everyone knows it's still there, buried in a shallow grave. Like the grim reaper, with his ghoulish claw lurking just beneath the surface. And what does our special prosecutor do? We're not sure, as his office has refused our calls and has made no official comment.

It would seem the citizens of this beautiful country now have to accept the ugly truth: that omertà, the Mafia's code word for silence and honor, also applies to our supposed saviors—our officers of justice.

Part 2 of this series will be continued next week.

W onderful. More stories about how inept he was and why his office is a colossal waste of taxpayers' dollars. No doubt his superiors' phones in Rome will be lighting up like the fireworks of Tropea's famous Red Onion Festival.

De Rosa and Testa's piece put the blame for the flagrant corruption squarely where they believed it belonged: the prosecutor who had not only lost his edge, but had backed down entirely—Nico Moretti. His anger turned to a slow burn as he recalled his colleagues' furtive glances when he'd returned from court that day. He'd wanted to shout, "And which one of you has a solid history of winning every case you've ever tried, except one?"

His feet hit the floor with a crash, his chair slamming upright. The article lambasted him for not standing up to the judge, who had cut him down to size before throwing out the case. For God's sake, he'd been prosecuting a known Mafia kingpin. One who happened to be married to the judge's sister. He rolled up the newspaper and hurled it across the room. Just what he needed, to be in a foul mood before he was to have it out with Ariana.

A fter a fitful sleep, Ariana had arisen early, the horrible evening with Nico weighing on her mind. On one of the many times she'd awakened in the night, she'd sent him a text, pleading with him to meet her in the morning. But he'd either been asleep, or had chosen to ignore her. It was an enormous relief when he replied, albeit with a terse message. She deserved his anger, but in Max's interest she needed to prepare Nico for what was to come. By this time tomorrow, the announcement she was preparing would be on every news outlet in Europe. Perhaps then, while he still might not forgive her, he would understand.

She was in the middle of amending her notes at the apartment when the internet went down. Did anything ever work properly in this damned country? With a sigh, she gathered up her things and walked the few blocks to Cannone Square.

"Hello, Sebastian," Ariana waved to the owner as she strode into the café and took her usual table on the waterside deck. "I'm meeting Nico, but my internet is down again. Do you mind if I work here for a bit?"

"Of course," he replied, wiping down the bar. "Your usual?"

"Yes, please." After settling in, she opened her laptop and resumed revising her notes for the sixth time that morning. In her usual acerbic style, she had entitled the announcement, *Government Officials Charged With Money Laundering and Corruption*. Soon, the cancer that had been a parasite on her country—one that extended from the upper echelons of government to the corporations that obscenely paid CEOs hid behind—would be over. Not even the senior members of her staff knew the exact nature of what she was about to expose. Of course, they'd played an integral part in the investigation, but she'd been careful that no one could know the sum of their work until she was ready. In part, it was for their safety as well as for the integrity of the case. This time, she would name names. This time, nothing could go wrong.

Forty-five minutes and two *doppio con lattes* later, a few more people had entered the restaurant. She looked at her watch and considered using the downstairs facilities. The area carved into the rock foundation beneath Cannone Square had been an air-raid shelter during the war. Now, it housed two restrooms for café patrons. But she put it off, wanting to finish up her notes before Nico arrived. She wanted nothing to distract her; this could be the last conversation she'd have with him for some time.

The previous night he had left in such a rage—so uncharacteristic for Nico—that he hadn't given her a chance to explain. Having a mother as a prosecutor who was both revered and hated, didn't bode well for Max's family life, so in order to keep both Nico and Max safe, she'd made the agonizing decision not to divulge her pregnancy. It was only going to be until things settled down and she'd put the diabolical individuals she was prosecuting in prison for life. When she thought of their names, she wished Malta still had the death penalty. Instead, taxpayers would have to foot the bill for the same people that had stolen everything from them.

But as her office had shut the book on one case, another one—even more egregious than the last—had come along. And the time to tell Nico about Max never came. She'd kept putting it off with each new prosecution. They became more complex, the perpetrators more dangerous. Max was only a few months old when the death threats started. When, as an enraged Nico had pointed out, eviscerated animals were left at her door. People spray-painted vile, disgusting things on the outer walls of her office building, and she'd panicked. She bought the house on Gozo, using an alias, and fled there with her baby boy. Francesca, one of only two people who had known of her pregnancy, offered to live on the tiny island during the week and look after Max. She was Ariana's research-assistant-cum-struggling-writer, and it was a perfect fit. There was no one Ariana trusted more than Francesca and Max adored her.

The other confidante who knew about Max was the one Ariana had entrusted to take her son out of the country just days ago. They'd both agreed it was best; just until this upcoming investigation was over. She needed to tell Nico who that person was and give him all the legal paperwork to obtain custody of their son if the powers that be made good on their threats to kill her. Ariana had named Francesca as guardian, but Francesca had always known who Max's father was. In fact, she'd begged Ariana to tell Nico. Upon her return to Valletta, she would explain why she was making a change to Max's guardianship; Francesca would understand.

Once her office made the announcement, the press would hound her mercilessly, and the barometer of risk to herself, Francesca and Max would skyrocket. No matter how Nico had lashed out when she'd told him, he would understand she'd had no choice but to do what she did. Their son would be safe and after the trial, together they'd figure out the rest.

She took one final look at her notes and mused over the government's likely reaction to her office's imminent announcement. *Thou doth protest too much, Prime Minister. The citizens of Malta are coming for you. And when they do, they will blow your private fiefdom wide open.* An image formed in her head: the prime minister, fear and guilt stamped on his face as the judge read out the guilty verdict. Those in the courtroom would heave a collective sigh of relief as they heard the clear message that their leader's corrupt reign over them was about to end.

She closed her laptop and sat back in her chair, the sun warming her face as she stared out at the Tyrrhenian Sea. Her gaze rested on a small boat bobbing on the calm water offshore, perhaps half a mile away. What would life be like, she pondered, when the cause she'd devoted herself to for so many years came to fruition? Freedom. She'd never let herself think of that possibility before. She prayed Nico would forgive her and they could pick up where they'd left off before she'd frozen him out. Even if they couldn't mend their relationship, she knew he'd love Max—after all, they were carbon copies of each other—and she would have to prepare herself for an equitable custody agreement.

But she was ready. She was tired of keeping secrets.

At precisely 10:50 a.m, Ariana pushed back her chair and was about to head to the downstairs toilet.

Simultaneously, the captain of the small boat that idled nearby received a phone call and sent a code to a second device.

With a deafening roar, the entire outer edge of the Cannone Square café plunged one hundred meters to the coastal road below. That sunny Calabrian morning, Ariana Delia Calleja became Malta's second anticorruption prosecutor to be assassinated.

Sixty kilometers away, a text was received.

The errand has been completed.

Nico was standing at the urinal in the men's room when he heard a muffled bang. What was that? It was as if the stone floor trembled beneath his feet. He zipped up his trousers and yanked open the heavy wooden door. Through the windows of the building's upper rotunda, he could see thick smoke billowing from the café across the street.

Oh my God, Ariana!

Heart hammering, he flew down two flights of stairs and tore across the street.

The scene before him was the closest thing to hell he'd ever come across. Outside the restaurant, facing the street, a section of wrought-iron fencing hung at grotesque angles, twisted like ropes of black licorice. The sections had simply disappeared. People lay bloodied and injured, strewn across the floor like discarded dolls. Others sat or lay on the ground in stunned silence.

Nico glanced toward the waterside terrace, but there was nothing left but a jagged edge. It was as if a mammoth shark had taken a bite out of the concrete deck.

He moved farther into the café. His foot hit something, and he stumbled. In his path, a woman, not Ariana, lay face-down on a bed of rubble. Tiny bits of stone were wedged under her nails as if she'd scratched and clawed her way across the ground. It was eerily quiet, like the void before a tsunami. Someone moaned, low and guttural, but Nico couldn't pinpoint the sound.

He blinked, trying to see through the dust and debris. More of the horrific scene came into focus. Tables and chairs lay upended as if tossed about by a tornado. Everywhere lay shards of china, glass, food, and things he didn't dare give thought to.

He shook his head and stared, his eyes straining to penetrate the acrid smoke that hung in the air. Then his gaze fixed on a body lying prone and bloodied on the restaurant floor, eyes wide open. Acid worked its way up his throat. He swallowed, fighting the urge to vomit.

Out of the smoke, Sebastian emerged, his face smeared with soot. Sweat had carved rivulets from his temples and down his cheeks. He frantically waved Nico away from the edge, babbling incoherently. "She was here . . . and then, she was just gone! Everything is gone—"

Both men leaped as an enormous chunk of concrete crashed to the ground behind them.

With disbelief, Nico scanned the café again. No, it wasn't possible. He'd been with Ariana last night when she'd told him she had a child. In the middle of the night, he'd received her text in which she'd begged him to meet her this morning. She couldn't be gone. Any moment, he'd wake up to find he'd just had a nightmare, and he'd have a second chance to work things through with her—to meet his son.

But then he heard another moan and sirens in the distance. He closed his eyes, hoping somehow that when he opened them, Ariana would appear at their usual table. He took a deep breath and opened his eyes. He saw the same devastating scene before him. The same caustic smell assaulted his throat and made him cough. As the sound of the emergency vehicles got closer, something moving caught his eye. A figure on the street outside the restaurant. Tall, in a hurry. A car screeched to a halt, a door opened, and the person jumped into the back seat. The door slammed shut and the driver gunned the engine and sped off.

Valetta Malta

"You have nothing to worry about—it's been taken care of. Now, make sure you follow through and do your part," he said. He ended the call.

In matters such as these, it was best not to involve himself in unnecessary details, but this situation called for extreme measures, and he couldn't afford a slipup. He'd be damned if he would cower to a female prosecutor whose personal mission was to reduce what he'd spent years building to rubble. Her brash persona and bald accusations were cutting significantly into his reputation with friends in high places. Friends who could turn into enemies in the blink of an eye.

And so, he had reached out to his contractor and had been adamant they strike while Ariana Calleja was off the island. They had been prepared for weeks, awaiting their moment. They had wiretaps on her phones and GPS on her car. Eventually, she would return to Calabria where she kept an apartment and visit her usual haunts. When she booked a ticket to Tropea, they were ready. Someone watched her from the moment she got off the plane at Lamezia Terme Airport until she arrived in Tropea. "I want it done cleanly," he'd instructed. "There can be no ties to us here."

The plan had been executed perfectly, and now he would be kept abreast of the investigation into Calleja's death. Not that he was particularly interested—the less he could think about that woman the better—but private surveillance showed she had been busy during her short stay in Italy. Despite her reported rigorous prosecutorial duties, the woman appeared to have found time for a personal life. She was seen at the market picking up supplies. It would have been easier to do it there, but there would have been too much collateral damage. After all, he did have a heart. He chuckled to himself. At least she'd had The Last Supper, so to speak.

Now, he no longer had to worry about what she was about to expose. He looked at his watch and smiled as his phone rang. This was the call he'd been waiting for. The one that would tell him whether he'd need to add another name to his list.

Chapter Four

May 8
Valletta, Malta

At the best of times, Francesca Bruno was a light sleeper. But after the devastating news of Ariana's assassination yesterday, she'd seen every hour on the clock. Each time she awakened, she prayed it had just been a horrible nightmare, but then the reality would hit her again. Her mind raced. It was as if she were watching a retrospective of her life in double time. Ariana's death had stunned her friends and colleagues, but none of them were surprised. In the past year alone, forty-seven of her peers worldwide, including some high-profile journalists, had been killed. Silenced, but their work not forgotten.

As her closest friend and confidante, Francesca knew Ariana had been threatened dozens of times, publicly and privately. Her dogged determination to expose the corrupt vices of those who wielded power in Malta—known members of the Mafia, lawyers, bankers, even current government leaders—meant there were dozens of people who could have wanted her gone. Over the six months prior to her assassination, Ariana had come home to find an eviscerated rabbit at her door; a pipe bomb, which thankfully didn't go off, had been delivered to her office; and her dog had been viciously slaughtered and left on the front seat of her car. Francesca knew her friend's life had been a living hell. And still Ariana had persisted. Until she couldn't. Until her bold attempts to change the country she so loved had killed her.

Someone had snuffed out the light of this lionhearted woman in the prime of her life. But ever the forward thinking woman, Ariana had ensured her relentless attacks on organized crime would not die with her. She couldn't bear the thought that her exhaustive investigations and her life's work would be in vain. When a female investigative reporter had been assassinated on the mainland, a group of those closely associated with their mission had formed a volunteer alliance called Journalists for Justice. Ariana had been distraught over the murder of the journalist she'd known and respected, and had made Francesca swear an oath that if anything happened to her, she would make sure that the group could continue her own work.

"I've sent copies of my investigative notes to three journalists I trust." She'd given Francesca their names and personal mobile numbers. "As you're my assistant, if anything should happen to me, I just need you to hold them accountable. Do this for me, Francesca, for all of us," she had pleaded. "We're so close to getting our beloved country back."

"Ariana, when has our country ever been different?" Francesca had asked. "When has Malta been anything other than what it is now: secrets and lies? Our citizens read your tweets and articles about you in the newspaper and *tsk-tsk* to themselves over their morning coffee. But then they shut the paper and get on with their day. Everybody knows about the curse on our Malta, the rampant corruption. And the sad fact is, we benefit from it, we all do. It's become our way of life."

Francesca remembered so well the passion and intensity in the eyes that stared back at her. The beautiful face she had envied since they'd met in boarding school. She'd prayed the time would never come when Ariana wouldn't be here and she'd have to make good on her solemn promise.

Then, just two days ago, Ariana had called to tell her she was going to Tropea to meet with Nico Moretti, and that she'd sent Max away for his safety.

"Are you going to tell him?" Francesca had asked.

"Yes, I must. My office is ready to move. Watch the news on Wednesday for the announcement. We've done it, Francesca! We know who these bastards are, and when I announce the charges, everyone in Malta will too."

But Francesca couldn't share in her friend's elation. She knew what it would all mean. "Ariana, please be careful."

"I will, but I have to tell Nico before it breaks. I'll explain everything when I get back."

But she never came. Nor would she ever return to her beloved country again.

And so, it was in the early hours before dawn, as Francesca let her body give way to the emotions that she'd buried during that last conversation. Her admiration and yet the fear she felt for her friend, how she was willing to risk everything for what she thought was—

A noise broke the early-morning darkness. It sounded like it came from downstairs. Francesca lay still, not moving a muscle, afraid to breathe. Then she thought of Ariana. She'd be damned if she'd die in her bed without putting up a fight. As quietly as she could, she pushed the bedcovers back and tiptoed to the edge of the half-mezzanine that was her bedroom. A sliver of moonlight illuminated the landing below. Nothing. She opened the door to the tiny adjoining bathroom and peered in. Only darkness.

With fear creeping through her veins, she reached out a trembling hand, and inch by inch slid out the bedside table drawer. She prayed it wouldn't squeak. When the opening was big enough, she put her hand in and closed her fingers around the cold metal of the handgun Ariana had insisted she have for self-protection. Weapon in hand, she crept to the top of the staircase that led to the first floor. With the stealth of a cat, she descended a couple of stairs. Her heart skipped a beat when the old wood creaked beneath her feet. She stopped, one foot suspended above the next step, afraid to breathe.

From her frozen position, she had a clear sight line to the front door.

A folded piece of paper sat on the tile floor inside the door.

Spotting Journalists for Justice's distinctive red-and-yellow sticker affixed to the note, Francesca exhaled and skittered down the last few steps. Depositing the gun on the foyer table, she bent down to retrieve the paper. She turned on the light and read the first line. In disbelief, she read it again.

Tell anyone what you know and you'll be next.

Clutching the note, she snatched the gun off the table and ran to the hiding place that contained the piece of paper and burner phone Ariana had pushed into Francesca's hand the last time they'd met. Her hands shook as she placed the call she'd prayed she'd never have to make.

Chapter Five

May 8
Tropea, Italy

Numb, Nico turned away from the window that overlooked the scene of the previous day's horrific incident. He faced the AISE's lead investigator. Reporting directly to the prime minister, Roberto Pezzente had phoned Nico's office to ask if it was too early for him to stop by. Nico himself had been at the office all night, catching a couple of hours of troubled sleep on his lumpy leather couch. As he'd tossed and turned, all he could think about was the terrible fight he and Ariana had had two nights ago. His last words to her. And about his son.

He couldn't believe she was gone. In a heartbeat, she and everything she stood for were literally blown off the face of the earth. Bargaining with God, he'd quizzed the police: Was there any chance she'd made it out alive? Was it possible she had changed her plans and hadn't been there when it happened? But of course, he knew differently. He recalled the shell-shocked expression on Sebastian's face as he'd told him he'd seen Ariana at the table seconds before it fell to the road below. Everyone had been kind, but they'd told him categorically Ariana had been there and could not have survived the blast.

He couldn't stop thinking about what her last moments on earth might have been like. That, and the image of the man he'd seen getting into a car in the blast's aftermath, haunted his brief attempts at sleep. He'd reported what he'd seen to the police, but his description was of little help.

Tall and authoritative-looking, Pezzente shook hands with Nico. "I'm so sorry for your loss. I understand you knew Ariana Calleja personally."

Nico swallowed a lump in his throat, unable to go there.

"Do you have IDs on the other victims?" Nico asked. Was it possible someone other than Ariana had been the target? He wondered if the woman he'd encountered lying facedown on the café floor had survived her injuries.

His grip wavered as he poured two cups of strong coffee on the sideboard. He hoped Pezzente didn't notice the tremor as he handed him a cup. But as Nico did so, it was impossible not to notice his Oyster Rolex watch. *They must pay agents well these days*, Nico thought. He drew his attention back to the room. "Do you have any leads as to who might have done this?"

Pezzente shook his head. "To your first question, the café owner gave us the names of the other customers who were seated at the waterside tables. Mostly, they were regulars, which at least makes identification somewhat easier. But we have no reason to believe they could have been targeted.

"To your second question, no one has claimed responsibility, however, it's still early." He shrugged. "We're assuming it was domestic terrorism. And highly professional.

They struck before the lunchtime rush, so only four besides Signora Calleja were killed."

Only, Nico thought, but he knew Pezzente was simply stating a fact.

"The force of the explosion, and the hundred-meter drop, guaranteed there'd be no survivors. It would have taken weeks to plant a bomb that would do that much damage without attracting attention. Someone knew exactly what they were doing and who they were after."

Nico's antenna went up. For several weeks, Sebastian had complained that every day the structural repairs to the underside of Cannone Square were delayed, he was losing money. Much to everyone's relief, the scaffolding had finally come down and the construction noise had ended. Nico and Ariana met there every morning for coffee when she was in town.

"You think Ariana was the target?" Nico asked, lowering himself into the chair behind his desk. It had happened mere minutes before he was to walk across the street to meet her for coffee. Could it have been connected to the case he'd just lost? Thinking of the individuals who could have been behind the bombing, he pushed the thought away.

Pezzente sipped his coffee. "You tell me." He put the spoon down and looked directly at Nico. "I understand Miss Calleja kept an apartment here. And that you were a frequent visitor. You would have known her schedule and what she was working on, correct?"

"What, exactly, are you suggesting? That I was somehow involved?" Though he kept a poker face, Nico's hackles went up. What exactly was this man insinuating? If the case hadn't been related to terrorism—domestic or foreign—it would be Nico's job as prosecutor to direct the investigation. By Italian law, both the police and investigators would be under his authority. This smug son of a bitch was enjoying the tables being turned.

"No, of course not," Pezzente assured him. "But we have CCTV footage of everyone who entered and left her building, and we know you were there the night before the explosion. It would be easier for you to get ahead of this and tell me your version."

Rather than the version you might make up, thought Nico.

Pezzente's current boss, the new prime minister, had promised to clean up the rampant corruption after his prede-cessor had eluded two prison terms stemming from fourteen charges of graft and money laundering. Nico had successfully prosecuted all the cases, but still the PM did no time behind bars. After they ousted him from office, the citizens of Italy heaved a collective sigh of relief. The trouble was many of the officials tasked with carrying out the new anticorruption initiatives had themselves benefited from the country's lais-sez-faire attitude toward white-collar crime. It was widely known department heads routinely awarded contracts to their friends or issued checks for bogus transactions. Nico looked at Pezzente's shiny watch again. Was Pezzente one of these beneficiaries? On one hand, staying on the good side of the investigator might help Nico find out who was responsible for the bombing that killed Ariana. On the other, depending on what Ariana had been working on, confiding in him could undermine whatever evidence she had amassed. Not to mention that he could be putting her child in danger. *Their* child.

What Ariana had told Nico the previous night, had hit a nerve so deep that he'd felt something he promised her he never could—hatred. Now it was too late. If he'd done the right thing and stayed instead of storming out of the apart-ment that night, she wouldn't have been at the café the next morning, no doubt hoping to smooth things over. No matter the outcome, he might have known where his son was. Instead, here he was discussing her death with the PM's personal lackey.

With those thoughts, along with the overwhelming guilt that threatened to smother him, Nico debated how much he should tell Pezzente about his relationship with Ariana. One that was now much more complicated.

N ico waited until Roberto Pezzente had closed the main door behind him before he returned to his own office. He'd done his best to hold it together while he answered Pezzente's questions. But by the time he finally left, Nico just wanted to go home and collapse. In his small private bathroom, he splashed cold water on his face. As he reached for a towel, he caught sight of himself in the mirror. He hadn't shaved since yesterday morning and his eyes looked as if he'd been on a bender the night before. All he could think about was that Ariana was gone and somewhere a little boy— his son—was without his mother.

He was packing up his computer and casework to take home when he heard a light rap at the door.

"Nico, I'm sorry to bother you," Gina said, peaking around the door. She looked at him with red eyes.

Over the years she'd worked for Nico, she'd got to know Ariana well. While there was a difference in the two women's ages, they'd become friends outside of work and Gina had been devastated by her death. "But there's a woman on the telephone and she sounds frantic. Says it's about Ariana Calleja."

Nico groaned. He downed two aspirin with a gulp of cold coffee, suspecting any hopes of getting out of the office early

—maybe even getting some sleep—were dashed. Trying to sleep would be futile, anyway. Whenever he closed his eyes, his mind could think only of Ariana and how he'd left things the night before she'd died.

"Have you reported this to the authorities?" Nico asked after he picked up the phone and listened to the woman's rapid-fire introduction and ensuing story.

"I can't. That's why I'm calling you."

Nico ran a hand over his stubble. "Miss Bruno, I'm a prosecutor." *And not a very good one*, he thought as he glanced at the furled-up newspaper that still lay on the floor. "Because of the strong possibility of terrorism, I am not involved in the investigation into the bombing. I can refer you to—"

"Call me Francesca. Ariana said if something happened to her, I was to call you. Please." Her voice rose an octave. "I know she told you about Max."

Nico shook his head and blinked several times. He had been without sleep too long, but he was instantly on edge. "I have no idea what you're talking about."

There was a long pause. When she replied, her voice had a ragged, almost hysterical edge. "Max lived with me at Ariana's weekend home."

His patience was down to a thin edge. "Miss Bruno, I don't know who you are or who you think you're speaking to, but I can assure you, I am the last person you want to be messing with right now."

"No, please, you don't understand. Please listen to me! Google my name. I've known Ariana since boarding school. I was her part-time researcher."

"And what would that prove? Anyone could get that information. I'm assuming I can't call you back on the mobile phone you're using? Do yourself a favor, Miss Bruno—if that's even your real name—and don't call me again, or I *will* call the police."

He was about to slam the handset back into its cradle when the woman cried out.

"Mr. Moretti, wait! Please don't hang up. Ariana told me she'd sent Max away. Her office is about to make a big announcement, and she wanted him somewhere safe. Do you have any idea where he might be?"

Now she had his attention. Ariana had told him the death threats had escalated, but she said nothing about an announcement. "Do you know what that is? The announcement, I mean."

"No. She just said that when it came out on Wednesday, everyone in Malta would know who was behind the government corruption. She was going to name names."

But today *was* Wednesday, and Nico had seen nothing on the news, which he had constantly running on mute in his office. Apparently, neither had Francesca.

"Mr. Moretti, Ariana recently sent envelopes containing her investigative notes to three senior journalists who are members of Journalists for Justice. I can tell you the names of those individuals and their private mobile numbers. Please—" Her voice broke. "Someone has threatened me, I have no idea where Max is, and I don't know who else to call."

As she had promised, Francesca Bruno knew everything there was to know about the three journalists to whom Ariana had sent copies of her investigative notes. They were to be her "insurance policy," she'd told Francesca. If Nico had known about Ariana's plans, he would have tried to talk some sense into her. Like, what would possess Malta's top prosecutor to share her investigative notes with the goddamned paparazzi?

Turning his attention back to his computer screen Nico scrolled through each of the journalists' online profiles. *Shit!* The first two were Ervio De Rosa and Vincenzo Testa. When not ridiculing Nico for having lost his edge, De Rosa's work focused on money laundering in the banking system. Testa, who was known for his brash but expertly researched exposés of the European pharmaceutical industry, was pursuing an ongoing investigation in the UK.

The last journalist Ariana had included in her inner circle was a woman. Elle Sinclair's online profile showed she had once been a well-regarded investigative reporter with the BBC. Now, she was a freelancer. He clicked on several of the images associated with her name. Tall and slim with an angular, square face and straight blonde hair that grazed her shoulders, Sinclair's glacial blue eyes suggested she was not a woman to be trifled with.

Nico put his head in his hands and rubbed the grit from his eyes. His first priority was to get some sleep. As worried as Francesca Bruno was, they both agreed there was nothing more they could do tonight. While he'd admonished her to report the threatening note to Maltese authorities, he understood her fear in doing so. Someone must have assumed Francesca knew sensitive information—perhaps what Ariana was about to announce. But why would they have used Journalists for Justice stationery?

He stuck his head out of his office. "Gina, I need you to book me on the first flight to Malta tomorrow. Use the influence of our office if you have to, but charge it to my personal credit card."

She looked confused but nodded.

In the morning, on the way to the airport, he would try to

find out more about Francesca Bruno. Next, he'd have Gina track down the three journalists that for some reason, Ariana had trusted with her work. Why she would go outside the prosecutor's office with such sensitive information, he couldn't fathom. From what Francesca had told him, it appeared she was on the brink of something big. Had she "named names" in the documents she'd sent to the investigative reporters? Would Ariana have told him the details the night before she died, if he hadn't shoved her out of his way and stormed from her apartment?

More critically, would she have told him where she'd sent their son?

Chapter Six

May 9

The next day, Nico awoke early, his thoughts and emotions weighing on him like a thick fog. All his thoughts, whether sleeping or awake, were of Ariana. Besides the overwhelming grief, the sense of guilt over their last conversation threatened to suffocate him.

Gina had got him on the first morning flight to Malta and booked him into a bed-and-breakfast in Valletta near where Ariana's office and apartment were situated. He needed to meet Francesca Bruno in person. Although she seemed credible on the phone, he wanted to read her for himself. So, after passing his court docket to his assistant prosecutor, he left a message for Gina to track down reporters De Rosa and Testa. He shoved some paperwork into his leather satchel and let himself out of the office, descending the stairs to the deserted street below.

The sun was trying its best to break through the gloomy predawn sky, but he could smell the impending rain. Just what investigators needed to further assault the already deso-

late sight of the bombed-out square. At least he wouldn't
have to look at the grim reminder for the next few days.

Nico arrived at Lamezia Terme Airport in plenty of time
for his flight. After getting through security and a brief wait
in the departure lounge, he buckled in for the five-hour journey, first to Sicily, then on to Malta. He sipped his espresso
and picked at the airline meal. After the flight attendants had
collected the meal trays and his fellow passengers prepared to
sleep or watch an in-flight movie, Nico opened the *Times of
Malta*.

His breath caught in his chest as Ariana's almost black,
almond-shaped eyes stared back at him from page two. He
studied her face: the clear olive skin and what one would call
an Italian nose, long and aquiline. Her smile was warm, open.
Unguarded. Did their son look like her? Or more like him?

The headshot looked like it had been taken some time
ago. In the article, Ariana was described as "the daughter of
an Italian socialite mother and a Maltese businessman."

Nico thought back to when he'd first met her at law
school. She'd been so passionate when she'd told him of her
intention to be the kind of lawyer who exposed the criminals
who were ruining her beautiful country and bring them to
justice. An interesting choice for a child who came from such
privilege. But true to her word, she left her comfortable
family home in Malta to attend law school in Milan. Her
mother had already started planning her daughter's coming-
out parties, but Ariana argued that she needed to get away
from everyday distractions to focus on her postgraduate
degree.

Nico had other reasons for wanting to get as far away
from his childhood home as possible. Geographically, Milan
was twelve hundred kilometers from where he grew up near
the tip of the boot of Italy. And for him, it was like being

transported to another world. He'd finally broken away from his father's business, and like a bird whose wings had been clipped, in the vast fashion and financial city he learned to fly again. But he never forgot his Calabrian roots. Back home, the pervasive but seldom talked about Mafia presence was always there beneath the surface of normal everyday life. Despite his parents' fear of judges and prosecutors having become targets, he knew he had to at least try to make a difference. The passion he and Ariana shared for exposing and punishing corruption in their respective countries had been the basis of their first date.

After graduating with honors, the Pubblico Ministero's Office recruited Nico, and he became their most valuable specialist in organized crime, and still was. Well, prior to his public humiliation by De Rosa and Testa, anyway. Ariana, too, had carved out a name for herself as a take-no-prisoners litigator who was on a fast track to becoming a magistrate. Her meteoric rise, one that put her on the minds of nearly half a million Maltese citizens, came after an exhaustive investigation that she and Nico had collaborated on. A kingpin in the widely feared 'Ndrangheta was purported to have run his vast organization from an underground bunker that served as his home for several years. When he was found to be the brains behind a complex operation that involved Malta, Ariana had successfully prosecuted the case. The rub? He didn't do one day of jail time—not in either country. However, Lady Justice meted her decision in a different way, when a rival clan killed him in a car bombing. But it was like cutting off the head of the snake of a terrorist cell; there were plenty more to take his place.

While Ariana and Nico kept in touch over the years, they had moved on to just being friends. The romance fizzled after they'd both graduated, and particularly when Ariana had to return to Malta after the tragic death of both her parents. When she returned to Milan to pack up her things, she was noticeably different. While Nico tried to be supportive, she was distant and refused to discuss her parents' deaths. He had hoped that as she dealt with her grief, they would pick up their relationship where they left off. At one point, he'd even hinted at marriage, but Ariana didn't see it the same way.

"I'm already married," she'd replied. "To my job. I have no time for a full-time relationship."

And yet, she had a child. Although Malta is the only country in Europe to forbid abortion, she could have had it done elsewhere or given him up for adoption. But she didn't.

Ariana had been notoriously private about her life outside of work, but she always made time to get together whenever she was in Italy. Respecting her preference for staying out of the public eye when she was in Tropea, Nico often went to her apartment for home-cooked meals, as he had the night before she died. On those occasions, they spent many a late night drinking too much wine and debating if they'd ever see their respective countries released from the grip of criminal syndicates.

It was during one of those evenings that Nico broached the subject of Ariana's personal life. The only concession to having a life outside of being a prosecutor was her purchase of a summer home on the tiny island of Gozo, a twenty-five-minute ferry ride from the mainland of Malta. He knew she'd purchased the property under an assumed name. He found it ironic that she'd used Malta's laissez-faire rules about property purchases to her own advantage. After receiving multiple death threats, she commuted from Valletta to Gozo every weekend and often spent the long hot summer months on the historic island. With its Neolithic Ġgantija temple ruins, rural hiking paths, beaches and scuba-diving sites, Nico thought

Gozo sounded like paradise. But she never invited him to visit. He'd put it down to her strict sense of privacy, but now he knew the real reason. But she'd let Francesca Bruno into her confidence, as well as whoever she'd entrusted with taking Max somewhere safe. And yet, not the boy's own father?

I t was mid-afternoon by the time Nico's taxi pulled up to Great Siege Square in front of Valletta's Law Courts. It was with some shock that the first thing Nico observed was a shrine to Maltese journalist Daphne Caruana Galizia. The investigative journalist and native of Malta had been assassinated in a car bombing on October 16, 2017. Another fearless woman crusader who had been one of Ariana's role models. Perhaps, Nico thought, she had been the reason Ariana had taken the three journalists into her confidence. Two years later, Galizia's family was still seeking justice for her murder.

His chest tightened as the grief rolled over him again in waves. It hadn't occurred to him, as he looked out his office window the day after the bombing, that there would be no closure. No place to visit her grave and lay flowers. To talk to her and tell her how much he loved her. In fact, he thought, there were no remains of Ariana to repatriate to her native country or with which to honor her in Tropea.

Francesca had said she'd meet him at his hotel. Unable to take him farther in the pedestrian-only zone, his driver had circled the location on a city map and pointed him in the general direction of his accommodation. Once he'd gathered his bearings, Nico ambled down Strait Street, the town's principal thoroughfare, and turned at Saint Lucia, the side street marked on the map. Two blocks down, he saw the green canopy of the inn's entrance.

A woman greeted Nico warmly as he entered the cozy foyer. It turned out she owned the four-hundred-year-old establishment, and was all too happy to show Nico up to his room personally. As this trip wasn't on Tropea's taxpayers' dime, he appreciated the inexpensive cost of the small but well-appointed room. A tiny Juliet balcony with French doors overlooked a verdant garden. With a modest bathroom and a small desk-cum-makeup table, he had all the amenities he required for what he hoped would be a brief stay.

He hung up the few clothes he'd brought. In addition to the black jeans he wore, he brought one pair in denim. One pair of dress slacks, a white and a blue linen shirt, and two T-shirts; one black, the other navy. Even though at home he had to have various dress shirts, suits and ties, he hated having to make a choice each morning. Packing minimally, it guaranteed that the need to deliberate would be minimal.

He'd just put his underwear and socks away when there was a quiet rap at the door. A young man stood on the other side of the door and handed him a white sealed envelope. "A lady is in the lounge to see you, *sinjur*. She wouldn't give me her name but asked that you come down to meet her when you're settled."

Nico thanked him, closed the door and tore open the envelope. It was a note from Francesca saying she was downstairs and was looking forward to meeting him.

He splashed some cold water on his face, ran wet fingers across his scalp, and grabbed his jacket off the back of a chair.

The inn's main staircase afforded Nico the briefest opportunity to observe Francesca Bruno as she waited by the front desk. The only person in the lounge besides an elderly man sipping a glass of mid-afternoon sherry, she sat as if hyperalert on the edge of an uncomfortable-looking baroque chair. It was difficult to ascertain her height sitting down, but she was of slim build and wore her auburn hair in a bob that just grazed her shoulders. She had on cream-colored trousers and a smart navy blazer. Her eyes darted toward the concierge desk, then back again. Nico saw her shake her head and give a polite smile when the gentleman put down his newspaper and offered to pour her a drink.

Nico descended the stairs and their eyes met. She all but leaped up to shake his hand. "Please, no names," she whispered. Despite her diminutive stature, the firmness of her handshake surprised him, although he was somewhat taken aback by her cloak-and-dagger comment.

"It's a pleasure to meet you."

"Have you eaten?" she asked. When he shook his head, she suggested they continue their meeting at a café nearby.

Once out of the inn, they turned right and continued up the road. "I hope your flights were smooth," she said, indicating they should turn down a side street. She led him to a vacant table that was situated on sloping steps that ran parallel to the café, facing the harbor. With a small metal table on one step, Francesca took the chair on the step above it, leaving Nico to sit on the lower one. While it was comical, he found the difference in their levels to be a bit off-putting. *Must be the lawyer in me*, he thought. *Always jockeying for the most powerful position.*

"Thank you for trusting me, Mr. Moretti," she said.

"Please, call me Nico."

She gave him a shy smile. "Very well, please call me Francesca. I'm sorry to have been so secretive back there. But given the manner of threats Ariana received before she died," she said, her voice lowering, "I thought it better not to reward listening ears. She was quite well known here, and not always favorably."

"The old man in the lounge?" Nico asked.

"I know, but as innocuous as he appears, one cannot be too careful, considering the unrest here since the journalist's murder—I'm sure you saw the shrine in the square. The people built it to honor her—and the government keeps tearing it down. Even though Ariana died in Italy—"

She paused when the waitress came out to take their order.

Nico knew he needed to eat something but making any decisions about food when he had so many questions about Ariana, seemed overwhelming. "What would you recommend?" he asked Francesca, leaving the menu unopened on the table.

"If you're very hungry, I can vouch for the daily soup and *piadina*. I'm going to have their *pastizzi*—traditional Maltese pastry made with filo dough and filled with warm, creamy ricotta cheese. And coffee."

"Sounds great." He turned to the waitress with a smile. "I'll have what Fr—" He stopped himself. "I'll have whatever the lady is having."

As soon as the server had left their table, Nico said, "What can you tell me about the investigation into Ariana's death? Even though it happened on Italian soil, she was Valletta's senior prosecutor. And yet, I've seen very little on the news." And absolutely nothing about what her office might have been ready to announce.

Francesca frowned, and put both hands on the table. "After the initial report of the bombing in Tropea, there has been virtually nothing more reported here. In fact, as it occurred outside of Malta, the authorities here appear to have washed their hands of the entire matter, referring questions to your jurisdiction in Tropea."

This was news to Nico. He had heard nothing specific from his office or Investigator Pezzente, other than they were still looking at the domestic terrorism angle. And to be fair, there were victims other than Ariana. "And there's been nothing in terms of the announcement from Ariana's office that she spoke about?"

Francesca shook her head.

That didn't make any sense. It should have been out by now. He decided to change tack, but their server arrived with their food, so he waited until she'd left.

"So, were you Max's nanny?" he asked.

"In a manner of speaking. I'm actually Ariana's personal assistant." She hesitated. "Or I was. I lived in her summer home, looked after Max and homeschooled him during the week. She came over every weekend and then I'd travel back to my place here. She felt he was safer there. But now . . ."

"Did you and Ariana ever discuss sending Max away somewhere if anything ever happened to her?" Maybe that would give him a hint of where she'd sent him.

"I . . . I guess we did, but never anything specific, and I didn't really take her seriously." Her sea-glass-green eyes filled with tears. "It just seemed overly dramatic, even with all the threats she'd received. But now it's happened."

"But she didn't consult you before she sent him away?" Nico said.

"No, the first I heard was when Ariana called to tell me she was going over to meet you, and that she didn't need me in Gozo."

"Is there any chance she could have left anything here that could point to Max's whereabouts?"

"You mean at her apartment?"

To Nico, it seemed like an obvious place to start. Even though it would still be a crime scene, he hoped his position would have sway with the Maltese authorities and he might be able to gain access to Ariana's home, if not her office.

Francesca put down her coffee. "A neighbor said the police swooped in within hours of the bombing in Tropea. She saw men carrying out Ariana's computers and boxes of files. But I suppose it wouldn't hurt for us to look."

Nico put down his coffee. "Isn't it still cordoned off for the investigation? It hasn't even been forty-eight hours. You and others are free to come and go as you wish?"

"Well, other than the building manager, I'm the only one who has a key. But in answer to your question, no, it isn't cordoned off."

Nico shook his head in disbelief as Francesca pulled several euros from her purse before he insisted on paying.

"Her apartment is only a few blocks from here."

A ten-minute walk from the café and down another cobblestone side street brought them to an inconspicuous entrance that led to a small brick courtyard. Francesca let them into Ariana's ground-floor apartment. Nico followed her into the arched stone entrance, but something, although he couldn't pinpoint what, kept him from venturing farther in. His chest tightened and his whole body felt heavy. It was as if something malevolent had accosted him when he stepped through the door. He had this strange sensation of the energy being sucked from his being. He wanted to turn and run, but Francesca looked back at him questioningly, and he felt stupid.

"*You're overly sensitive*," his old-school Italian father had ridiculed him.

Embarrassed, he shook it off and followed Francesca into a sparsely furnished living room. But from where he stood, all he saw was chaos. It was as if a tornado had swept through the room, scooped up its contents and dumped everything on the floor. Although Francesca's expression appeared strained, she didn't seem surprised.

Nico stood aghast. "The police did this?"

She shrugged. "I presume so."

Stunned, he ventured farther into the apartment. Every room had been tossed, but none more so than what he assumed had been Ariana's office. Filing-cabinet drawers lay empty and turned on end, having taken huge gouges out of the wood floor. Books had been ripped from wall-to-wall shelves and were scattered across the room. Stubs of telephone and internet wires poked out from the wall like little clusters of flowerless stems. His heart sank. Nothing in here gave a hint of Ariana's essence, or that she had once occupied this space. There were no dark squares on the faded walls where pictures might have hung. If there had ever been any photographs or mementos on the furniture, they were absent. This is what Ariana's life and work had been reduced to. A vandalized, hollowed-out shell.

Among the papers strewn across the floor, Nico's eyes fell on a tiny piece of red paper. It looked as if it had been torn from an envelope. He picked it up and turned it over in his hand. In a childish scrawl, the word *Omm*—the Maltese term for *Mama*—was written on it. It pierced him like a dagger through the heart. Had it been part of a card written by his son?

He turned to show it to Francesca, but he'd been so lost in thought he hadn't noticed her leave the room. He tucked the paper in his pocket and threaded his way back through the apartment until he spotted her through the open French doors off the kitchen. Outside, on a small iron-railed terrace, every-thing there looked undisturbed. Pots of herbs and colorful flowers occupied every square inch. Magenta bougainvillea covered the red-brick walls and moss-lined baskets hung from the railings. In the center of the tiny oasis sat Francesca, perched on a metal chair, tears streaming down her face. The woman who'd given him a firm and confident handshake now looked tiny and frail, like a lost child.

Nico pulled out a chair opposite her. "May I?" He felt guilty he'd even questioned her honesty when she'd first contacted him. The pain in her eyes said it all. "I'm so sorry, Francesca. What can I do?"

She stared at him for a few seconds, blinking back more tears. Then something changed; she seemed to grow taller in her chair and she set her jaw.

"Put an end to this, Nico. Someone needs to stop these people. Ariana lost her life trying to rid our beautiful country of its curse." She shook her head. "You were deprived of knowing your son because she was so scared of putting you both in danger. She wanted to protect us, but we owe her to see this to the end."

Nico's thoughts hurtled around his head like a pinball machine. He wanted to help, more than anything, but this wasn't his jurisdiction, he had no power here; he had no choice but to leave it to the Maltese authorities, as inept as they appeared to be. It sickened him.

But then he thought of Ariana. She had indeed lost every-thing. The legal world had lost one of its strongest crusaders. Her young son had lost his mother. He had lost his dearest friend. He knew what he had to do.

"What can you tell me about this group, Journalists for Justice? Do you know what was in the envelopes Ariana sent to three of them?"

Francesca shook her head, then pulled a piece of paper from her bag and handed it across the table. On the front was a logo of a person's finger held to their mouth. He hesitated to touch it, although it was unlikely there would have been anything useful, like fingerprints. It would be too late now. He took it and turned it over.

Tell anyone what you know and you'll be next.

"And you have no idea who could have left this?" he asked.

Francesca didn't answer. At first, Nico thought she hadn't heard him. Gazing out toward Grand Harbour she seemed lost in a world of her own. Did the note refer to her going to the police, or did she know more than she was letting on? She seemed like a decent person, but putting his lawyer's hat back on, what did he really know about this woman? He was just taking her word for it as to how close she was to Ariana and Max. It seemed odd if that really was the case, that Ariana wouldn't have confided in Francesca. Or even have *her* take Max somewhere safe.

"Could it have been someone other than the police who did this?" Nico prompted again, sweeping his hands toward the chaos inside the apartment. "From what Ariana told me about her work, she appeared to be working on several cases before she died. Maybe this is unrelated?" Although even he didn't believe his own words.

"That is true," Francesca replied without turning her head from the view. "But they all circled back to the same thing. What we here refer to as the 'Ghost of Malta.' Our shame. The way of life that has allowed greed to take hold of this country.

"First, there's our pay-to-play passport tragedy. Our prime

minister travels the world, recruiting anyone who has the money to buy their way into Maltese citizenship—Russian oligarchs, dictators of countries with atrocious human-rights violations. Then there is our largest private banking empire, run by a multigenerational family from old Maltese money. There have been rumors they've laundered money for those same despots. Then, there is the cronyism in the government. I could go on, it's a never-ending loop that always comes back to what our country has become: a haven for criminals pretending to lead respectable lives."

Ariana had railed against the corruption of her homeland to him so many times. He also knew that the alleged banking fraud extended across into his own jurisdiction of Calabria.

"What else can you tell me about what Ariana was about to announce?" he asked.

"A year ago," Francesca said, turning back to face him, "some kind of secret report was leaked about corruption within the government. Then a second one emerged. It was thought to have come from a member of parliament in our Nationalist Party."

Malta's ruling party. The party Ariana despised. "Do you know who the mole was?"

She steepled her hands together, her index fingers touching her top lip.

Nico looked into her eyes and saw fresh tears ready to escape. "Francesca," he said as gently as he could. "You have to trust someone. Is that why they killed Ariana? Was she about to expose someone in the party?"

Her brows knitted together, and she spread both hands on the table. "She told me it was safer if I didn't know." She shook her head and her eyes filled with tears. "There's a Nationalist Party MP by the name of Lydia Rapa. Ariana met her after she bought her home on Gozo—she lives there as well. Most weekends, they both commuted on the ferry that went from Ċirkewwa. That's how Ariana got to know her well."

"So it would be fair to say she was supportive of Ariana, despite the obvious political differences?"

Francesca nodded.

"So, if Lydia Rapa *was* the leaker, do you think she knew what Ariana was about to expose?"

Nico felt the familiar buzz of adrenaline. "Francesca," he said, "I need to speak to her."

Francesca looked at her watch. "It's Friday, she will be on the five o'clock ferry to Gozo. That's the one she and Ariana always took."

Chapter Seven

B y Nico's calculation, he had a good two hours before he had to be at the ferry terminal. To get to the car rental place, he had to walk past the slain journalist's shrine again. He tried to just walk on but something pulled him toward it. In the midst of the multitude of flowers was a portrait of the woman so many still mourned. The photograph had been in all the papers in Italy at the time. Dozens of candles illuminated her doe eyes and serene, beatific smile. But this time, it was Ariana he saw looking back at him. The growing sense of what these two remarkable women had stood for suddenly overwhelmed him, and he swallowed back the ache in his throat. He should have done more.

"Please, Nico," Ariana had pleaded months ago. "You must help me. I can only do so much from inside the country, but if Malta sees Italy hitting back, it will force our own justice system to do something about it." Even as she gave voice to those thoughts, Nico had questioned if she really believed it.

"Everybody knows this is happening, Ariana," he'd said to her. She had lost more weight and looked thin and gaunt, older than her thirty-two years. He'd been concerned at the time, but hadn't said anything. Why hadn't he done something then, before she took an even more dangerous path?

"Yes, everybody knows we have lost the monopoly of truth. But nobody does anything about it, including you. You all sit in your comfortable offices and go home to your comfortable lives. Lives made possible by greed and corruption. And you do nothing. *Nothing!*" She'd looked him directly in the eye and her words cut deep. "You're sworn to uphold justice, but you're just like the rest of them."

He'd thrown his hands in the air in protest, responding with anger rather than hurt, as they'd sat at the very table she'd been at only a few days ago.

Now, as he drove out of Valletta's city limits, he remembered the utter frustration etched on her face. Could he ever forgive himself for ignoring her desperate pleas?

W hile sitting in his car waiting for the ferry to board, Nico caught up on some emails. He checked in with Gina, who'd had limited success finding the reporters Ariana had sent her notes to.

"Testa's wife said he's somewhere on assignment," she reported. "And both De Rosa's and Sinclair's voice mail is full."

He thanked her, making a mental note to try them himself when he got back to the mainland. In the meantime, he rehearsed how best to approach Lydia Rapa. Once on the ferry, passengers were required to leave their vehicles and go up to the passenger deck. With a photo he had downloaded to his phone, he hoped finding the politician wouldn't be too difficult.

It helped that Francesca had told him she almost always traveled with her dog, a white shih tzu.

Sure enough, upon arriving on deck, Nico saw a woman who resembled the one in the photo, accompanied by a little mop-faced dog. Wearing little or no makeup, and with mousy blond hair tied back, the woman had an air of not being particularly concerned with her appearance. Rapa was pouring water into a collapsible rubber bowl and the dog wasted no time in lapping it up.

Nico reached down to pet it. "And what's your name?" he asked as he ruffled its ears.

Its mistress smiled at Nico. "Her name is Gabriela."

He smiled back. "She's sweet."

"Do you have one of your own?"

OK, get on with it, Nico thought. *Otherwise, you're going to look like a disingenuous schmuck.* "Nico Moretti," he said, handing her his card. "You must be Ms. Rapa."

The smile vanished. She ignored his business card. Instead, she tightened the dog's leash and reached to pick up the water bowl. Nico was sure that in a heartbeat she would be gone.

"Please, I wish you no harm. I'm a friend of Ariana Calleja. I simply want to talk to you."

If it were possible, the woman turned a whiter shade of pale. Her eyes darted to either side, and then behind her. "We mustn't talk here. Meet me on the other side," she whispered. "A bar called The Fishing Eagle. I'll wait for you there."

Before Nico could respond, she scooped up the dog and disappeared down the stairs that led to the car deck. He resisted the urge to follow. Clearly, he had spooked her.

. . .

O ne could only describe The Fishing Eagle as dingy. It looked more likely to be a watering hole for the locals rather than the island's multitude of sun-seeking tourists. It took a few seconds for Nico's eyes to adjust from the bright sunlight to the interior darkness. He looked around, observing a handful of patrons, but no Lydia. Perhaps he had arrived before her.

"What can I get for you?" a man asked without looking up from wiping the bar.

"Lydia Rapa?"

He looked up with a scowl. "Who's asking?"

"Nico Moretti. She's expecting me."

There was no mistaking the once over the bartender gave Nico as he tilted his head toward a partly open door. "Through there," he said, then went back to cleaning the pitted countertop.

Nico made his way toward the back of the bar and through a set of wooden double doors painted the same azure as the harbor beyond. Outside, the view was stunning. In the shadow of an imposing cathedral perched several meters above, the bar's rough stone deck with a single iron bench sat high above the boats of the marina below. And on the bench sat Lydia Rapa and Gabriela.

"May I?" Nico asked, rounding the bench.

Lydia nodded. The dog wedged itself between them like a mini sentry.

"I can't stay long. What do you want?" Lydia demanded.

Where to start? He had so many questions, but he sensed her skittishness. "I understand you knew Ariana Calleja. Could you tell me a little bit about her?"

"How did *you* know her?" she said.

OK, this is how it's going to go. "We met in law school, and we've worked together on several cases. I'm —"

"I know who you are, Mr. Moretti. What exactly is it you want to know?"

A friendly bunch they are here on Gozo. Nico tried changing tack. "I wondered if you might have any clues into her death." *And did you know she had a son?*

"Why would I? It was a shock to me as it was to everyone else." Her tone was abrupt.

Jesus, this woman seems made of stone, Nico thought as he considered his next question. He was only going to get one shot at this.

"I understand you were supportive of her work and investigations." He paused. "And that you might have been the one to leak a report regarding alleged corruption inside your government."

Rapa whirled to face him, startling the dog who leaped to the ground. "Where did you hear that?" Her knuckles were white as they clutched Gabriela's leash, even though the pint-sized canine didn't look to be going anywhere.

"Someone Ariana trusted," he replied. "A woman by the name of Francesca. Do you know her?"

Lydia let go of the leash and put a hand on the seat of the bench as if to steady herself. She breathed out slowly. "Yes, I know Francesca. She sometimes came with Ariana to see Gabriela. To play with . . ." She halted.

"To play with Ariana's son?" Nico ventured.

"You know about Max?"

Not until recently.

"Do you know where the boy is? Is he safe?" The urgency of the woman's words startled him. When he looked over, her expression had softened into concern, bordering on maternal.

"I don't know. That's one of many things I'm trying to

find out. Do you know what Ariana was working on before she—"

Nico could practically feel the tension emanating off her as she clutched her handbag to her chest just as her phone pinged. She glanced at the screen, then jumped up from the bench. "I'm sorry, I must go. Give me your card. I'll be in touch."

She took his card and reached into her handbag, searching for something. She fished out a small spiral-bound notebook, scribbled something down before ripping out the sheet of paper and handing it to him. "This person might be able to help you. Tell her I sent you. She lives in the UK, but I heard she came here following Ariana's death." She picked up her handbag. "I really must go. Good luck."

Rather than going back in through the blue doors of the bar, Lydia and the dog disappeared around the side of the building and down a set of stairs, presumably to where she had parked her car below. Nico leaned over the railing and just moments later, saw a green Audi speeding away up the hill.

Annoyed, he walked back to the bench, the Maltese sunshine warming his skin, and focused his attention on the note. The name Lydia had written was Elle Sinclair, the British journalist and one of Ariana's three most trusted confidantes. And a phone number. And Lydia had said Elle was "here."

W hile the Malta police didn't seem to bother about drinking and driving, using a mobile phone, even hands-free, was strictly prohibited. But Nico desperately wanted to speak with Elle Sinclair, so as soon as he had cleared the city limits of Mġarr Harbour and was on the two-lane coastal road heading north, he dialed the number Lydia had given him. He felt a surge of adrenaline when the journalist answered on the first ring.

"Miss Sinclair," he said, "you don't know me, but my name is Nico Moretti. I'm a prosecutor in Calabria... and a friend of Ariana Calleja. I was given your number by Lydia Rapa. Do you have a few minutes?"

"Oh, thank you for calling, Mr. Moretti." She sounded relieved. "It's devastating," she said with a perfect English Oxford accent. I came to Gozo the minute I heard of Ariana's death."

"It is," Nico agreed. "I'm here on the island as well. Is it possible for us to meet?"

"Yes, of course. I don't know why I thought there would be something I could do by coming to Gozo. It didn't even happen here, did it? And the Maltese police are useless."

There were so many questions Nico wanted to ask her, but he preferred to do it in person. "Do you have time today?" he asked, hopefully.

"Actually, I was preparing to catch the ferry back to the mainland this afternoon. I need to file a story at our office in Valletta. There really doesn't seem to be much I can do here."

Nico felt the same way. He'd only come to meet with Lydia Rapa and as she was less than forthcoming, he couldn't afford to waste valuable time just hanging around waiting for her to contact him again. As she'd given him Sinclair's contact information, she must have thought Sinclair could be helpful.

"I'm also ready to go back," he said. "What ferry are you planning to catch? I can meet you there."

He was so intent on trying to take a mental note of where and when to meet Elle that he didn't notice the vehicle behind him, practically glued to his rear bumper.

"I can make the three o'clock," Sinclair said. "Does that work for you?"

Nico heard the roar of an engine as he looked into his rearview mirror. A white van pulled out from behind and into the oncoming lane. *And I thought we Italians were aggressive.* He dropped back, letting the driver pass.

He'd have to kill a few hours but what Sinclair was suggesting would work. "Yes, I can make that. Where shall—"

Without signaling, the speeding van swerved back into Nico's lane between him and the car in front. Staying at the speed limit, he watched it roar up behind the next car. They were on a straight stretch and he could see both vehicles approach a curve in the potholed road, guarded only by a low stone wall. His heart beat faster, and he was only vaguely aware that Sinclair was still speaking. He watched in shock as the van bashed into the back of the vehicle ahead of it and pushed it careening across the oncoming lane. Toward the cliff's edge. As Nico raised his foot to brake, it crashed through the wall and over the edge. The pursuing car kept going and disappeared around the next bend.

Nico jammed on his brakes. He looked both ahead and behind him before making a U-turn so fast that his tires squealed, laying rubber on the pavement. After doubling back, he pulled off the road where he'd seen the car crash through the wall and down the hill toward the sea. As he ran from his vehicle, he heard Sinclair's voice over the car's hands-free mobile phone speaker. "Hello, hello? Mr. Moretti, are you still there?"

He smelled it before he saw it. Grabbing a handful of scrubby tree branches for support, he looked down at the raging fireball. He let go of the branch and half ran, half slid toward the burning wreck. But as he got closer, the intensity

of the heat drove him back. He wiped his eyes with his shirt-
sleeve and tried from another angle, but it was impossible.
Sliding a few feet to another shelf on the cliff's side, he dug
his feet into the rubble for purchase and pulled his phone
from his pocket and punched in 112— *grazie a Dio*, there
was only one digit difference between the Italian and the
Maltese emergency services number. When the dispatcher
came on the line asking whether he needed fire, ambulance or
police, he shouted, "All of them. There's been a car wreck!
Get here as quickly as you—"

An explosion rocked the ground and flames shot higher.
The azure sky had turned to a thick, oily curtain of opaque
black. Nico strained his ears, praying he'd hear sirens soon.
But, wait . . . That wasn't sirens. An almost inaudible
mewling sounded again. Is that a child's cry? Oh dear Lord,
please not a child!

Something moved in the long grass near the wreck where
the fire hadn't yet singed. Nico stared at the spot, hoping to
see it again. Seconds passed. Nothing. Then, from the thicket
of grass, a small white animal emerged, dragging one of its
hind legs. It cried again and pulled itself another few inches
before stopping. It lay pitifully in the grass, keeling over on
its side, whimpering.

Nico's heart plummeted. It was Gabriela, Lydia Rapa's
little dog. How was that possible? Lydia had at least a five-
minute head start when she'd left the bar before him. She
must have stopped for something.

The next movements were automatic, running over to the
animal and lifting her up and out of harms' way. He tried to
move closer to the burning car, but the heat was too intense.
Was Lydia still inside? There was another explosion, and he
jumped back, Gabriela cried in his arms, as if she too was

trying to see if Lydia was okay. But there was nothing either of them could do.

Somewhere in the recesses of his mind, Nico was aware of encroaching sirens. He wasn't sure how long he'd been sitting on the ground with the dog in his arms, having moved a safe distance from the inferno. Gabriela opened her eyes, gave a sad little whimper and licked his hand.

He heard shouting from above. But he just sat there, in shock.

"Sinjur, are you all right? We need to move you and your dog away from here."

Nico wasn't sure if the man who appeared beside him was a paramedic or a fireman.

"It's . . . she's not mine," he stammered. "She belongs to the woman in the car."

But the man didn't hear. "Please, sir, you must come with me."

Together they moved up the hill to the myriad of emergency vehicles parked on the road. He was ushered over to an ambulance, as another first-responder held out his arms for Gabriela. "Can I take your dog while we look at your injuries?"

'I keep telling you, she's not my dog.' Nico said, while a medic applied something to some scratches and minor lacerations on his arms and hands. Behind him, in the treatment part of the ambulance, someone was splinting little Gabriela's broken leg. All he could think about was that Lydia must have perished in her car. She couldn't possibly have survived the crash and the explosion. Yet, somehow, her dog had. The emergency responders surmised she must have been thrown from an open window before the car landed and caught fire.

"If you're sure you don't need to go to the hospital," the EMT continued, "there's a vet on the way back into town. If you'd like, we can drop your dog off for you while you go to the police station. You should be able to pick her up after your interview."

"I told you, it's not my dog." Nico wanted to scream. "The woman in the car was her owner. Lydia Rapa."

"Well, we can take her to the pound, then. They'll have a vet who will fix her leg."

The pound.

"What happens to her then?" Nico asked.

"If she's lucky, someone will adopt her."

Otherwise? He was afraid to ask.

"If you feel you're all right to drive your car, sir, we will follow you to the station where someone will take your statement."

As Nico drove back toward Mġarr Harbour with a police car following behind, he thought about Elle Sinclair. He remembered her frantically calling his name as he ran from his vehicle toward the crash. Was it mere coincidence that Lydia Rapa had been run off the road right after meeting with him? He didn't believe in coincidences; by planning to meet with Sinclair, could he be putting her in danger? If Lydia was targeted, the last thing he wanted was for the journalist to be next.

Calling Sinclair again, even hands-free, was a calculated risk. He'd taken a chance the first time he contacted her and was about to do it again with the police right behind him.

He hit Redial. Again, Elle answered on the first ring. "Mr. Moretti. What happened? I thought I heard an explosion. Are you all right?"

"Listen carefully," he said. "I only have a minute. Lydia Rapa is dead."

"Oh my God! How?"

"About an hour ago. Someone ran her off the road, right in front of me. I'm on the way to the police station to give my witness statement."

"I'll come and meet you there and then we can go to the ferry. Poor Lydia, I—"

"No, I want you to stay put. I have to assume whoever killed her will be watching me and I don't want to lead them to you." Nico couldn't know with certainty that whoever had killed Lydia hadn't come back for him, only to have been foiled by the emergency vehicles arriving.

"When will I hear from you?"

"I'll contact you as soon as I can." He was approaching the city limits and conscious of the police car behind him, he needed to get off the phone. "Wait until the news of her death comes out in the media. Otherwise, don't say a word to anyone." He didn't want to alarm the woman, but better safe than sorry. "For now, I advise you to stay off the roads, and if you have to go out, keep to public places." With that, he disconnected the call.

I n the hour and a half he'd spent inside the Mġarr police station on Coast Road, the warmth of the sun had cooled and a slight breeze had whispered in from the sea. The night air was fresh and a sweet relief from the stuffy confines of the interview room.

At first, the two officers responsible for taking his statement had seemed congenial enough. While professional in their questions, they asked several times about his well-being and offered to get him water or coffee, both of which Nico declined. He gave them everything he knew about the car that had run Lydia off the road, which wasn't much. It had all happened so fast that without a license-plate number, he doubted much of his witness statement would be helpful.

About forty-five minutes into the interview, however, it occurred to him he had become a bit like a frog in water; the police had been turning up the heat so gradually, that he hadn't noticed the interview become an interrogation.

"How do you know Lydia Rapa and why were you following her?" one of them had asked.

"I had just met her on the ferry, and I wasn't following her. As you well know, there's only one road leading away from the harbor." As he felt the tables turn, he decided not to tell them he and Lydia had met at The Fishing Eagle before the car crash. Although, he suspected it would only be a matter of time before they realized there was a time discrepancy between when the ferry had docked and when she'd been run off the road with him behind her.

It also depended on whether the bartender who'd seen Nico go out back to meet Lydia was a friend or foe. If it was the latter, it could have been him who tipped off the killer.

Porca miseria! Nico wanted to scream. For God's sake! "I've already told you, I came to Valletta following the murder of Ariana Calleja."

"Why would you come to Valletta?" the other officer enquired. "You don't have jurisdiction in Malta."

Because your idioti on the mainland aren't doing their damned job. Nico bit his tongue. After going round and round, and Nico making a point of looking at his watch ever more frequently, he was told he was free to go but to leave his contact information in the event they had further questions.

"I assume you'll be returning to your job in Calabria, yes?" The one that had been the "good cop" smirked.

"Yes, more than likely," Nico said through a clenched jaw.

But Nico had every intention of staying in Malta. Yes, the island was small, and the police could easily check the ferries and flights from the mainland, meaning he wouldn't be able to remain below their radar for long. But he still had a short window of time, and he planned to make the most of it.

Chapter Eight

Nico kept checking his rearview mirror as he drove away from the harbor, traveling back along the stretch of the road that had claimed Lydia's life. He still couldn't figure out how he came to be right behind Lydia's car when she'd left The Fishing Eagle before him. He was lost in that thought when he saw the sign for the animal shelter and realized he'd forgotten all about the little dog. She'd been so helpless, limping away from the burning wreck, and yet still determined to look out for Lydia as he held her. . . Screw it, she wasn't *his* problem; somebody would adopt her. Finding out who was responsible for Ariana's murder, and where Max might be were top of mind and he didn't need a four-legged tag-along getting in his way.

Dammit! His conscience wouldn't let him leave her there, especially in that he may have been responsible for her mistress's murder. He had almost passed the exit when he swerved the car to the left and, a few meters down a gravel road, found himself in front of the SPCA.

"She's all ready for you." A young woman pushed a prescription bottle across the counter after Nico signed the paperwork releasing Gabriela into his care. "She needs to have the cast and stitches removed in ten days. In the meantime, give her two of these tablets a day to prevent infection, and she should be as good as new."

After he'd made a donation for the dog's treatment and medication, he waited while the attendant slipped into the back to retrieve her. In a moment, she came out holding Gabriela and handed her to him. "She'll be a bit dopey for another hour or two, so it's best if you keep her quiet for the rest of the evening."

The woman must have noticed Nico's stunned expression. He felt like she'd just handed him a baby that he hadn't the faintest idea what to do with.

"Do you have her lead?" she asked.

Nico shook his head.

"Food?"

He gave her a blank look, feeling completely pathetic.

She put her hand up. "Hold on, I'll be right back."

When she returned, she had a bag of sample-sized tinned and dry dog food, a collapsible rubber dish and some bottled water. "This should tide you over until you can get to the shops tomorrow."

"Thank you." He knew nothing about Lydia's personal life. What if her family came looking for her dog? He wrote out his contact information and received the woman's assurance that the shelter would provide it should someone come looking for Gabriela and want her back.

"She seems to like you." The woman smiled as she watched the little dog lick Nico's neck.

Once outside, Nico bunched up his jacket on the front seat of the car and gently placed the dog in the center. Before he had re-entered the highway, she had curled up, as best she could with her hind leg sticking out, and was fast asleep.

. . .

U ntil he could contact Sinclair again and rearrange their meeting, Nico needed to find a place to stay on Gozo, hopefully one that allowed dogs. A little further along the highway from the animal shelter, he saw a sign for a historic inn, and confident that he wasn't being followed, he left the highway and ventured up the long driveway. The building would have originally been the ruins of an ancient castle and, like so many buildings in both Italy and Malta, it had been repurposed into an inn. He couldn't for the life of him understand why tourists chose to stay in the characterless high-rise hotels when they could sleep in the same spot in which history had been made. He parked the car and went inside, Gabriela in his arms, immediately basking in the warmth of the crackling fireplace that blazed in the corner of the exposed brick lounge. A woman sat behind a single desk that served as the reception area.

She didn't seem the least bit curious that he had no luggage and offered him a complimentary toiletry kit, as well as a dog biscuit for Gabriela, who was stirring.

"Many prefer not to travel back across our roads at night," she said. She took back Nico's guest registration form. "Ah, you're from Calabria. First time on Gozo?"

"It is, I've come to . . . I'm here to do a little sightseeing."

She smiled and handed him a heavy, old-fashioned brass key. "You have time to take a nice hot shower if you like before we start serving dinner, but you're welcome to take a glass of wine and some cheese and crackers to your room. A little something to tide you over."

Music to Nico's ears. His teeth felt furry, and he hadn't eaten since he'd shared pastries with Francesca in Valletta. He'd meant to stop at a restaurant on the drive along Gozo's coast, but got distracted as he'd debated how best to contact Elle Sinclair. After his experience at the local police station, he couldn't be sure how much he should trust the authorities. Two women were already dead; he'd be damned if he'd be responsible for another. However, he desperately needed to find out what Ariana had sent to the journalist. And although Max was safe for now—or so he hoped— Nico needed to find him, and quickly.

Despite the late hour, he pulled his mobile from its charger and made the call. Again, she answered immediately.

"I'm sorry if I've disturbed you," he said.

"No, not at all, Mr. Moretti. Where are you?"

"I'm at an inn here on Gozo," he said, sufficiently vague.

"We must meet. Are you familiar with Yandex?"

Nico's ears perked up at the mention of the secure internet browser, lesser known and more private than the commonly used Tor. He'd become familiar with this technology while working a covert investigation last year. "Yes," he replied.

"Good, I'll send you a message where to meet tomorrow. Check online in about ten minutes and confirm to me you got it." Elle paused. "And, Mr. Moretti, please don't consider contacting me either by phone, text or a regular internet connection again. Do you understand?"

Her friendly tone of earlier had changed to one of absolute authority. The journalist wasn't stupid; she could do the math. Two women she knew well were already dead. That didn't bode well for her.

After hanging up, he opened his computer bag and lifted Gabriela from the bed to the floor. Although a little clumsy at first, once he'd put down a bowl of the food the shelter had given him she bumped and scraped her way across the carpet, oblivious to her cast, and happily tucked in.

Nico absently nibbled on some cheese and crackers. What

a colossal loser he was. First, he turned his back on Ariana's plea to help her drive the last nail in the coffin of those she'd tried in vain to prosecute— which potentially was the catalyst for her murder. Then, he gets Lydia Rapa killed and ends up with her dog. Perhaps De Rosa and Testa were right; the tiger *had* lost his edge.

A fter a quick breakfast and a hobble outside for Gabriela the following morning, Nico bade the inn's proprietor goodbye. He and Elle Sinclair had agreed via encrypted message to meet on the ferry returning to the mainland. From studying Elle's byline and social media, he knew what she looked like. He was going to leave the dog in the car but, thinking she'd make a great foil, he scooped her up and brought her on deck.

As they'd agreed, Nico took his seat next to a lifeboat on the ferry's starboard side. The wooden bench was tucked away by itself, where they wouldn't be easily observed without their knowledge. He sipped on the coffee he'd picked up at the terminal and waited.

Within minutes, a tall, blonde woman walked past him and stood at the railing as if admiring the view. He was admiring her long, tanned legs before she turned toward him. "What a sweet little dog," she said. "What's her name?"

"Gabriela," Nico replied.

"My friend Lydia has one just like her." She gestured to the space beside him. "May I?"

"Of course," Nico said, scooting over a little on the bench.

There they sat, side by side. He waited for her to take the lead.

"Would you like a piece of the paper?" Elle asked, offering a section of the island's daily newspaper.

"Thank you."

"I don't know if you follow football, but Malta has made it into the World Cup. There's an article on page three."

Nico casually turned to the page. There was a small manilla envelope taped to the page above the fold. In pen, she'd written, *Read this in your car for further instructions.* He looked out to sea, glancing over at Elle at the same time.

She had bent down and was ruffling Gabriela's neck. "Well, I must go. It was nice talking with you." Then she vanished around the corner of the ship.

Nico waited until the announcement came over the loud-speaker for passengers to return to their vehicles. He had been one of the first on board, meaning he'd disembark last, which gave him time to read Elle's message in the car.

It's imperative that you ensure you aren't being followed. Meet me at Dingli Cliffs. I will wait until quarter to the hour, and if you're not there, I'll assume you're being followed and will leave.

They threatened Ariana multiple times prior to her death. Lydia Rapa was the whistleblower, and I believe I know who may have killed her, or at least who ordered it.

Now we're getting somewhere. He waited impatiently to drive off the ferry.

Scanning the light traffic behind him and doubling back twice, Nico was certain he hadn't been followed to the cliffs at Dingli. As there were no other vehicles in the parking lot, he assumed he'd arrived before Sinclair. He parked his rental car in a small turnout overlooking the sea, and while he waited, he let the dog out to do her business. A few minutes later, a blue Fiat drove in and Elle Sinclair parked beside him. Nico turned on the ignition and rolled down all the windows so the dog had fresh air, then followed Elle toward a weathered sign at the entrance to the trailhead. It promised an easy walk via Buskett Gardens, which was supposed to come out in the village of Dingli.

It would seem though, Elle had other ideas as she took the alternate trail that hugged the side of the cliff. Though he wasn't afraid of heights, Nico found it difficult not to be distracted by the sheer drops of the route she'd chosen. They stood side by side, the spectacular view of the Mediterranean stretching out before them. As breathtaking as it was, he was anxious to find out what she knew.

"How long did you know Ariana for?" he asked.

"Gosh," she said as she looked over the expanse of water. "We met at a charity fundraiser in London. That must have been what...?" She counted on her fingers. "Eight, ten years ago?"

So, she would have known about Max, Nico thought. Yet she hadn't mentioned him. "Did you know Lydia Rapa?" he asked.

"I never met her in person, but I spoke to her on the phone when Ariana asked me to interview her. Lydia agreed if I guaranteed her complete anonymity, which of course I did." They walked on. "As you're no doubt aware, she was a member of Malta's government. Two weeks before Ariana was assassinated, someone leaked a report that members of Lydia's party, and several top government officials, were threatening Ariana. The report named names, payments, and to whom—everything. It was quite damning."

"Lydia was the whistleblower, then," Nico said, "but why would she turn against her own party?"

"She and Ariana were once fierce adversaries. As you can imagine, they came from opposite ends of the political spectrum." Elle touched Nico's elbow, steering him left on the trail. He hoped she hadn't heard him exhale with relief as it took them away from the cliff's edge for a bit. "But Lydia was seeing the cracks in her party: the dishonesty, the corruption. Kickbacks were routine to certain MP's family members.

"But," Elle continued, "when Ariana bought her home on Gozo and both women took the ferry back and forth every weekend, they developed a friendship. Ariana had been working on so many cases of corruption, it was hard to keep track. In addition to a pay-to-play passport scheme— I'm sure you've heard about it…"

Nico nodded.

"Well, the passport scheme was bringing all kinds of rich people into the country from outside the EU. Russians, Iranians, members of countries run by dictators—some very unsavory characters. Ariana alleged Malta's largest private bank was money-laundering for several of them. It was a mess."

So far, everything matched with what Francesca had told him. "Rumors to that effect have been circulating for years," he said, frustrated that this was all information he knew already. "I understand Ariana sent copies of her investigative notes to you before she died."

Elle looked surprised. "Did she tell you that?"

Nico wasn't sure why, but at this point he wasn't sure he wanted to name Francesca as his source. He also chose not to ask about the other two journalists for now. He nodded his head. "She didn't tell me what was in her notes," he said. "But she did tell me that her office was about to announce something significant the day after the bombing. Do you know what it was?"

Elle pointed to an exposed tree root before he tripped over it. "Not specifically, no. However, six months ago, things took an interesting turn."

"How so?" Could this finally be the lead he needed?

"Malta's finance minister was in Amsterdam on government business when Ariana got a tip that the minister had been photographed in a rather compromising position with someone who wasn't his wife. She was going to use it to drive one more nail into the corrupt government's coffin." Elle stopped at a small lookout and pointed out a massive white-domed cathedral that gleamed in the distance.

"Beautiful," Nico said, admiring it. "And did she? Use it for her investigation?"

"She did. But that turned out to be the least of the story."

Nico turned to look at her, intrigued.

"After extricating himself from the liaison in question, the minister was later caught on video meeting two men, one a known gun-for-hire. A long-angled camera lens caught them shaking hands and the man accompanying the minister passing over a thick envelope, no doubt filled with cash."

"Do you know who the individuals were taking the money?"

Elle shook her head. "In Ariana's notes, she made reference to Alesandru Baldisar. Current president of the decades-old, family-run Baldisar Bank. But honestly, it could have been anyone. There are so many players in Malta's lucrative underground economy it's hard to tell one from the other."

"So, let me get this straight," Nico said as he and Elle sat on a bench on a small outcrop at the base of the cliffs. A faint breeze wrinkled the otherwise serene sea. "Lydia Rapa was cooperating with the European Central Bank's investigation into her party's organized threats against Ariana."

"That, and she was also the source that provided the details of what the British banking authorities needed to nail Baldisar Bank in the UK."

"That's where you come in," Nico said.

"Correct. Two years ago, the bank opened an office in London. Under the 'passporting regulations,' the UK granted them permission to operate there, but they were not permitted to open accounts for UK residents.

"As part of Ariana's investigation, she discovered Malta's anti-money-laundering agency was about to come down on the bank for their lack of regulations and controls. I picked it up from the UK end and worked the story while Ariana pieced together her case."

The steely blue eyes Nico had first seen on Elle Sinclair's bio during the flight over to Malta were no less penetrating in person. He imagined the woman would be like a pit bull once she got her teeth into something. Or someone.

"Anyway, I happened to be at a society wedding at an estate in Kent—as a guest, not a reporter," she added. "And who should be there but Mr. and Mrs. Alesandru Baldisar. I tried to keep a casual eye out for him in particular, but I lost him in the crowd of guests.

"Later in the evening, I needed to use the loo. The outside portable ones they'd brought in for the wedding were all occupied, so one of the catering staff directed me to a lavatory in the main floor of the house—I later found out that was strictly verboten. However, on my way to the toilet, I passed by what looked like a study. The door was partially open, and I saw Baldisar engaged in a heated discussion with someone."

"What did you do?"

"What any self-respecting reporter would do," Elle said with a smirk. "I ducked around the corner and listened."

"Did you hear what the other person said?"

"No, but he had an accent—Eastern European, I think, maybe Russian—I'm not sure. He was angry about something. I don't know what exactly, but I know it had to do with Baldisar's bank."

"How do you know that?"

"Because he said if Baldisar didn't cooperate, he would go to the authorities and tell the FCA—Britain's Financial Conduct Agency—everything about what was going on, and they would shut the bank down in both countries."

Nico squinted into the sun. "Were you able to see what the other man looked like?"

"Well, I might have." Elle turned to look at him. "Except that a bloody butler came along and gave me a right dressing-down. Said I had no business being in there and promptly closed the door to the study and escorted me out. Still having to pee, I might add."

O nce again, it had proven useful to have the chief of Gozo's police force on his payroll. Upon being told of Nico Moretti's presence on the island, he'd had the Italian prosecutor followed, which in turn led him to Elle Sinclair. He'd never heard of the damned woman, but it had been brought to his attention that as a journalist with the UK press, she was nearly as lethal as the Calleja woman. What the hell was she doing in his territory and why was she meeting with Moretti?

"You should have taken them out while you had the chance," he said into the phone. "Both of them. I know that

trail that runs along the bluff. It's steep. It wouldn't have taken much for them to lose their footing . . ."

"Too risky—both at the same time. We don't know what she might have told Moretti."

"Exactly. That's why we should eliminate them."

"Trust me on this. It isn't the right time."

With a sigh, he hung up. He couldn't abide incompetency, and he wouldn't tolerate his orders being questioned. Once more and he'd have to take action.

Chapter Nine

Nico followed Elle back along the road to ensure she wasn't being followed—or worse—and returned to his room at the hotel in Valletta. He'd come in from taking Gabriela for her last outing when his phone rang. Roberto Pezzente.

"I wonder if I might ask you a few more questions, Mr. Moretti." This time, the investigator seemed more conciliatory and less confrontational as they spoke via secure video conferencing.

"Certainly," Nico replied.

"*Grazie*. It would appear that apart from Signorina Calleja, the other victims were locals. No one significant in any way."

I wonder how their friends and family would feel about that, Nico thought.

"You met with Signorina Calleja the night before she died. A neighbor said he saw a man leaving her apartment very angry. Would that have been you?"

Nico surmised the investigator already knew the answer

to that or he wouldn't be asking. What exactly was he intimating?

"Would you mind telling me what you were so angry about?"

Nico made the decision not to tell Pezzente about Max. He didn't know why— he might have actually been able to help find him— but he still wasn't sure that he could trust him.

"I was angry that she'd taken on the role of senior prosecutor, which I felt would put her in more danger," Nico said.

There was a pause where they held each other's gaze on the screen.

"I see. Would you happen to know what she might have been working on just before she died?"

Why was he asking him? Pezzente could easily find that out on his own.

"Not specifically, no."

Now it was Nico's turn to ask a question although he doubted Pezzente would be forthcoming. "Have you found out any more about who was behind the bombing?" he asked.

Surprisingly, the man appeared willing to share what he knew. Despite the pissing contest, they were supposed to be on the same side.

"Yes, we've determined the type of device used to detonate the bomb in the square. It may sound complicated," Pezzente explained before Nico could ask. "While it would have taken some time to plant the explosives without detection, the mechanism itself is actually quite simple, using something as basic as two mobile phones. The first device is a generic handset, which sends the bomb's activation code by text. The second device has a SIM card installed. It receives the code and then detonates the bomb remotely. Such a device was planted under the waterside deck of the Cannone Square restaurant." He paused. "It's not the first time it has been used."

Nico tilted his head and raised his eyebrows.

"It appears it was the weapon of choice for two other assassinations. One in 2016. Another earlier this year. In the most recent one, this exact method was used to kill three businessmen thought to be connected to a money-laundering scheme. Word on the street is it was an execution ordered by certain individuals who control much of the private banking system."

Nico's ears perked up as he recalled bits of his conversation with Elle. "Where?" But he already knew the answer.

"Malta."

Bingo.

Pezzente shared his screen, and a video clip appeared. It showed a lineup of people waiting for cabs, Ubers and the like, in front of what looked to be a hotel.

"OK, so this is CCTV footage of around the time of the blast from the attack in Malta earlier this year. Now watch carefully."

Nico glued his eyes to the screen as Pezzente zoomed in on three men standing at the curb outside the hotel. A black SUV pulled up in front. One man appeared to say something to his companions, then stepped forward and opened the car door. The driver stayed in the vehicle while the men climbed in, and the car pulled away.

"Where was this taken?" Nico asked.

"Outside the Hilton in Saint Julian's, Malta." A high-end hotel known for businesspeople and conferences.

"I gather you were able to get identities on the victims," Nico said.

"Eventually," Pezzente replied. "It took some time, but Forensics managed to get DNA from scattered remains at the scene. Unfortunately, there weren't enough for their families to give them a decent burial."

Just as with Ariana. Nico's stomach turned.

Pezzente pulled up two photos onto the screen. "These are the men in the video. On the left is—or was—a research scientist from the UK. Another was a Canadian businessman."

"And the third?" Nico asked.

"A Maltese banker."

"Do you know why they were all together in Malta?"

"We didn't at the time, but after viewing the hotel's security video, my people looked into how they were connected. As soon as we got confirmation of the victims' identities, local investigators interviewed the families in London, Vancouver, and here in Rome."

"Were they able to tell you anything?"

"Not at first. It appeared the wives knew little about their husbands' extracurricular affairs, if you get my drift." Pezzente winked and a sly smile crossed his face.

Nico didn't dignify the comment with a response.

"But after further investigation, it appeared the Brit and the Canadian were part of a long-running money-laundering scheme. We tied the one in the UK to the pharmaceutical industry—turns out his wife was also a researcher. The one in Canada was laundering planeloads of cash in the casinos in and around the Vancouver area. Couriers brought the cash in on their persons, got on the rapid train from the airport, went into a nearby casino for forty-five minutes to an hour, then handed off the cleaned money."

Nothing new there. This type of activity went on all over the world. "But why assassinate them?" he asked. "Particularly if they were getting the job done."

Pezzente clicked off the images, and his face reappeared

on-screen. "That was the problem. They were doing *too* good a job. Seems they had a private deal going with certain casino dealers. Essentially, they had doubled their efforts from what they were contracted to do, running enough dirty cash through the casinos that they could start skimming. In order to launder the money during such brief visits to the casinos, there was a certain percentage of loss built into the system. Whoever hired them was aware of that."

"But?"

"They got greedy. By playing at specific dealers' tables, their actual losses could be mitigated. Even after cutting the dealers in for their percentage, they were taking bigger and bigger shares off the top."

"What about the third guy? The banker from Malta. Which bank was he with?"

"The biggest private bank in the country," Pezzente replied.

Nico had a sense of déjà vu.

"Baldisar Bank."

Chapter Ten

Since the video call with Pezzente the previous night, Nico's mind had raced with so many unanswered questions. Frustrated, that he couldn't do anymore until the morning, he'd got out of the same clothes he'd been wearing since his unplanned overnight stay in Gozo. When he'd emptied his pockets of loose change, he realized he still had the note Francesca had given him for safekeeping. With Lydia's death and his subsequent meeting with Elle, he'd forgotten all about it.

Smoothing it out, he laid it on the desk.

Tell anyone what you know and you'll be next.

That it was written on the Journalists for Justice distinctive red-and-yellow stationery was deeply disturbing. Was it a reporter who'd gone rogue? Someone out there posing as a trusted member of the group who was anything but? Most importantly, what was it they thought Francesca knew?

It had been late, but he'd tried to call Francesca to tell her about Lydia's death. It would be a shock if she heard it on the news. He also needed to tell her he intended to take the note to Valletta Police Station in the morning. As someone sworn to uphold the law, he couldn't in clear conscience not report such a threat.

But when he'd rung Francesca's number several times, there was no answer. He'd sent her a text asking her to call him, no matter the hour. Then within minutes, he'd collapsed into bed beside a gently snoring Gabriela.

Now he sat watching the news about Lydia Rapa's "accidental death." He couldn't believe the audacity of the police, knowing there was a witness to what had happened, and they were passing it off as an accident. One more reason to go to the police in Valletta. Or not. Were the police on Gozo covering up the cause of the MP's death? And if so, why? Even more alarming was that Francesca hadn't called him back. He'd dialed her again, only for it to go to voicemail. He'd been preparing to leave a message when he was told her message inbox was full. Great, now what?

He knew the general vicinity of her apartment—close to Ariana's—but nothing more. However, he recalled Francesca's familiarity with the waitress at the café she'd taken him to when he'd first arrived, and so he'd headed back to the café.

"Francesca? No, I haven't seen her since you were here together," the waitress told him as she wiped the dew off the tables and put out menus. Initially, she appeared reluctant to provide Francesca's address until Nico handed her his card and hinted that he was worried about her.

Armed with an address and directions, Nico set out. He recalled some of the side streets he'd passed when Francesca had taken him to Ariana's apartment. Two blocks down on the right, he turned into a side alley. There were no numbers on the doors, but a woman whisking a broom back and forth in front of her doorway smiled warmly when he asked if she knew which unit was Francesca's. Her eyes lit up, and she pointed to the door across the alley.

The old woman watched Nico as he knocked a few times and waited patiently. No answer. He knocked again. Again, nothing. Where was she? He pulled out a pen and his business card and wrote a hasty message telling Francesca to call him as soon as possible. He began to slide it between the doorframe and the door for Francesca to find later, when the door yawned open with a creak. She had left her door open. Perhaps she'd only popped out for a moment. Maybe he ought to wait and catch her on her return. Nico looked over his shoulder as he considered whether he should enter. The lady and her broom were nowhere in sight.

But something felt odd. With everything that had happened over the past few days, would Francesca have left her door open and vulnerable like that? A tingle started at the base of his neck and rippled all the way down his spine. He should really contact the police and wait for them before entering. Then he remembered the shambles of Ariana's apartment and Francesca's expression of disgust when he'd asked her if the police had done it. He slipped in the door and closed it behind him.

The apartment was stifling. The shades were drawn, but they did little to lessen the heat. "Francesca? It's Nico. Anybody home?"

Out of his peripheral vision, a curtain rippled ever so slightly. Was there a sliding door behind it? Perhaps Francesca was out there. He pulled back the curtain but there was only a window. Closed.

Hesitantly, he took a few more steps into the apartment. He really shouldn't be in here without Francesca's knowledge. To the left, there was a set of wooden stairs. He looked up and saw they led to a half mezzanine floor. "Francesca, are you up there? It's Nico." Should he go up? "I'm sorry to have come in but your door—"

As he took a step forward, there was a whoosh of air before he felt as if a freight train had hit him from behind. In one rapid movement, he landed face first on the floor, the air punched from his chest. He tried to yell, but only a low grunt came out. Nico's one-hundred-and-eighty-pound frame was no match for his attacker, but he was agile and hadn't yet forgotten his amateur boxing skills from his college days. He scrambled to grab a handful of the rug just inches from his nose and tried to drag himself out from under the deadweight. Except it wasn't a deadweight. Whoever had him pinned to the floor was very much alive and seemed laser-focused on making sure Nico wasn't.

Behind them, the apartment's front door squeaked. *God, no, Francesca, don't come in. Run!*

"Sinjur?" the elderly woman he'd just seen called out. "I've brought muffins for Francesca. Is it all right if I—?"

Whoever had been on top of Nico clambered off him and charged toward the open doorway. The little woman was literally lifted off her feet before landing with a sickening crack against the concrete entrance. By the time Nico had found his breath, she lay on her back in a pool of blood, twisted legs splayed across the threshold, half in, half out. Her eyes were closed, and he couldn't tell if she was breathing.

D espite her profusely bleeding head wound, Francesca's muffin-bearing neighbor regained consciousness and was taken to the local hospital. Hearing the commotion, another neighbor had come to the rescue and called for an ambulance. Nico told the attending paramedics he would call the police himself and wait for their arrival. And he would, but for now he needed to use the time he had to his advantage. He determined that he'd better take as cursory a look around Francesca's apartment as he dared and get the hell out of there. Especially if there was any likelihood of the human tank returning to finish him off.

From the apartment's ground floor, his gaze fell on a short flight of stairs that appeared to lead to a loft. Nico took the stairs two at a time before he pulled up short when he reached the landing. Francesca had struck him as the type who would make her bed and keep her small apartment neat and tidy. The downstairs certainly had looked that way in the short time he'd seen it before being bowled over by the fast-moving ton of bricks. Upstairs, however, was a different story. Her bed was not only unmade, but the mattress and sheets looked as if they'd been dragged off it and left to lie in a heap on the rough wooden flooring.

He rounded the bed and pushed open the door to a tiny adjoining bathroom. Other than a sink and toilet, it contained a shower enclosure so small a grown person would have to step outside to change their mind. And yet someone had ripped the plastic shower curtain from the railing and it lay in tatters on the floor, sprinkled with shattered glass shards. The rest of what would have been a water glass sat on the edge of the sink, its jagged edges tinged with what looked like blood. Nico's stomach dropped. Surely not...?

Nico turned back to the bedroom area. Except for the bed, nothing else looked out of place. Francesca's dresser drawers were closed, and when he slid a couple of them open, nothing looked amiss.

As he pieced together the clues, Nico came to a sickening realization. The man who'd attacked him had clearly not been alone. He must have had an accomplice who took Francesca with him. Had the one who tackled him stayed behind to search her apartment and Nico interrupted him? But what would someone hope to gain by snatching Francesca? Or were they looking for something they assumed she knew about what Ariana was about to expose?

Tell anyone what you know, and you'll be next.

He dropped to the edge of the exposed spring bed and ran a hand across his scalp. Someone thought Francesca possessed information they wanted. *Ariana. God. Please, someone, give me a sign before it's too late. What's happened to Francesca and where did you send my son?*

With Francesca gone, Nico headed straight for the police station on Archbishop Street. Although he had his doubts they'd be any more efficient than their counterparts on Gozo, he knew he had to at least make a missing person report. Instinct had told him he could trust Francesca when he met her in person; nonetheless, something niggled at the back of his mind. Even though he understood her reticence, why hadn't she reported the threatening note to the police? At the same time, he was hardly beyond reproach. That he'd entered Francesca's apartment illegally could implicate him in her disappearance. Further, as an officer of the law, he should have called the police immediately after he was attacked.

He did a quick replay in his mind: What had he touched when he was there? *The door handle for starters, you idiot.* And, of course, the elderly neighbor had seen him, as had those who'd come to her aid. Given that she'd been taken to hospital, the police had probably questioned her already. One way or another, it was going to come out that he was there, so there was no point delaying the inevitable.

Nico approached the neoclassical building that said

Pulizija Valletta on the front. He took a deep breath and pulled open the green wooden double doors. A woman in uniform behind the security desk asked the nature of his business.

Nico handed her his business card. "I'd like to register a missing person."

"Certainly, please sign in here and I'll find someone to assist you."

After receiving a visitor's badge, possibly expedited by his title of Calabria's special prosecutor, Nico was ushered up a flight of ancient stone stairs and into a small meeting room. *Here we go again,* he thought as he waited for a good-cop-bad-cop duo to arrive and take his statement. Or, more likely, interrogate him.

The door opened and a man, not wearing a police uniform, came in carrying a bottle of water and two glasses. Not disposable cups, Nico noted. Glasses that DNA would adhere to if he were naïve enough to accept a drink of water.

After depositing the water and glasses on the table between them, the man held out his hand and smiled. "I'm Inspector Mifsud. I understand you'd like to report a missing person."

A detective inspector, on a first interview for a missing person? Now, Nico was certain his title had upped the ante. Mifsud gestured for him to be seated, then took a seat across from him. He removed a small notebook and pen from his breast pocket, then placed Nico's business card on the table in front of him. "It's a pleasure to have you in our midst, Sinjur Moretti. Please accept my deepest condolences on the loss of our most prominent prosecutor, Ariana Calleja. I followed a number of the joint cases you worked together."

Well, that didn't take long. *That's* why they'd sent in the big guns. "Thank you."

"I understand you wish to report a missing person. How long has he or she has been missing?"

"It's a woman by the name of Francesca Bruno." *Shit, what date had they met at the café?* "It was Friday. I'm sorry, I can't remember the date."

Mifsud looked at his watch. "So that was May tenth. And you haven't seen or spoken to her since?"

"No."

"With due respect, sinjur, then how do you know she is missing? Were you due to meet her?"

Nico swallowed hard. *Madonna!* "Because I . . . I called on her and she wasn't at home."

"You mean you phoned her, and she didn't answer?" The detective's pen was poised for Nico's answer.

"Well, I did that, too. But no, I went around to her apartment." God, he could do with a drink. The water sat on the table. It would taste so good right now.

"I see." The detective smiled. "Perhaps she had just gone out."

"She wasn't at home, but her door was open." That wasn't completely true, but it was close enough. "And I went in."

Inspector Mifsud's pen stopped moving, and he looked up.

"Without her being there?" The officer reached for the jug of water and offered Nico a glass.

Here goes nothing, Nico thought. "I, uh . . . I had just gone partway into the apartment when I was attacked."

"By someone already inside?"

What the hell—having his prints and saliva on a glass of water couldn't be any worse than the incriminating fingerprints they'd find at Francesca's apartment. Nico accepted the glass and took a large gulp of cold water.

He thought back to the gentle ripple of the curtain inside

the apartment right before someone had flattened him like an ant. "Yes, I'm assuming my attacker was already inside. But I suppose he could have come in behind me." He fished in his pocket and produced the note Francesca had found slipped under the door of her apartment. He put it on the table between them.

The formerly relaxed atmosphere was suddenly charged with tension. The detective sat back in his chair. "Where did you get this?"

"Francesca Bruno gave it to me the first and last time I saw her."

Mifsud frowned, then rose from his chair and made for the door, taking the note with him. "Wait here."

Ten minutes later, the inspector returned to the room with a fresh pitcher of water. He offered to refill Nico's glass and when he shook his head, he resumed his seat across the table and opened his notebook.

"Mr. Moretti, as I consider you to be the victim of an assault, and possibly a witness to Miss Bruno's disappearance, I have not offered you a solicitor. And there is no need to record this interview. However, I'm sure you understand the importance of telling me everything you can. Are we clear?"

Abundantly, Nico thought, resisting the urge to squirm under Mifsud's gaze. "*Si.* Yes, sir," he replied.

"Good. Now can you please tell me how long the note you gave me has been in your possession?"

Nico cleared his throat. "As I mentioned, Miss Bruno gave it to me when I met her for the first time on Friday, May tenth. It was the day after I arrived in Malta."

"And you met with her for what reason?"

"To see what more she could tell me about the last days before Ariana Calleja's death. Miss Bruno was Ariana's close friend and personal assistant. "

"And you didn't see her again after that?"

"No."

"Why did you go to her apartment this morning?"

Where should he start? "I couldn't reach her by phone after my return from Gozo. I needed to tell her about Lydia Rapa, who Miss Bruno had referred me to."

Mifsud stopped writing and looked up from his notebook. "The MP that died in the automobile accident?"

"Yes. Miss Bruno thought she could give me information that might be important in Ariana's assassination." Nico paused. "But what happened to Lydia wasn't an accident."

The inspector gave Nico a quizzical look. "Why do you say that?"

"Because I witnessed it happen. Someone deliberately ran her off the road."

Mifsud wrote something in his notebook and then put down his pen. "That's a substantial claim, Mr. Moretti. Did you tell this to the Gozo police?"

Nico nodded and proceeded to explain everything that had happened, including the interview, a.k.a. interrogation they subjected him to.

A n hour of intense questioning later, the inspector put away his notebook. He'd given the note threatening Francesca to an officer to put in an evidence bag, but Nico knew there was little likelihood of it providing any clues to her disappearance. He'd been on the verge of telling Mifsud about Max, but given the shoddy way the police had handled the investigation into Ariana's death—or *not* handled it—he didn't know if he should trust him. While still polite, it was obvious the deference with which Mifsud had initially treated him had turned to something more. Skepticism? Nico wondered as he gathered his things and followed the inspector down the corridor and into the elevator.

"I've already dispatched a forensics team to Miss Bruno's residence," Mifsud said. He paused, as if weighing what he was about to say next. "Mr. Moretti, I understand your desire to protect your own culpability, but as an officer of the law, well . . ."

Nico finished the detective's sentence in his head. *I should have contacted the police immediately, and he was well within his rights to report me to my superiors.*

The elevator doors opened on the ground floor and Mifsud stepped aside for Nico to exit. "I'm assuming you plan to remain in Malta for the time being?"

In other words, don't leave town.

Nico removed his visitor's badge and deposited it in the basket at reception. "You have my card, Inspector. I'll be at your disposal."

Chapter Eleven

With nothing more he could do regarding Francesca's disappearance, Nico returned to his hotel to catch up on some emails. At the top of his inbox was Gina's email advising him she still could not reach either Ervio De Rosa or Vincenzo Testa and she was needed on an urgent case. The burning question on his mind was why neither reporter had come forward after Ariana's murder. Given their mutual investigative interests into corruption, Nico assumed they would be obsessed with discovering who might have ordered her assassination. And possibly wondering if they'd be next. Perhaps that would explain their unavailability.

With Gina otherwise tied up, Nico resumed the search for the journalists. At last count, they had eight mobile numbers between them. So, it was with some surprise when Nico's second call hit pay dirt. Sort of. A woman answered the phone. After he asked to speak to Ervio De Rosa, she replied in rapid Italian that he had the correct number, but she didn't know where he was or when he'd be back. The more Nico peppered the woman with questions, the more agitated she got, until she hung up on him. But not before he heard children screaming in the background. The journalist had a family. Was that why he'd disappeared? To keep them safe.

After several more fruitless dials, Nico gave up and called the editor of the newspaper both men worked for. Another abrupt conversation ensued, during which the editor said he'd have to check Nico's credentials before giving him any information and then hung up. *Stronzo!* He couldn't have done that by doing a quick Google search while he was on the damned phone? Frustrated, Nico shoved his mobile in his pocket and headed down to the front desk.

He'd been well into his extended time with the police when Nico realized he'd left Gabriela in his room, and Inspector Mifsud had permitted him to call the hotel. A housekeeper had already cleaned up the poor thing's accident and had taken her to the reception desk where she'd remained ever since. Nico found her curled up in her new bed—a leftover from the innkeeper's beloved late labrador, Monty. He inquired if he might take her for a walk and couldn't explain his disappointment when told she'd just returned from one. The canine didn't even open an eye at the sound of his voice.

With no dog to walk and still needing to kill time in the slim hope he'd receive a callback from the wretched newspaper editor, Nico walked up the road that led to the main square. This time, when he arrived at Daphne Galizia's shrine, it looked slightly disheveled. As Francesca had said: the street sweepers had torn it down the previous night—at the behest of the government—only to have the residents rise in arms and resurrect it again. *Only in Malta.*

When his mobile rang, no caller ID came up on the display. Nico gazed at the framed photograph at the center of Galizia's shrine as he took the call.

"*Ciao*, Nicoló Moretti speaking."

"Signore Moretti? Ciao. This is Vincenzo Testa. I believe you've tried to get in touch with me. Several times."

"Ah, Signore Testa, thank you for calling me back."

The journalist's tone was warm and apologetic. "I'm sorry I can only speak a minute or two. I'm about to board a flight. My editor said this is about Ariana."

"It is." Nico spoke quickly. "I understand that before her death she sent you a copy of her investigative files." He still couldn't wrap his head around Ariana sharing her prosecutorial notes with journalists. Albeit ones with impressive credentials.

Testa said nothing. If it weren't for Nico hearing various flight announcements in the background, he would have thought he'd lost the call. "Signore Testa, are you still there?"

Testa finally spoke. "How do you know that?"

"She sent copies to you, Ervio De Rosa and one other journalist. I've tried to reach De Rosa, but the woman I spoke to wouldn't tell me his whereabouts."

"I asked you how you know that?" Testa's tone was now frosty. "And who might the other journalist be?"

Was he really not aware the other journalist was Elle Sinclair, or was he testing Nico?

"Look, I have to go," Testa said. "They're announcing last boarding for my flight. I'll try to call you when I get to my destination."

Before Nico could protest, Testa hung up. *Merda.*

He stood gazing at the photograph of Daphne Galizia, her face illuminated by candles. Again, he saw Ariana's face staring back at him. Pleading him to do something.

.   .   .

W hen the editor no longer accepted his calls, and Testa hadn't called back as promised, Nico called his second-in-command.

"There were flight departures being announced while I spoke with him," Nico told Sergio on the phone. "Find out what flight he boarded." If they could nail it down to one or two strong possibilities, Nico's prosecutorial authority allowed him to pull the passenger manifests from the airlines. In the meantime, he attempted several calls to Ervio De Rosa's other numbers, each time reaching voicemail. Which, as Nico's assistant had said, was still full. With each dead-end, his frustration mounted.

Even though Nico was undoubtedly under scrutiny by Valletta's police, he was legally free to return to Calabria, though doing so would be ill-advised. Inspector Mifsud had been appropriately deferential at the start of the interview. However, his tone changed dramatically after Nico admitted to entering Francesca's apartment illegally as well as the threatening note he hadn't reported. Regardless, returning home wasn't an option until he found her. Dead or alive. Meanwhile, all Nico could think about was a five-year-old little boy somewhere in a strange place without his mother. Nico prayed Max hadn't seen the news about her death. *Why couldn't you have told me, Ariana? Even if you didn't want to be with me, I could have kept him safe.*

It had occurred to Nico several times that the subject of Max had been noticeably absent from his conversation with Elle at Dingli Cliffs. He assumed if she had known about him, she would have said something. Then again, perhaps she was wondering the same thing about him. Somehow, he'd have to figure out a way of finding out. If only he could ask Francesca about her.

. . .

Nico sat in the passenger seat as Elle maneuvered the rental car out of Valletta's city limits and headed toward the ancient walled city of Mdina. Admiring the scenery as they drove through the picturesque countryside, he pondered how best to question her about the other two reporters. And Max. She'd had ample opportunity to bring them up in conversation, but she hadn't.

"Do you know if Ariana sent her files to any members of Journalists for Justice other than yourself?" He hoped he sounded casual.

Elle shook her head without taking her eyes off the road. "Not that I'm aware of, but I suppose it's possible. We all pledge to carry on each other's work if anything were to happen to one of us. Why do you ask?"

He hesitated. It was unethical, if not illegal, for a prosecutor to share information with journalists, no matter how highly regarded they might be. So why had Ariana done so? But he didn't want to risk offending Elle. "Do you have specific names of others who are members of Journalists for Justice?" he asked.

"You mean is there a formal list somewhere?" She shook her head. "I haven't a clue, but I know there's a lot of us working on these corruption stories worldwide." She took her eyes off the road briefly and looked over at Nico. "Do *you* know who Ariana might have sent her notes to?"

Nico scratched his head. "Not for sure, but Ervio De Rosa or Vincenzo Testa come to mind. Do you know either of them?"

"Not personally. We don't travel in the same circles, but I certainly admire their work." This time, she looked over at him, her expression relaxed. "Is there something you'd like to ask me, Nico? I get the feeling you're on a fishing expedition."

He felt his face flush. "No, not at all. Like you said, you knew of their work and I thought one of them might have contacted you after Ariana's murder, that's all."

"Well, they might have tried to, but as you know, I left London for Gozo immediately after I learned of her death."

If she'd been to Gozo in the past, maybe she knew about Max after all.

"Back at Dingli Cliffs you asked me if I knew what Ariana was working on before her death. As I said, she was juggling several investigations at once and all had significant implications for those alleged to be involved. As you undoubtedly know, Ariana never did anything half-way.

Nico nodded, remembering back to his heated discussions with her.

"As I mentioned," Elle said, breaking into Nico's thoughts, "I was working a story about Baldisar Bank in the UK while Ariana investigated in Malta. We discovered the bank was in bed with a pharmaceutical company, Heritage Pharmaceuticals, that had a revolutionary new drug that could inhibit cancer cells." She paused as she swerved around a slow-moving truck carrying farm equipment.

Nico surreptitiously fastened his seat belt. "I thought that Britain's FCA didn't permit the bank to sign up UK accounts. Did that only apply to individuals and not corporations?"

"No, that very much applied to corporations. But the Heritage Group is registered in Malta and they own Heritage Pharmaceuticals. That loophole made it possible for them to do business with Baldisar Bank. They were one of the bank's most lucrative clients."

A vehicle tried unsuccessfully to merge into their lane. Elle sped up to prevent it from cutting in. Nico was grateful the Maltese drove on the left side of the road, and it wasn't the passenger's side that would take the brunt of a side-on collision. Elle seemed oblivious to the rude hand gesture from the driver she'd just cut off.

"That is," she continued, "until someone in the university's lab discovered that some of their research that had been applauded in the medical journals had been falsified."

"That couldn't have been good," Nico agreed, "but it wasn't the bank's fault. They'd have no liability."

"Except that it wasn't just the bank backing the pharmaceutical company, but several of Alesandru Baldisar's shell companies were heavily invested too. If it got out that the research was in question, he would stand to lose millions. And the losses the bank would suffer could have gone into the billions."

Nico let out a low whistle. "What happened to the person who had the inside information?"

Elle took her eyes off the road and looked over at him long enough to make him clutch the edges of his seat. "He was blown up in a car bombing. In Saint Julian's, if I recall."

Nico thought back to his video call with Pezzente. The three businessmen were killed by the same type of remote device that had killed Ariana. Pezzente had said one victim had worked for a pharmaceutical company. But that they were killed for skimming from a money-laundering scheme. Mulling over that apparent discrepancy, and nervous that Elle would take her eyes off the road again, he remained silent for the rest of the drive.

Once they had parked the car and walked into Mdina's historic city center, Nico suggested they get a bite to eat. He hoped some food would steady his nerves, which still jangled from her driving. Not to mention his unease about how her story differed quite significantly from Pezzente's.

They found a café half a block off the main square. As Nico sat across the table from Elle, the intensity of her pale blue eyes struck him again. But rather than refreshing pools that you'd want to swim in, they were deep, icy, as if you'd drown. "So tell me again why we're here," he said.

"The ground-breaking cancer drug I was telling you about?" Elle said. "The lead PhD responsible for developing it for Heritage Pharmaceuticals was a woman by the name of Dr. Anna Braithwaite. She's originally from Malta but she took her husband's surname when she married. She still keeps an apartment here. Anyway, once her research came to light she got a ton of media coverage—quite unusual for a scientist in the UK—because the drug could target and kill the rarest and most aggressive cancer cells without damaging the healthy ones. It wasn't a cure for cancer, but it was the next best thing."

She paused while their food was delivered. Nico unwrapped his cutlery from his napkin, then raised his water glass. *"Buon appetito."*

Elle cut into her fried rabbit livers, pink and nestled on a bed of wild mushrooms and fennel. As she chewed with gusto, all Nico could think about were the hares and rabbits he'd observed running freely on the grounds of his hotel. He speared an olive from his plate of *ftira*, a traditional Maltese dish of tuna, sun-dried tomatoes and capers. And tried not to think of little liverless bunnies. Prematurely balding with geeky round spectacles, he was also pescatarian.

"Anna's husband, Clarence Braithwaite, was also a highly regarded postdoctoral research scientist who was on the fast track to becoming a professor at Cambridge. He worked with Anna, supervising part of the team that was developing the drug. Word in the research community, however, was that there was some professional jealousy between the two of them."

"Between a husband and wife on the same team." Nico shook his head. "That really happens?"

"More often than you'd think. Clarence was working his ass off trying to get the trials approved so the drug could go to market, and when some of the data was found to be faulty, rumors abounded that Anna Braithwaite was trying to pin the blame on him. Clarence allegedly complained to a colleague that thanks to her, his future career was ruined."

Nico raised an eyebrow. "And you know this, how?"

Elle put down her fork and knife, having finished her lunch while Nico was only halfway through his. "Give me some credit. I didn't get to be where I am without excellent sources. Now, I need hard evidence. And that, to answer your question, is why we're here."

"What, because two scientists were having professional and marital problems?"

Seemingly unaware Nico hadn't finished eating, Elle threw some euros on the table and got up to leave. "That car bombing I told you about? One of the victims was Clarence Braithwaite."

T hey stood outside the bistro, having finished lunch. Well, at least Elle had.

"Anna Braithwaite's apartment is here in Mdina? Even if she was responsible for the drug trials going awry, surely that's a matter for the UK authorities? What are you going to do, walk up to the woman's front door, ring the bell and ask if she fiddled with the drug trials and tried to pin it on her husband?" Nico berated himself for not asking for specifics when Elle suggested he come with her to Mdina.

"I wouldn't have brought us up here unless I knew she wouldn't be at home. I happen to know she's not even in the country at the moment."

"So why did we come if she's not here . . . ?"

Then the penny dropped.

Nico shook his head. "Oh, no, we're not. We are *not* breaking into her apartment."

"Suit yourself." Elle shrugged. "Ariana would have done it. With or without your help." And she strode off.

Porca miseria! While his prosecutor's conscience shrieked in protest, Nico took off down the narrow cobblestone street just in time to see Elle disappear around the corner.

I f anyone had told Nico he'd be standing on a landing, keeping an eye out for unexpected guests while an investigative journalist broke into a respected researcher's apartment, he would have said they were delusional. While he had caught up with Elle as she marched determinedly down the road that led to Braithwaite's apartment, he flatly refused to take part in the break-in. One illegal entering in two days was more than he had an appetite for. Nonetheless, he kept his mobile in hand, ready to text her if anyone showed up. She seemed a bit fickle about when he was only permitted to use Yandex versus instant messaging.

At the fifteen-minute mark, he texted her.

N: How much longer?
E: Almost done.

Five minutes later, she emerged with her handbag and mobile in hand. Nico saw a pair of blue Latex gloves peeking out of the bag as she checked the door had locked behind her. He didn't even want to venture a guess as to how she got inside Braithwaite's apartment without damaging the lock. For a journalist, the woman certainly came prepared.

They walked in silence back to the car. While Elle seemed in no hurry, he was more than anxious to get the hell out of the walled city in case someone had spotted them. Once back in the car, Nico let out a sigh.

"You're wound tighter than a piano wire," Elle said as she started the car. "We should have stopped for a drink on the way out. You look like you could use one."

"I don't need a drink." His lunch roiled in his gut. He wished he had some water. Then he wished he hadn't thought about that, as it reminded him of his meeting with Mifsud. The detective had probably dropped Nico's water glass into an evidence bag before he had even left the building.

"Aren't you going to ask me if I found anything?" Elle said as she maneuvered the car out of the parking area and onto the main road.

When Nico didn't reply, she handed him her phone. As she checked her side mirror and merged into the traffic, he scrolled through the photos. There must have been a couple dozen. Some were obviously rooms in Braithwaite's apartment, the rest looked to be scientific papers. His antenna went up when he got to the last two, which looked like stills taken off a video.

"These look like surveillance shots. Do you know who the subject is?"

"Now you're asking the right questions," Elle replied. "I shot those two from an envelope of original photographs I found locked in Braithwaite's desk drawer."

Nico cringed. Elle had broken into the woman's desk.

"That, my friend, is Dr. Clarence Braithwaite."

"Why would—?" He looked at her. "You think Anna had something to do with her husband's murder?"

Elle shrugged as she sped up to pass a car in front of them. "You never know what someone might do given the right circumstances. She had incredible stature in the research community. If he knew she was responsible for the faulty research... well, her career would be over."

"Jesus."

"Speaking of which, what do you really know about Francesca Bruno?"

What? Nico hadn't seen that coming. He swallowed his surprise and again tried to sound casual. "Apparently, she was Ariana's assistant, but they were lifelong friends, going all the way back to boarding school. Why?"

"Ariana never talked about her, that's all."

Nico had to admit she'd never mentioned Francesca to him either. But then again, she hadn't mentioned she had a child either. *His* child. "Never?"

Elle shook her head. "Who knew you were on Gozo when Lydia Rapa was killed?"

Nico looked over at the sharp outline of her profile. Elle kept her eyes on the road.

His heart sank. Francesca had told him what ferry Lydia would be on and how to spot her. She knew there was only one route from the ferry and how long it took to drive it. But that didn't make any sense. She would have had no way of knowing Lydia would stop off at The Fishing Eagle. Unless she had eyes on the ground. But what possible motive would she have to do harm to the woman who could have helped solve Ariana's murder?

Chapter Twelve

With his mind still reeling from his trip to Mdina, Nico needed to do what he did best when he was at an impasse: map things out on paper. When he returned to the hotel, he asked one of the staff if they had any butcher paper. The man looked confused. After further explanation that it was used to wrap food, Nico saw a spark of recognition light up the young man's face.

"We don't have such an item, Sinjur Moretti, but my friend has the delicatessen down the road." He snapped his fingers. "Give me ten minutes and I will get some for you."

In less than that, he arrived at Nico's door with an enormous ream of brown wrapping paper. He seemed delighted, even as he refused a tip, that he could be of help. He'd also obtained the felt marker pen and adhesive tape Nico had requested.

He closed the door, then ripped a length of paper from the roll and taped it to the wall at eye level. On it, he drew a circle. Around its perimeter he wrote the names of all the people he'd met or knew of during his investigation into

Ariana's death. Next, he drew lines between the people he knew to be connected to others. Then, as he would do in the boardroom of his prosecutor's office, he paced his tiny room, muttering to himself.

Ariana trusted three people: Francesca Bruno, Elle Sinclair and Lydia Rapa. One, allegedly a friend that dated back to boarding school, another an investigative journalist, and the last an MP who, despite their political differences, became a close friend and confidante. All the other names had a straight line running toward the center. They all had connections to Ariana, but did they have a connection to each other?

He stood back, trying to gain some perspective. Obviously, Francesca and Lydia knew each other because it was Francesca who'd told Nico how to find the MEP on the Friday afternoon ferry. And Lydia admitted Francesca had visited her with Ariana and Max on several occasions. Next, he moved to Elle Sinclair. She said she hadn't met Francesca and that Ariana never mentioned her. That was odd, given that Lydia Rapa had met Francesca several times.

Nico put the cap on the felt pen and tapped it against his chest. Elle and Ariana had been friends and colleagues since meeting years ago at a charity fundraiser in the UK. Wouldn't Elle have known about Max? And yet, she hadn't mentioned him. And wouldn't Francesca's name have come up in relation to the boy if anything were to happen to Ariana?

Drawing another line, Nico connected Elle to Alesandru Baldisar. She knew him, both from her investigations into his bank and the society wedding at an estate in the UK. She had thought the man Baldisar was arguing with was possibly Russian, but given the ilk of the bank's clients both Francesca and Elle had told him about, that could mean anything. Right now, possible money-laundering wasn't Nico's top priority. Finding out who ordered Ariana's assassination was the only thing on his mind. Not to mention finding his son.

Nico drummed the pen against the desk. He was missing something. But what? Absently, he reached out to stroke Gabriela, forgetting she was snuggled up in her new bed downstairs. He dropped to the end of the bed and sat stewing in the growing darkness.

Then there were the two other journalists. Sergio had been unsuccessful in finding out what flight Testa had boarded, and there was no answer when Nico tried calling him back. He never did manage to track down De Rosa. Obviously, both had gone into hiding. But from whom? Ariana's killer?

So much for the Journalists for Justice code to continue the work of a fallen comrade. It looked increasingly like they had ditched Ariana's memory in favor of their own well-being. But then again, who could blame them?

He needed to talk to Elle and find out what more she could tell him about the journalists' organization. After sending her an encrypted message for her to contact him, Nico sat at the tiny desk in his room and reviewed the notes he'd tacked to the wall. Four women, two of whom were dead, the third was missing and could well be dead. They all knew about the existence of Max. Was Francesca snatched because they thought she knew what Ariana was about to expose? If so, if she did know more than she'd let on, that could be the one thing that could save her. But after that? Nico's blood ran cold. If she couldn't or wouldn't tell them what they wanted to know, then all bets would be off.

He rose from his chair and paced the small room. A ping from his computer signaled a message from Elle.

E: Turn on the news!

N: Why?

E: Just turn it on!

He found the remote buried under a pillow and clicked on the local news station.

The banner along the bottom of the screen read, *Breaking News*. He hit the button to unmute the sound.

"*We're just now learning that a few hours ago,*" the female news anchor announced with great drama, "*police staged simultaneous raids on Malta's most prestigious family-run private bank and several of its clients. FBI and Europol agents jointly launched what sources tell us was a highly orchestrated siege on Baldisar Bank branches in the UK and Malta, as well as at the home of the bank's CEO, Alesandru Baldisar.*"

Nico sat down heavily on the bed. There was a close-up of what were apparently the banker's wife and children standing in their nightclothes outside a house, shielding their eyes from the television camera lights. His heart went out to them. But where was Baldisar himself? He wasn't there among his terrified family. Out at a "meeting" in the wee hours of dawn? Or had someone tipped him off and made sure he wasn't there for the police raid? Leaving his family to take the brunt of the police and media assault.

The anchor was back on-screen, and she took a quick breath as if even that might rob her audience of life-sustaining information. "*The bank has often been cited for having dragged their heels in implementing stringent FINTRAC regulations. The charges leveled against Baldisar Bank include money-laundering, conducting business ille-gally in the UK, and not providing financial regulators with proof of adequate oversight in a timely manner. On a personal level, Mr. Baldisar has been charged with fraud, corruption and bribery.*"

Again, the camera swept away from the reporter's face and a grainy video clip appeared on-screen. It showed someone reported to be Baldisar exchanging an envelope with a second man. Nico's throat went dry. Elle had told him of this exact exchange at Dingli Cliffs.

He leaned forward and squinted at the screen. The tall man accepting the envelope looked familiar. Wait, no, it couldn't be . . . ? In reaching for the package, the man's shirt-sleeve rode up and on his wrist was a distinctive Rolex Oyster watch. Exactly like the one he'd observed Investigator Pezzente wearing.

As the reporter's voice faded into the background, Nico's thoughts ran amok. Surely the PM's investigator couldn't be behind this? He felt sick. From Lydia Rapa being deliberately run off the road to Francesca's disappearance—Pezzente had known Nico's whereabouts the entire time he'd been in Malta. And from what Elle had said on the drive to Mdina, he'd lied about the car bombing outside the hotel in St. Julian's. He said they'd been killed for skimming off a money laundering operation. The only thing Nico prayed Pezzente *didn't* know was where he was currently staying.

He flipped through the TV channels again. Nico was beginning to fear that it was more than a coincidence that only a day after he'd been attacked and Francesca had disappeared, news of Baldisar Bank was breaking.

After turning off the television, he remained perched on the end of the bed, in the dark. He was ready to call Pezzente and tell him what a son of a bitch he was and report him to the authorities. But then the reality of what he'd just seen sunk in: When it came to investigating Ariana's murder, Pezzente *was* the authority. The shocking realization that Pezzente could be both the investigator and the *investigated* hit Nico like a sucker punch to the gut.

He unclenched his fists and shook the tension from his neck and shoulders. As angry as he was, he had bigger fish to fry. The authorities could deal with Baldisar and Pezzente if, indeed, they were connected. At this stage, he didn't really give a rat's ass about two men in a sea of corruption. The authorities in both countries could sort that out. Or not. It appeared to have nothing to do with Ariana's murder, or Max.

If he was going to find his son, he needed to play his cards close to his chest. Francesca had said she didn't know where Max was but based on what Elle said driving back from Mdina, Nico was no longer sure. While he didn't know either woman very well, he was inclined to trust an accredited journalist over a part-time assistant cum nanny. If there was even a remote possibility that Francesca had lied to him, he needed to find her alive and well. She could be the sole person who could tell him what Ariana was about to announce before she was killed. And Max's whereabouts.

Early the next morning

"Where the hell have you been?" demanded the man's wife. "I've been trying to reach you all night!" Her voice was so shrill he held the phone away from his ear as he paced the deck of his private yacht. "And that cheap tramp the paparazzi caught you with. I don't care about your affairs, we passed that bridge a *long* time ago, but your children. How do you think they feel?"

"Settle down, Paola. I've got this." When has the woman ever worried about being shamed? His frequent affairs were public knowledge. They'd been going on for years—behind her back for a while, but now he didn't even bother hiding it. All that mattered to her was that her place in Malta's high society was sustained, and he'd given her that and more. Secretly, she was probably happy to be written about in the society papers.

"Take the children and go to the country house," he said. "You'll be safe from prying eyes there."

"We can't go anywhere, you stupid man! There are photographers everywhere."

He sighed. This was not how things were supposed to be.

"Did you hear me?"

He gave a huge sigh. "Just do it, OK? I don't have time for this."

Mercifully, his other phone rang. "Paola, I have to go—"

"Don't you dare hang up on me, you miserable piece of shit—"

She was still screaming when he hung up and picked up the other mobile. "It's about time. What's taken you so long?"

"Ah, so you've been expecting my call," a robotic voice said.

Abruptly, the man stopped pacing the deck. "Who is this?"

"That's not important. What's important is what I know about you and Heritage Pharma, among other things."

He frantically looked around the vast sea that surrounded him. Despite the miles of ocean around him, his spine tingled as if he were being watched. No, they couldn't be. There wasn't another vessel in sight.

"Are you still there? This is just a friendly conversation. But we can make it more difficult if necessary."

"What . . ." The words caught in his throat. "What do you want?"

"That's much better." The voice was monotone, with no distinguishing accent. It was impossible to even decipher the sex of the speaker.

"I believe you have received some photographs, yes?"

So, this was his blackmailer. Baldisar walked toward the bow and stared out across the deserted stretch of water. They had some intimate photos of him. Big deal. "That's old news, my wife already knows about that. Why should I care?" he said, more emboldened.

"Tsk, tsk, you underestimate me. Your wife might care about those photos. Perhaps even your superiors. But me? The documents I possess have much more significance, I assure you."

His antenna went up. *Documents*? They had something other than embarrassing photographs.

"I know you had a research scientist killed. The one who was about to blow the whistle on the faulty drug trials at Heritage Pharma."

He sunk heavily into a nearby deck chair. "I have no idea what you're talking about," he said with all the calm he could muster.

"You were heavily invested in Heritage. I believe the recent dumping of your personal Heritage shares would be referred to as insider trading."

It must be someone associated with the company he used to make his stock trades. Some low-life scum who had seriously misjudged him.

"I don't know who the hell you think you're dealing with, but—"

"No, *you* don't know who you're dealing with. Now, shut the fuck up and listen to me very carefully. I'm only going to make this offer once. After that I go to the authorities."

The abrupt change in tone had him rooted to the spot. "What do you want?"

"Very good. Now, isn't it easier to do this in a friendly, cooperative manner?"

Chapter Thirteen

In his private stateroom, he poured himself a stiff drink and considered his options. Whoever was blackmailing him knew precise details about the car bombing that had killed Clarence Braithwaite—the whistleblower who was about to expose the faulty Heritage trials. They also knew about Heritage Pharma and the proliferation of shell companies he'd used to clean the proceeds of crime that ran the gamut from drug dealing to international terrorism. And he wasn't the only one.

He tugged his fingers through his hair. Everything had been running perfectly—like clockwork—for years. How had it all gone so wrong so fast? He'd thought himself invincible. Now, his churning gut told him otherwise. Grimacing, he picked up the phone and hit the speed dial.

"It's me," he said when she answered. "We need to talk, but not on the phone. Can you contact me via our usual means?"

He detected a slight edge to her voice, but she agreed and hung up. He flipped open his laptop and waited.

It was a few minutes before her encrypted message came through.

What's up?
Someone knows about the Heritage.

Through the portal glass he could see storm clouds gathering to the west. He called up to his captain as he waited for her reply.

How do you know?
I'm being blackmailed. We are being blackmailed.
What do you mean "we"?
Can you meet me at our spot at 6 p.m.?
Is that wise? The police are looking for you.
They won't find us there. I'll send the helicopter for you.
All right.

And she signed off.

A s they cruised into the cove of his private island, he couldn't help but admire the view from the boat. High atop a hill, and only accessible by a secure underground elevator, sat the house he had built for his retirement. For the days he'd been counting down to when he could liquidate his formidable assets, cleanly. Before everything had gone so horribly wrong.

The house, though aesthetically pleasing, was built like a fortress. By design, there was no dock. The yacht's captain would anchor out and then, as he had ordered, no crew were to accompany them; only his bodyguard would pilot the launch that would deliver him to the beach.

Likely hearing the noise of the engines, she had come out onto the patio off the main salon. She had on a short dress of some sort and held a drink in her hand. Despite everything on his mind, he felt a familiar stirring in his body.

"Idle off," he said when they reached the shore. "I'm not sure how long I'll be staying."

The bodyguard nodded.

Dusk was falling as he made his way through a fragrant grove of pomegranate and carob trees. The helicopter sat on its pad with the pilot and co-pilot inside. He gave them a nod, then looked into the retinal scanner that would open the elevator. He arrived on the main floor, deposited his bag and laptop and made his way out to the deck.

She turned when she heard him, champagne flute in hand. Under his tutelage, she'd blossomed from a plain, timid researcher to a woman who could hold her own, both intellectually and now, thanks to a little help from his friends in the fashion and beauty industries, the looks department. Her highlighted strawberry-blonde hair was piled in a messy knot on top of her head. The long, tanned legs beneath the filmy shift she wore were the toned limbs of a runner. Since he'd seen her from the boat, she'd put on a loose linen blouse which she'd tied at the waist. He felt another flush of arousal as he stepped toward her.

"Champagne?" she asked, extending a glass toward him.

He took a sip, but the cool liquid did little to assuage his anxiety. She had returned his kiss and embrace, but he could feel the tension in every sinew of her body.

"Who contacted you? How much do they know?"

"I don't know who, but they know everything." Even things he'd conveniently forgotten. He picked up his glass and drained it in one gulp.

"What will you do?"

"It's what *we* must do, my dear."

She froze, her champagne glass clutched in her hand. "What do you mean?"

"They know I found out about the faulty research in the cancer drug trials and that's how I was able to dump my stock before it went public."

Her face shone pale against the darkening sky. "How could they know that?"

They moved inside and he refilled their glasses. She sat on a bar stool watching him while he forced himself to take his eyes off the dark V he could see where her thighs didn't quite meet. That warm spot he knew like the back of his hand.

"It no longer matters *how* they know. What matters now is what we are going to do about it." Was it his imagination or did he detect her wince at the second mention of "we"?

He pulled her into an embrace and started to untie her overblouse, but she wriggled free, taking her champagne with her.

"Clarence Braithwaite was in charge of the particular drug trial that went wrong," she said. "It was awful the way he died in that car bombing, but thankfully that secret died with him."

"Yes, well you have me to thank for that. I had an insider in the lab on my payroll. One that was quite willing to throw you under the bus."

She took a step closer to him. "What are you talking about?"

"He was about to blow the whistle on the faulty research before I could dump my stock. I couldn't let that happen."

"*You* were behind that car bombing? Jesus, what have you done?"

"For Christ's sake, between him and that Calleja woman, they were about to expose us."

Her hand flew to her mouth. "What do you mean, the Calleja woman?" She stared at him, her eyes wide, her expression horrified. "Please don't tell me you were behind her assassination!"

He tamped down the slow rage and indignation that threatened to explode. But he didn't confirm or deny her question. "What matters now is making this go away. Then we can get on with what we've been planning all this time."

"*We* haven't been planning this for a long time. You were corrupt long before I met you. If it wasn't for me, you wouldn't have had that chance to divest yourself of your Heritage holdings."

His blood, which had run hot at the mere thought of having sex with her, now coursed through his veins like ice water. Yes, they were in deep, but he was not going to be sold down the river by this tart. "For which they can put you in prison for a very long time, my dear."

Her eyes narrowed. "You bastard. How dare you!"

He softened his tone. Brought it down a notch. "Look, I can pay the money, then it will all be over. If we don't cooperate, we will both go to prison for the rest of our lives."

Standing ramrod straight, she hugged her arms as if suddenly chilled. She fixed him with a piercing stare. "I'm done. I'm going to the police." Her voice was so quiet he had to strain to hear her.

He sighed and shook his head. "You stupid bitch. As you said, the proof died with Clarence Braithwaite. All you have to do is deny everything and we'll be fine."

Like a rocket, she crossed the space between them and slapped him hard across the face. "Don't you goddamn use 'we' again. I am highly respected, for God's sake! It will be your word against mine." Her eyes were wild. "I will not do this."

She glared at him while he fought to keep his fists at his sides. He would not stoop to hitting a woman. He thrust his hands into his pockets.

A few moments later, he heard the soft ping of the elevator opening behind him.

The blood drained from her face and her eyes widened. "You wouldn't," she whispered, turning to him. "Please, no!"

"You know what to do," he hissed as he walked past the newcomer and the elevator doors shut behind him.

F ollowing his boss's orders, he took the woman to the cavernous basement that served as a safe room should it ever be needed, where he bound and gagged her. He locked the solid steel door behind him and made his way up to the next floor.

He looked around. *So this is how the other half live.* The opulence was astounding. From behind the sheer netting that covered the floor to ceiling windows, he could see his superior under the lights of the beach waiting for the launch that approached the shore. He waited until he'd seen both men board the yacht, the launch had been winched in, and the boat headed out to sea. Then he went downstairs and opened the steel door.

Chapter Fourteen

After their trip to Mdina, Nico had arranged to meet Elle for breakfast. The only place he could think to suggest was the café he and Francesca had gone to the day he'd arrived in Valletta. It was set on a quiet side street close to the hotel. The unhurried walk gave him time to reflect on what it might have been like to be here with Ariana in her native country. Despite her misgivings about the rampant corruption that reined over Malta, he knew it was a place she still loved. If not for the tragic circumstances that had brought him here, he could have walked for miles in the freshness of the early-morning peacefulness. And thought about her and all the memories he treasured.

Soon, the streets would be engorged with tourists, interspersed with locals weaving their way through and around them, no doubt cursing under their breath. In a city so beautiful, it was difficult to remember that its denizens still had to live and work here. Not unlike Tropea.

As he rounded the corner, he saw Elle had secured a table outside and was deeply engrossed typing something on her phone. It was a beautiful morning with the temperature already pleasantly warm. Elle had shrugged off her jacket and was basking in the sun. Nico couldn't help but notice her well-toned arms as she raised her coffee cup to her lips.

She looked up as he approached the table. "I've just ordered, do you know what you'd like?"

Nico turned to their server. "I'll have whatever the lady is having." He'd hoped to run into the waitress who'd given him Francesca's address, but she didn't appear to be working today.

"Catching up on work?" Nico pointed to an open note-book and Elle's mobile phone on the table.

"Somewhat. Actually, I was looking into flights back to the UK."

Nico felt a brief twinge of something—surprise, disappointment? He wasn't sure which. "Oh?"

"Mm. I'm not sure how much longer I can stay on here. Much as I hate to say it, the investigations are in the hands of the authorities now, aren't they? As incapable though they might be. I'm thinking I should get back to London to finish the exposé on Baldisar. Somebody needs to nail that bastard. With the news of the raids fresh in people's minds, it would be perfect timing. I know it sounds a little self-serving but now that I'm freelancing, I can't afford not to scoop the story."

"How soon would you leave?"

"Well, I have a few things to clear up here, but I was thinking of catching a flight tomorrow."

That certainly changed things. It also provided some urgency for him to get off the fence and find out what, if anything, she knew about Max. But how?

Their breakfast arrived, and he was pleasantly surprised to

see they each had a steaming plate of eggs, fried potatoes, toast and sausages, the latter of which he offered to Elle. When she happily scooped them onto her plate, he was reminded of the gusto with which they'd dug into her plate of rabbit livers in Mdina.

"I know it might feel a bit like I'm abandoning ship," Elle said as she stabbed a piece of sausage and chewed it. "But I thought I might actually be of more help from London."

"How so?"

"With my contacts there, I can dig deeper into the whole thing with Dr. Braithwaite's late husband, the whistleblower. And Heritage Pharma. She's apparently taken an indefinite leave of absence, but they still support her lab at the university. But I need to be there on the ground to do that." She took a sip of her coffee. "How much longer will you stay on?"

Come to think of it, Nico wasn't sure how much more time he could take away from his job either, given that he was essentially in Malta for personal reasons. On his last phone call, Sergio had indicated there were rumblings from the higher-ups, questioning Nico's extended absence. He wasn't sure if Mifsud might have reported his inaction to Nico's superiors, but either way, he couldn't imagine leaving Malta until they found Francesca, and he'd located his son.

In that moment, he made his decision. He waited until they'd both finished their breakfasts and the waiter had topped up their coffees before he fingered the worn piece of paper in his trousers pocket. "I know you and Ariana were often investigating the same cases from different angles, but how well did you know her personally?"

Her eyes narrowed. "We were close, why?"

"Did she live alone on Gozo, do you know?" That sounded pathetic, like he was asking about Ariana's love life.

Elle sat back in her chair and stared at him. "Exactly how well did *you* know, Ariana?" she asked, rather sharply. "I would think you, of all people, would have known that."

Checkmate.

"Did she ever mention a little boy to you?" It sounded open-ended enough. He could have been asking about a nephew.

Elle's jaw dropped. "You know about Max," she whispered. Her expression softened, and she leaned across the table. "I'm sorry, Nico, I wasn't sure if you did, hence why I didn't say anything. I've been worried sick about him. Is he all right?"

So it wasn't Elle who Ariana had entrusted with his son.

"I'm sorry, too. It's just that . . . When did you last see him?"

Elle visibly relaxed and took a sip of her coffee. "Oh, that's easy. Ariana brought him to London for his fifth birthday. Twenty-sixth of January. Unfortunately, it was typically filthy, wet weather, but Max didn't seem to notice."

"Did they stay with you?"

"Of course, they always did when they came. We took him on the London Eye," she said. "Ariana insisted on taking Max to the London Dungeons, which I felt wasn't the best choice for a five-year-old, but he was all right. I think we could have left him at the zoo for the day, though— he loved it there so much he wouldn't have noticed we'd gone. We practically had to drag him out even though he was falling asleep." Her eyes lit up as she gave Nico a blow-by-blow description of their days together.

"Ariana always insisted Max write me a thank-you note whenever they'd visit. I've kept every single one of them."

"How did Max address Ariana?" Nico asked.

"What do you mean? She was his mother."

"Yes, but did he call her 'Mummy' or 'Mama'?"

"Oh, 'Mummy.' Always." She looked puzzled. "Why do you ask?"

"The night before Ariana died, she told me she'd sent Max somewhere for his safety. Do you have any idea who she might have entrusted him to?" Nico took a deep breath. "Could it possibly have been Max's father?"

Elle shook her head. "I don't believe so. Ariana never confided in me who Max's father was. As you know, she was very private. But as far as I know, he's never been involved in Max's life."

"Did Max ever stay with her at her apartment here in Valletta?"

"Absolutely not. For security reasons, even her mailing address was a post office box. Very few people knew she had a son."

"So you have no idea where he could be?" Nico asked.

Elle looked as frustrated as Nico felt. "It doesn't make any sense that she wouldn't have at least told *me*." She drew in her breath and fixed him with her glacial stare. "Unless . . ."

"Unless?"

"Well, it's obvious, isn't it? That Francesca Bruno woman must be involved. You said she told you she and Ariana had been friends since boarding school." Elle gave a sniff of disdain. "Personally, I find that suspect, given that I never heard Ariana speak of her."

Nico's heart sank. Was it possible Francesca could have staged her disappearance to look like an abduction? And then gone to be with Max wherever she'd taken him before Ariana died?

It appeared Elle was thinking the same thing. She closed her notebook. "All right, I'll put off returning to the UK until we find out what that bloody woman did with Max."

N ico left Elle at the café, relieved she had decided to stay on in Malta. He was conflicted about his feelings for her. Ariana's death had left such a cavernous hole in his heart. Was he transferring his feelings to Elle? Like Ariana, she was formidable. And she seemed to love Max. Could something grow between them over time? He pushed the thought from his mind.

Elle said she had some errands to run and then planned to return to her hotel to work on the next installment of her exposé on Heritage Pharma. While chatting over breakfast, she admitted to Nico that she had some regrets about leaving her newspaper to go freelance.

"I left the BBC because I refused to abide by their personal safety requirements," she'd said. "But to be honest, I sometimes miss it."

That hardly surprised Nico, but it was the first time he'd observed any sense of apprehension in this otherwise steely woman. He wondered if she had a lover, or a close circle of friends in the UK. Someone she might let her guard down with and show her softer side to.

T here was still no news from the police about Francesca Bruno's disappearance. However, Inspector Mifsud had told Nico that Mrs. Cilia—the elderly woman who'd been hurt during the attack at Francesca's apartment—had been treated and released from the hospital. It was a long shot, but Nico hoped she might shed some light on the comings and goings at Francesca's apartment in the day or two leading up to her disappearance. And whether she had ever seen Max in Francesca's presence.

But instead of Signora Cilia, a young woman in her late twenties or early thirties answered the door.

"Excuse me," he said, offering his card. "I'm Nicoló Moretti. I'm a friend of Francesca Bruno. Is Signora Cilia in?"

The woman smiled warmly upon hearing Francesca's name, and she opened the door wide. "Yes, yes, come in. Please follow me."

Nico followed her down a short hallway and into a small but well-kept living room. Signora Cilia was sitting in a reclining chair, reading. "Sinjur Moretti has come to see you," the younger woman said.

The signora pushed the throw from her lap and began to struggle out of her chair.

"Please don't get up." Nico advanced toward her quickly, offering his hand. "I apologize for popping in unannounced, but I didn't know how to reach you by phone."

The elderly woman took Nico's hand in hers. They were cool and dry to the touch, her fingers gnarled from arthritis. But her eyes, bracketed by decades of lines, burned bright, her expression warm and animated. "I'm so glad you came, sinjur. Please, sit down. Esme, dear, put the kettle on for tea. There are biscuits in the tin above the stove."

"Is Esme your daughter?" Nico asked when she had left to make tea.

"Oh my!" the elderly woman laughed, and her hand flew to her cheek. "You flatter an old woman. No, she is my granddaughter. My daughter—her mother—unfortunately passed some years back. Esme lives with me. I don't know how I would manage without her." She pointed to the bandage still covering a part of her head. "Especially now."

"Yes, I came by to see how you're feeling."

"How kind of you, but it takes a lot more than a bump on the head to keep me down. Soon I will be as right as rain."

Esme arrived with a tray of tea and biscuits, milk, sugar and lemon slices. She laid the tray on the coffee table. "Sinjur, is there anything else I can get for you?"

"No, thank you. This spread looks wonderful. But please, won't you join us?" Nico hoped he didn't appear disingenuous. He had come to check on Signora Cilia's health, but now that he knew Esme lived with her grandmother right across the lane from Francesca's apartment, he was eager to talk to her as well.

Esme looked to her grandmother.

"Yes, bring your tea from the kitchen, dear, and join us. Perhaps you could answer some questions for Sinjur Moretti." She winked at Nico. "At nearly eighty, my memory is not as sharp as it once was. Anything we can do to help find dear Francesca. I was shocked when the police told me she'd gone missing."

"I was wondering if you might have seen anything unusual in the days prior to Francesca's disappearance," Nico said when Esme returned.

"I didn't." Signora Cilia turned to her granddaughter. "Did you, Esme?"

She shook her head. "Not before, no. But afterward, I thought it odd when that man came to the door asking about Francesca."

"What man, dear?" Signora Cilia asked before Nico could.

"You were still in the hospital, Nanna. I thought I'd told

you." She turned to Nico. "A man came to the door and asked if I had a key for Francesca's apartment."

"Was it the police?" Nico asked.

"No, he said he was a friend of Francesca's and she was expecting him. He was to stay a few days and he couldn't understand why she wasn't there. He thought perhaps he could wait inside for her to return."

"My God, child, you didn't give him the key, did you?"

"Of course not, Nanna. I'd never do that. But I did give him her mobile number when he asked for it." Her brow furrowed. "Since then, I've been thinking, if he was that close a friend, he would have already had her number."

Nico agreed. "Can you tell me what he looked like?"

"Swarthy, about five ten. And now that I think of it, he would have been much older than Francesca. Not one of her peers, or a boyfriend, if you know what I mean."

Nico's brain was racing on fast-forward. "Esme, do you think you could give an accurate description to the police?"

She hesitated a moment, looking to her grandmother for approval.

"*Pupa*, tell Sinjur Moretti. Could you give enough of a likeness?"

"Yes, I believe I could."

Nico left Signora Cilia with the promise that either he or the police would be in touch with her shortly. Esme said she had to do a few errands but would be back within the hour.

On the walk back to his hotel, he called and left a message for Mifsud. Like Signora Cilia's granddaughter, Nico highly suspected that the man she'd described was no friend of Francesca's. But if he had anything to do with her disappearance, why would he have gone to her neighbor requesting a spare key? Why not break in like before?

The answer to his question came via a return call from Mifsud. After Nico told him what the young woman had related to him, the detective promised to send a sketch artist around to Signora Cilia's residence that afternoon.

"It's a pity he *didn't* go into Miss Bruno's apartment, legally or otherwise." Mifsud said before hanging up. "After your attack, and her disappearance, we installed a silent alarm inside her apartment. It would have activated our surveillance camera, and we'd have caught him on video. Possibly, he would have stayed there long enough for us to capture him."

Nico's opinion of Valletta's police department, and Mifsud in particular, went up a notch. As he hung up, he couldn't help wishing Signora Cilia's granddaughter had gone against her better judgment and given the swarthy man the key. At least they'd finally have something to go on.

As he continued his walk back to the hotel, he placed several more calls, including one to his office.

"I hate to say this, boss," Sergio said, "but I'm not sure how much longer I can keep making excuses for why you haven't returned from Malta."

Nico felt guilty for putting his second-in-command in such a position, but he cared more about finding Max and Francesca than he did about returning to Tropea. While the timing wasn't ideal, if need be, he'd put in for vacation time. "Leave it with me, Sergio. I'll see how quickly I can tie things up here, or let the brass know if I'm going to take some personal time." Nico put his phone in his pocket as he entered the back lane that was a shortcut to his accommodation. He'd just gone a few steps in when he heard someone call his name.

"Nico Moretti?" a male voice said from behind him.

Startled, Nico turned to see who it was. A man he didn't recognize stood at the entrance to the laneway.

"Yes, what can I do for— "

The words had barely left his lips when a second man darted out from behind a green industrial garbage bin. It happened so fast. Nico felt a rough push from behind, sending him right into the fist of the first man. Someone kicked his feet out from under him. There he lay, with the breath knocked out of him, facedown on the rough cobblestones. He tried to look up to get a better look at his attacker, but before he could gather his wits, two pairs of steel-toed boots pummeled his lower back and sides.

"We've had enough of the likes of you, Mr. Moretti," one of them said. "If you know what's good for you, you'll go home where you came from."

What was he talking about? Nico was trying to make sense of what was happening, but he felt like his head was about to explode. A wave of nausea started in his belly and threatened to make its way up his throat.

The pummeling continued, each kick landed with more force. He tried to roll out of the way, but his feeble effort was met with more blows from the other side.

"Please, I don't—" Another hit.

When he thought he was about to black out, a fist grabbed his hair, lifting his head from the pavement.

"This is a warning. Next time, we won't be so gentle," one of them said.

Nico felt the hot breath in his ear as whoever was kneeling close to him let out a guffaw. He felt a sharp twinge in his neck as it was ratcheted sideways.

A door banged open. "Hey! What are you doing?" someone shouted.

Nico was vaguely aware of a long white apron and a set

of feet standing in an open doorway just down the alley from where he lay. "Get away from him before I call the police!"

Whichever of his attackers had a death grip on his hair released him, and he heard the unmistakable crunch of his nose as his face met the pavement.

Then everything went black.

Chapter Fifteen

Elle gasped when she entered the hospital room. "Jesus, Nico, what the hell happened? You look awful."

Nico turned his head and the pain shot up his neck and into his skull so fast he thought his head would explode. Elle winced.

"It appears . . . two rather large men mistook me . . . for a punching bag in an alley near my hotel." It hurt to breathe and his voice had a nasal quality to it. Judging from the tightness he felt in his nose, he assumed it was broken. He lifted his hand, which was attached to an IV, to touch his face. *Well, there goes my good looks*, he thought sardonically. "How did you know I was here?"

"I called the hotel, and the proprietors told me the police found a receipt from there in your pocket and called them to ask if they knew your next of kin."

Nico couldn't remember anything except praying he wouldn't die alone in a squalid back alley. Then, as the pain intensified, he prayed he would.

As Elle pulled a chair closer to the side of his bed, the door swung open and an amiable-looking man in a white coat entered. "Sinjur Moretti, I'm Dr. Camilleri. How are you feeling?"

Probably as bad as I look, Nico thought. *Maybe worse.* "I've been better."

Elle made to get up. "Would you like me to leave?"

"I'm fine if Sinjur Moretti is." Nico indicated that Elle should stay. Then he wished he hadn't moved his head. The pain brought tears to his eyes.

The doctor flipped through some pages on his clipboard. "We've got the results of your X-rays. I'm sure it will come as no surprise that you have a broken nose. And a couple of lacerations on your face that required stitching. You also have two cracked ribs. You took quite a beating to your lower back and torso, causing a lot of soft-tissue damage."

No shit, Sherlock. Nico could have sworn a fully loaded bus had used his body as a parking spot. He hurt in places he didn't even know he had.

"Although your right kidney is swollen, it doesn't look like there's any serious damage."

Nico raised his eyebrows. Even that hurt.

"As in, it hasn't ruptured," the doctor explained. "We see this type of injury quite commonly in athletes. Even after abdominal blunt force trauma, you should fully recover with conservative management alone. That means staying in the hospital while we monitor your output." He looked at Elle. "Are you family?"

"Yes," Nico replied before Elle could answer.

"Then you won't mind me speaking frankly. You have a catheter." He pointed toward the side of the bed. Nico didn't dare move his head to look, but he assumed a bag containing his most personal bodily fluids hung over the side. It was more than he felt comfortable sharing with Elle at this stage in their professional relationship.

"There is quite a bit of blood in your urine. That's normal and should start clearing in the next few days to a week."

A week! Nico didn't have a damned week. Francesca and Max might not either.

As if reading his mind, Dr. Camilleri continued. "If there is no infection or complications, I could release you within the week, but I must warn you, recovery can take as long as a month. And you will need to be very moderate in your activities or exercise for possibly six or eight months."

He flipped the pages of his clipboard closed. "Now, if you have no further questions, I believe the police are outside and wish to speak with you." He addressed Elle as he left. "The best thing you could do for him is to make sure he doesn't overdo it. Rest and obeying orders will get him out of here faster."

No sooner had the door swung closed than it opened again. Nico was disappointed to see an officious-looking, middle-aged man in plainclothes rather than Inspector Mifsud walk into the room. Without introducing himself, the man looked at Elle. "And you would be?"

This time, before Nico could speak for her, she catapulted from her chair and gave the cop an obvious once-over. Standing directly in his personal space, she towered over him by at least four inches. "And *you* would be?"

"*Sergeant* Panetta." He looked over at Nico. "Inspector Mifsud asked that I see you until he can return to Valletta. I'd like to ask you a few questions." He took a couple of steps back from Elle. "In private."

Mifsud had been here in Valletta when Nico called him minutes before he was attacked in the alley. How long ago was that? How long had he been in the hospital?

"Do you have a card?" Elle asked, as if reading Nico's mind.

The officer reached into his pocket and handed his card not to Elle, but to Nico. "As I said, I need to question you in private."

"Nico, I'm going to run," Elle said. "I have a few things to check out." She flicked the card, making no secret that the officer might be one of them. "I'll be back this evening. Let the nurses know if you'd like me to bring you anything."

She pushed past Panetta, then turned around and addressed him. "By the way, Dr. Camilleri has given strict orders for Mr. Moretti to rest. I'll be asking a nurse to make sure that you don't keep him too long." With that, she yanked open the door and charged out of the room.

W hen Elle returned to the hospital later that evening, she seemed wired. By dinnertime, Nico was running on nothing more than painkillers and some watered-down, nondescript soup. Elle, on the other hand, seemed to have energy to burn.

Half-heartedly, Elle asked if she could remove any of the lids of the rest of the foul-smelling hospital food, to which Nico declined. Judging by her look of relief, he suspected tending to sick people wasn't her strong suit. Seemingly eager to share where she'd spent her day after leaving the hospital, she shoved the meal tray to one side of the table and made room for her laptop. "How was your interview with Sergeant Numbnuts?"

"Nothing earth-shattering. Apparently, he was sending someone around to question the restaurant worker who, fortunately for me, came out for a smoke while I was being attacked." Based on what Francesca had told him about the lack of follow up by the police following Ariana's murder, Nico doubted it would provide anything fruitful. "Other than that, I guess we wait until Inspector Mifsud returns." Somewhere in his room at the hotel was Mifsud's card, but Nico had no idea where it was, or even if it would have the inspector's direct mobile on it.

Elle was so focused on something on her computer that Nico doubted she was even aware he'd answered her question about Panetta.

"Look at this." Elle spun her laptop to face Nico. With the aid of some extra pillows, he could sit up in bed for short periods of time. However, the pain was telling him that time was closing in. While he envied Elle's frenetic energy, he considered suggesting she switch to decaf.

She pointed to the computer screen. "In what appears to be a colossal public-relations move—no doubt a thinly veiled effort to win back the support of Valletta's citizens—the local police have just announced that two people have been taken into custody in connection with Ariana's murder."

Nico sat bolt upright, then winced at the pain. PR stunt or not, at least the authorities finally seemed to be taking her assassination seriously. "Are they holding them at the Valletta police station?" That must be what was holding Mifsud up.

"Not exactly, no," Elle said with a smirk. She tapped a key, and a video started playing. She turned up the sound.

Nico watched closely at what appeared to be a police raid on a bar as it unfolded on-screen. The background was dark except for a few bobbing lights. Flashlights? There were some loud pops like gunfire and the night air lit up. The camera then focused on the front of the building. Seconds later, the doors flew open and people swarmed out into the street like locusts. Police lights illuminated the sky and Nico heard sirens in the background. With the extra light, he could now make out the building clearly.

He leaned forward and squinted. It couldn't be. "Can you

back it up a few seconds?" Elle pressed Pause, slid the red bar at the bottom, then pressed the arrow for play. Nico knew this place. It was a well-known bar frequented mostly by commercial fishermen down by the Port of Tropea. "This is in Calabria, not Malta. I don't understand—"

Elle raised her hand. "Wait, it gets better." She clicked on another link and a second video came up.

Against his better judgment, Nico sat bolt upright and pulled Elle's laptop closer. He pushed the searing pain to the back of his mind. Caught in the lights of the marina's main dock, a stocky man hastily untied the bow and stern lines of a launch before jumping on board. A second man was at the helm. He turned to look over his shoulder, presumably to make sure they were untied before gunning the engine and taking off into the dark. Something about him seemed familiar to Nico, but it was too fast and the video too grainy to make out either of the men's faces.

"It's been all over the news," Elle said. "'Calabrians behind Ariana Calleja's assassination. Malta exonerated of any ties to her death,'" she quoted. "It goes on—do you want me to read more?"

Nico leaned back and closed his eyes.

"I'm sorry, Nico. I know this isn't what you wanted. Sadly, it looks like the two thugs they've apprehended are Italians. And things aren't looking too good for your new prime minister either. The one that was voted in on a vehement anticorruption platform, I might add."

Nico sensed Elle's body as she sat on the side of his bed. His eyelids felt like lead, but he willed them to open.

"From everything I'm getting from my media sources, neither of the arrested men are purported to be that bright." Elle picked absently at some lint on the hospital blanket. "In my opinion, the two thugs that police rounded up at the bar might have detonated the bomb, but they most certainly weren't the masterminds behind it. I think they were working for someone. The question is who.

"I don't believe in coincidences. I think it's highly likely that someone involved in that police raid paid them to take care of Ariana."

A fter an endless night of listening to hospital alarms and nurses waking him to take his vitals, the only thing Nico wanted to see less than another hospital breakfast was Sergeant Panetta. But in he strode, a cup of takeout coffee in hand.

"I thought you might like something other than hospital swill," he said, depositing the coffee on the table beside Nico's bed. "My wife said the only thing that's worse here are the mushy peas."

"Your wife is in the hospital?"

Panetta shook his head. "She works here. She's a nurse on another floor. I was hoping she could quit," he said, rubbing the stubble of his beard. "But after the birth of our third child, that has proven to be impossible."

For some reason, that added a touch of humanity to the man Nico had otherwise disliked at first glance. The cost of living was much higher in Malta than in Nico's native Italy. Feeding three children on a police officer's salary would be a challenge. On the other hand, Nico thought as he inhaled the pungent aroma of dark-roasted coffee, it could also mean the sergeant might be on the take.

"Thank you," Nico said. "Any word from Inspector Mifsud?"

Panetta shook his head. "I haven't checked in with my office yet. I came straight here."

Just to bring me coffee?

"As you are aware, the alley where you were attacked is only minutes away from your hotel. Who knew where you were staying?"

"I don't understand. What do you mean?"

"With the attack so close, your assailants would have had to have known you were staying at the hotel."

Nico considered that for a moment. "Unless I was followed." He instantly wished he hadn't said that.

"Unless you were followed," Panetta agreed. "Where did you say you were coming from?"

I didn't. "I was out doing some errands. You know, the usual things: the pharmacy, the newsstand . . ."

Panetta consulted his notebook. "Your journalist friend, Sinjorina Sinclair. She knew where you were staying, correct?"

He'd checked up on Elle. "Well, yes, but so did several others I've met since arriving in Valletta."

"That's a good place to start." Panetta clicked his pen. "Can you give me a list of names?"

Nico went through everyone he'd met since arriving in Malta. "The hotel staff, obviously." There was the waitress at the café, but he didn't remember telling her where he was staying. Now he felt foolish; he couldn't think of anyone else.

"What about Miss Bruno? I understand she met you at your hotel the day you arrived from Tropea."

How the hell did Panetta know that? He remembered Francesca's warning against using names until they got outside. He'd thought it ridiculous at the time. But someone knew they met. Perhaps he shouldn't be so cooperative with the sergeant for now. "Well, as she has disappeared under suspicious circumstances, I would rather doubt she had anything to do with my attack. Have the police made any progress in their search for her?"

The officer didn't look up from his notebook. "Not that I'm aware of, but possibly Inspector Mifsud can shed more light on that. So there's no one else you can think of who knew where you were staying?"

Nico was racking his brain for anyone he might have forgotten when the door opened, and Elle burst in. She pulled up short on seeing Panetta, and the pair eyed each other like startled cats.

"Sinjorina Sinclair." He gestured to the chair beside Nico's bed. "Please come in. We were just speaking of you."

She ignored the invitation to sit. "Really? And why would that be?"

"I understand you'll be leaving us to go back to London."

What? Elle had told Nico she'd put off her plans for now.

"I hope it's nothing I've done to chase you away from our beautiful city." Sergeant Panetta smiled. It didn't suit him.

When Nico looked at Elle, her cheeks were pink and her eyes had turned a steely glint.

"Sergeant . . . what did you say your name was?"

Nico suspected that Elle never forgot a name, and she was just yanking the officer's chain. Trying to make him feel less important than a flea on a dog.

"Panetta."

"Yes, well, Sergeant Panetta, you overestimate your influence. I'm well acquainted with your captain and I can assure you, if you had done anything to upset me, he'd be the first to know."

The blow sat between them like a sheet of ice. Nico suspected the first one to skate across it would be the loser.

. . .

"**M**iserable man," Elle said to Nico when Panetta was barely out of earshot.

"Do you really know his captain?"

"Yes, of course." Elle winked and gave him a sly grin. "Though I only met him once at a police ball I attended with Ariana."

"Ariana attended police functions here in Valletta?" That surprised him.

"Oh, yes. She never missed the opportunity to stick it to them. She was often quoted in articles about all the criminal activities that the upper echelon of the police maintained they had no knowledge of."

"And she was still invited?"

"Of course not, but when did that ever stop Ariana?"

Good point, Nico thought. And no doubt one of the many traits that might have got her killed. "So, what's this about you leaving to go back to London? I thought you'd changed your mind for now." There it was again—a feeling he couldn't describe—but he wanted her to stay.

Elle didn't make eye contact as she fussed with something in her bag. "You're going to be laid up for a while, even when you're released from the hospital. And there's nothing further I can do here. Now that the thugs who carried out the bombing are in custody, I need to get back and tap my sources for what's going to happen with Baldisar and Heritage Pharma. Their stock price has hit the floor and I'm sure it will drop even further.

"I ran into Dr. Camilleri in the hall," Elle continued. "He expects you to be released by the end of the week but advises against travel for at least two weeks. So, with you here in Malta and your relationship with the local police inspector, I feel comfortable the investigation will go on without me."

It wasn't lost on Nico that she had said nothing about Francesca, but what about Max? He remembered the light in her eyes when she talked about his visit to London. It was the only time he'd seen any hint of a soft center to this hard-nut journalist. "When will you leave?"

"Today, on the four-o'clock flight. But I'll keep you posted." She picked up her bag. Then, seemingly unsure of what to do, she leaned over and grasped Nico's hand. He thought she was about to kiss him when Dr. Camilleri walked in.

"I can come back," he said with a smile.

"No need," Elle said. "I was just leaving. Take good care of him." She blew Nico a kiss. "I'll call you when I get back to London."

Chapter Sixteen

E ven though Nico's physiotherapy session was brief, his entire body ached. Frustrated, he wondered if he'd ever regain his strength. He felt like one enormously tender bruise, inside and out. Feeling miserable, he tried to distract himself from the fact that the time was nearing seven o'clock. Another half hour and Elle's plane should land at Heathrow.

Surer than ever that he'd been run over by a bus, he collapsed into the chair beside his hospital bed and tried to recall the notes he'd left taped to the wall in his room at the hotel. He wondered if it would be a huge imposition to call and ask if the young man who'd brought him the butcher paper and markers could bring his notes to the hospital.

He was mulling that over when Inspector Mifsud walked through the door. At last. Hopefully, that meant he didn't have to deal with Panetta again. He still wasn't sure if he trusted him. But before he could ask the inspector about Francesca, the look on his face caused a chill to run up Nico's spine.

Mifsud slowly and purposefully closed the door behind

him. He turned to face Nico. "Sinjur Moretti, I'm afraid I have some bad news."

Oh, dear God, please, no. Max? Elle?

"There has been an incident on St. Nicholas Street."

The street name sounded familiar, but Nico couldn't put his finger on it.

"I'm sorry to inform you that we found the body of Esme Agius two blocks from her home a few hours ago."

Signora Cilia's granddaughter. Nico was stunned. "What?"

Mifsud indicated the side of the bed. "May I?" Nico nodded, and the inspector sat down opposite him.

"They found her with her throat slit in a laneway near her home. Unlike the men who attacked you, this was professional. They knew exactly what they were doing."

Madonna . . . Nico had led the killer right to her by going to visit the old woman. Signora Cilia . . . ? He was afraid to ask. "And Esme's grandmother?"

"She was the one who reported her granddaughter missing," Mifsud replied. "As you can imagine, she is extremely distraught."

Nico *couldn't* imagine. The old woman's grown daughter had died young, and now her granddaughter had been taken from her.

"As you're aware, someone came to Sinjura Cilia's door asking for a spare key to Francesca Bruno's residence. After you'd been in her apartment and Sinjorina Bruno had disappeared." Mifsud checked something in a spiral-bound notebook before continuing. "That would make it the eleventh of May."

"We think whoever killed Sinjorina Agius did so because they knew she could identify at least one of them—the one that went to her door asking for a key."

"That makes no sense," Nico replied. "She didn't give him a key, and while I agree it was odd, he could have simply broken into Francesca's apartment. Obviously he didn't, or he would have activated the surveillance camera."

Mifsud dropped his eyes to the notebook in his lap. He closed it, then looked at Nico. At that moment, the man looked more like a puppy who'd just wet the floor than he did a police Inspector.

"I'm afraid that's where we have discovered a bit of a problem. It would appear that he did break into Miss Bruno's apartment."

"I don't understand. Then why would he have gone looking for a key?"

"He broke in sometime *after* that."

"But you said there was a silent alarm—"

"Something tripped the alarm, but it appears to have been . . ." With a pained expression, he cleared his throat. "It appears that no one in the station observed that there had been a break-in."

The potential killer was right there. Valletta Police could have caught him red-handed, and no one noticed an alarm being activated? A mounting sense of rage crawled its way up Nico's spine and tightened across his already bruised body. He clenched his fists in his lap. Words he knew he'd soon regret spewed forth.

"What kind of police department are you running? Not only could you have caught him in Francesca's apartment, but he might have led us to her." Nico gulped for air. "Not to mention the fact that Esme Agius would be alive today. *Figlio di puttana!* Son of a bitch!"

Inspector Mifsud sat with his head down, absorbing the tirade in silence. When Nico had exhausted himself, Mifsud placed his notebook on the bed beside him. He caught Nico's angry glare and held it.

"Sinjur Moretti, I don't expect this to provide much comfort, or for you to even believe me. You are correct on all counts and it is something I deeply regret." He steepled his hands together as if in prayer. "But I give you my personal assurance that the matter of Sinjorina Agius's murder, and the disappearance of Sinjorina Bruno will be my top priority— my *only* priority from this moment."

"You're right, I don't believe you. Why should I?" Nico knew he was pushing his luck, given his own transgression in not reporting Francesca's disappearance sooner. "What assurance can you give me that the morons—your colleagues whom you have the audacity to call police professionals—won't screw up again out of gross incompetency? You at least have the footage of whoever triggered the alarm, correct?" Nico hoped these idiots at least knew how to press record, let alone the brains to put out an all-points bulletin. How hard could it be to find someone they'd captured dead to rights on camera?

Mifsud stood and cleared his throat again. "The surveillance footage is missing. It's been erased from our main computer. We have a technician trying to recover it as we speak."

Santo cazzo Madre di Cristo! "You call yourselves a police force?" Nico railed. "How can anyone be this incompetent?"

Mifsud's expression turned grave. "The oversight of the silent alarm being set off in Miss Bruno's apartment wasn't caused by incompetency."

"Oh, really? What would *you* call it, then?"

"Corruption. I'm ashamed to tell you that the team member who was tasked with monitoring Miss Bruno's apartment deliberately didn't report that someone had broken in and tripped the alarm. Not to me, nor my superiors."

Like that was supposed to make him feel better? It reinforced what Nico and so many others knew: Malta was rife with corruption. As Elle had said, it was no surprise it extended to the capital city's police force.

"However," Mifsud continued, "the officer in question has been removed from his duties and is being held pending charges. His wife, who works here at this hospital, has also been suspended until the authorities can determine if she had knowledge of his connections to organized crime."

"Wait. Officer Panetta?"

"I'm afraid so. We have linked him to the two men police arrested in your jurisdiction of Tropea. He appears to have been the one who tipped off whoever killed Miss Agius and attacked you in the laneway. Now, we need to determine who they were working for."

Livid, Nico was about to tear another strip off the inspector when his mobile phone vibrated on the bedside table. He had set an alarm for the approximate time Elle would land at Heathrow, wanting to check that she arrived safely. Or maybe he just wanted to hear her voice.

Still glaring at Mifsud, he snatched the phone off the table and stopped the alarm. Then he hit speed dial. Three rings, four. On the fifth it went to voicemail. "Elle, call me the minute you get in," he said. "No matter the hour. It's urgent." He was about to hang up, then put the phone back to his ear. "And, be careful."

Chapter Seventeen

By 9 p.m., an hour and a half after Elle's plane landed in London, she'd still not called Nico back. He was starting to get worried. When he'd raised his concerns with Inspector Mifsud, he'd requested a police officer meet her at the arrival gate—"assuming she actually boarded the flight," he'd cautioned. When no one resembling Elle's description was spotted, he had her paged numerous times. And still nothing.

"So let me get this straight," Nico said on the phone to Mifsud from his hospital bed. "Her name wasn't on the manifest?" *Could something have happened to her on the way to the airport?* "Did you have someone double-check it?"

"Of course." Mifsud sounded indignant. He may not have said "I told you so," but the sentiment was evident in his promise to look into it further and keep Nico posted.

Gingerly, Nico swung his legs over the side of the bed and let out a massive sigh. Elle Sinclair was officially missing person number three. And the last thing he intended to do was languish in bed waiting on someone to find her.

He gritted his teeth as he packed the last of his belongings into a hospital-issue plastic bag. A nurse had alerted his attending physician when she discovered her patient had unhooked himself from his IV and was almost fully dressed.

"Sinjur Moretti, I must caution you, it's too early to leave the hospital," Dr. Camilleri said when he burst in. "While your injuries are healing well, you have a long way to go. You need to rest at least until the end of the week, and then ongoing therapy after that."

"I appreciate your advice, Doctor, but I'm afraid that isn't going to happen."

"I will refuse to sign your release papers."

Nico shoved his laptop into the bag and pulled the drawstring closed. "Well, that's certainly your prerogative, but it isn't going to change anything."

"You at least need to come back for outpatient physiotherapy!" was all Nico heard as the door swung closed behind him.

N ico managed to snag a taxi from the hospital to Valletta's central square. While he'd thought it quaint that no cars were allowed on the main street, now he cursed to himself as he hobbled back to his hotel on foot. When he finally made it in the door, the proprietor looked up. Judging by the shocked expression on her face, Nico assumed he must have looked like the walking dead. She'd insisted on sending a tray up to his room and while he appreciated it, he had little appetite. Instead, he reached for a glass of water and knocked back a couple of painkillers.

"Shouldn't you still be in the hospital?" Sergio asked when Nico called. "We expected you to be on sick time for at least another two weeks."

"Yes, well, that's another story. Right now, I need you to

get me everything you can on Special Investigator Roberto Pezzente. And while you're at it, see what you can find out about Francesca Bruno."

That could prove more challenging as Bruno was a Maltese citizen, but if anyone could get the lowdown on her, it would be Sergio. "This is top priority. Pass off anything you're working on that's urgent to Ferraro. I've already given him the heads-up."

"Yes, sir. I'll get back to you as soon as I have something."

"Sooner," Nico snapped and hung up.

Since the drive back from Mdina, he couldn't get Elle's comment about Francesca out of his mind. There was no doubt Francesca had been devastated when she'd pleaded with him that day at Ariana's apartment, to find her killer. But now he was seriously beginning to contemplate the possibility that she had staged her own kidnapping and had actually been the one to have taken Max away before Ariana was murdered.

He'd dozed off when Sergio's call came in. "I've sent you my summary findings by email. I'm leaving the office shortly for my little girl's birthday party, but if you have any questions after you've read it, I'll make myself available."

"Thank you, Sergio. I appreciate it." As Nico hung up the phone and booted up his laptop, he thought of his own son, who he hadn't even met. He berated himself for not knowing Sergio's daughter's name or how old she was turning. It was something he needed to change when he eventually got back home.

As he read through the confidential dossier, it became

abundantly clear that the Pezzente family's wealth could easily account for the flashy Rolex watch and the vintage Maserati the special investigator apparently drove. But those appeared to be his only concessions to being anything other than a paid government employee—albeit it one who, until recently, had been in the exclusive employ of the Italian government. Pezzente lived in a working-class section of Vibo Valentia, where he owned a modest apartment and lived alone—no wife, no kids. Not even a steady girlfriend, according to the report.

Nico scrolled through the attachment, scanning its contents. A lengthy entry that dated back almost ten years was followed by a more recent one. After reading them thoroughly—twice—he sat in shocked silence, struggling to digest the implications.

It would seem the current administration had chosen Roberto Pezzente as the new PM's most trusted assistant for a good reason.

The dossier outlined how, as a young investigator, Roberto Pezzente had earned his chops rousting several Mafia bosses out of bunkers buried in multiple locations beneath small towns in Rosarno, Calabria. Some had built elaborate underground homes where they could live for years, surfacing only in the dead of night to order executions or plan elaborate operations in a handful of countries, including Malta. By 2010, Pezzente and his team were responsible for two of the largest busts ever made on Italian soil. One involved laundering 8.5 million euros buried in the form of three hundred tons of chocolate. The other involved several tons of cocaine hidden in wholesale flower orders on the way to the Netherlands.

The busts put Pezzente on a career trajectory that read like the who's who of criminal investigations. In short, it brought him the kind of attention that the Mafia could no longer tolerate. They decided to teach him a lesson. Eight years ago, he lost not only the wife who had been his childhood sweetheart, but twin nine-year-old daughters who looked like mini-clones of their stunningly beautiful mother. The investigator's family had been killed, in cold blood, in front of him. But first, he'd had to watch while his wife was raped and brutally beaten. Mercifully, the bastards who did it shielded Pezzente's children from witnessing the horrific scene, but eventually they, too, were paraded out in front of him. Each child died by a single bullet to the head.

After a leave of absence, followed by an unblemished record of criminal investigations, Pezzente's tenacity put him squarely in the sights of the soon-to-be prime minister.

When Italy's former prime minister was ousted, his successor made it widely known that he would be the one to finally take on the rampant corruption that trickled down from the top. That meant attempting to rein in the infamous 'Ndrangheta—the Mafia clan who also happened to be the ones responsible for the killing of Pezzente's family.

Roberto Pezzente was the first major hire of the new administration. The PM's office couldn't have recruited anyone better than a man who would have the strongest of reasons for bringing the criminals responsible for the deep-seated corruption to justice. A reason that was likely predicated by a long-simmering, all-consuming desire for revenge. A top member of the prime minister's inner circle, Pezzente was known as *il Toro.* The Bull.

Nico scrolled through the files on his computer for the photograph of the man who it seemed fairly certain was Pezzente receiving an envelope of money.

He sat back and stared at the images until they were

indelibly etched on his brain. Was it possible that The Bull had turned?

Nico's thoughts were interrupted by his phone ringing. He grunted his greeting.

"I hesitate to ask you this," Inspector Mifsud said to him down the line. "But we have a possible lead regarding the disappearance of Sinjorina Bruno."

Though the pain thrummed through his body, Nico was instantly alert.

"I can't discuss it over the phone," Mifsud said, "but do you feel up to—"

Nico interrupted. "What time should I be ready?"

Chapter Eighteen

"How are you feeling?" Mifsud asked as Nico gingerly lowered himself into the passenger seat of the unmarked police vehicle. He winced as he did up his seat belt. And thought about his bruised kidney.

"Not like running a marathon, that's for sure. But I'm doing better, thank you."

Mifsud looked at him with a raised eyebrow, then pulled out into traffic.

"So here's what we know," he said. "A confidential informant has told us that in the past few days, there's been people coming and going at a disused vineyard in Ta Qali. It's about ten minutes from here."

Like Tropea, Nico thought, in Valletta, nothing is very far from anything. "Do you think it's a credible tip?"

The inspector shook his head. "One can never be sure, but we can't afford to ignore it. He recognized the vehicle of one of the men he saw entering the property. Then, after watching it for a day or two, he saw a woman being driven in by another man, and neither of them came out again."

"Did the woman fit Francesca's description?" Nico asked.

"We showed him her photograph, but he couldn't say with any certainty. Just that it was unusual to see people coming or going from the property."

Puzzled, Nico looked over at Mifsud. "I know. It's tenuous at best. Though he won't admit to it, we're fairly certain our informant has been using the property."

"You mean living there?"

Mifsud laughed. "Not exactly. I suspect if we did a flyover, we'd see a sizeable marijuana crop in among the old grapevines. I don't know why we don't just legalize the damned stuff, it's not as if—." He tapped the communications feed in his ear. "Excuse me."

Mifsud listened, then punched a button on the dash. "There's been a positive sighting. It could be Sinjorina Bruno."

Sirens wailed and lights flashed, transforming the unmarked car into an official police vehicle. The previously mild-mannered inspector floored the gas, and they sped down the highway, flying past signs so fast they all melded into a blur. By Nico's estimation, they'd gone about twelve kilometers when Mifsud turned onto a gravel road. Without decreasing speed, he expertly swerved around potholes and ruts in the road. The car flew momentarily as it hit a mammoth bump, then bottomed out in a hollow on the other side. Nico clenched his teeth and hung on to the hand rest each time, trying to minimize the pain to his ribs.

"Sorry," Mifsud said. Nico just nodded and hoped they were close to their destination.

A dilapidated wooden structure came into view, which Nico thought might have been a barn or possibly a farmhouse in better days. Mifsud killed the siren and came to a screeching halt on a makeshift driveway. Judging by the flattened weeds and bushes, someone had used the access recently.

Mifsud pulled his firearm from its holster and opened the car door. "Stay in the car until backup arrives. They have our location."

No worries, pal. I think the siren and lights might have tipped off the bad guys, anyway. They were probably long gone by now, but if Francesca was there . . . Nico gazed out past the vast fields of overgrown hay, a sea of golden waves rippling in the gentle breeze. Beyond that was a solid row of trees, likely built to protect the vineyard from more robust winds. The dense cypress hedge would make a great hiding place for anyone who might have gotten that far before he and Mifsud had arrived, like the circus coming to town.

He watched the inspector creep along one edge of the building, his back snugged up to what was left of the sun-bleached wooden wall, firearm held in both hands. Then he disappeared out of sight. Nico strained to hear if sirens were approaching. Nothing.

Then he heard it. The unmistakable sound of gunshot.

Nico launched himself from the car, running—as best he could with two cracked ribs—in the direction he'd last seen Mifsud. He could smell the cordite in the air, but everything was eerily quiet as he mimicked what he'd seen Mifsud do. Crouched low, he hugged the wall, sliding along it. He was all too aware that the difference was he had no weapon and his right side throbbed with pain.

He advanced slowly, inch by inch. What was he going to do when he got to the end? If he stuck his head out, it was entirely possible that whoever had just shot Mifsud would pick him off in an instant. One more step forward and he'd run out of wall. With an enormous inhale, he forced himself to dart his head out and look around the corner. Mifsud lay facedown on the trampled grass. Dead? Or just injured? He'd been hit either way, and having heard only one shot, that meant whoever shot him was close by. He darted his head back in and exhaled as quietly as he could.

Nico's pulse thrummed in his ears as he debated whether he should expose himself by going to check on the downed cop or hope backup might arrive within the minutes Mifsud had promised. Instinct told him he only had seconds to decide. As his pulse reached deafening proportions, he squatted low to the ground and half waddled, half crawled to the inspector.

The instant he reached Mifsud's side, he knew he'd made a fatal mistake. A tall dark figure stepped from a doorless entrance mere feet away from where Nico remained frozen on the ground, a gun pointed directly at him.

The man stepped out from the shadows. "Don't even think about it." The eyes were hard, his expression devoid of emotion, but the voice said otherwise. This was someone teetering on the edge. Someone Nico was sure would make good on his threat.

He slowly stood up and put his hands in the air. The pain shot down his side. "I'm not armed."

"Take off your jacket and throw it toward me. Then put your hands up and turn all the way around."

Nico did as he was told. As he turned his back on the armed man, his scalp prickling with sweat, he prayed he'd remain alive long enough to circle back around. Any second, he expected to feel the heat of a bullet smash into his spine. He prayed it would be his head and that it would be over quickly.

Instead, something whizzed past Nico's shoulder at break-neck speed. The bullet hit the gunman square in the middle of his forehead. At least that's where Nico thought it hit. It was hard to tell. His face had become a bloody pulp before he pitched backward and fell to the ground.

"Put your hands up!" Cops in full sniper gear converged on the scene like a colony of hornets. Nico whirled around. All guns were pointed in his direction.

"That means you," one cop bellowed. "Put your hands in the air. Now!"

While one cop checked the man they'd just shot, another kneeled at Mifsud's side with a hand to his neck. "He has a pulse, get an ambulance!"

Nico paced the floor outside Inspector Mifsud's hospital room. Dr. Camilleri, the same surgeon who had cobbled Nico back together, came out into the hallway.

"He's lost a lot of blood, but we've removed the bullet. Fortunately, there was no damage to any vital organs. Now our biggest factor is the risk of infection."

"Can I see him?"

"You may, but only for a few minutes."

Nico shook the doctor's hand. "I promise, I will only look in on him. No questions."

"You should be worried about yourself, too. You left the hospital far too soon," Camilleri said. Nico didn't reply. "There's a room off the doctors' lounge you can use if you need to rest. I will have a nurse wake you when he comes around."

Nico had popped another pain pill and was in a deep sleep when he was awoken by a repeated nudge to his shoulder. Irritated, he pulled the thin blanket around him.

"Sinjur, Dr. Camilleri asked me to awaken you. The inspector is conscious now."

Nico opened his eyes and blearily remembered where he was.

Guns. Those eyes. Mifsud shot. Lots of blood.

Instantly awake, Nico pulled back the cover, dragged himself off the cot and limped down the hall to Mifsud's room.

Dr. Camilleri was there, along with a nurse who was monitoring the inspector's vital signs. "Five minutes with him, that's all. And if I see him becoming agitated, you stop. Are we clear?"

"Completely," Nico said, and the doctor stepped back to allow him access to Mifsud's bed. He had taken it upon himself to learn the inspector's first name, Mikel, and what family he might have. His wife and three children were en route to the hospital. His face was pale, his eyes closed. He reached out and touched his forearm. "Mikel, it's Nico Moretti. How are you feeling, my friend?"

No response.

"Your wife is on her way. She should be here soon."

Nico thought he saw Mifsud's eyelids flutter, but he suspected it was fruitless to try to get anything from him for now. And he had promised the doctor. He gently patted the detective's hand. "I'll come back when you're feeling stronger. In the meantime, focus on getting well and seeing those beautiful little girls of yours."

As Nico pulled his hand away, Mifsud grasped it. Weakly, but he held on to it. "Sinclair," he whispered.

"Don't worry, your colleagues are doing everything to find her," Nico assured him. "You just get well."

"No, *no*." Mifsud's voice was hoarse, and he became

more and more agitated. The nurse who had been watching the monitor looked at the doctor over her shoulder.

Dr. Camilleri stepped forward. "That's enough for now."

"*She* has him," Mifsud said, barely above a whisper.

Nico put his arm out to hold the doctor back. "Please," he whispered to him, "one more minute."

The doctor backed off.

"Mikel, do you mean Francesca?" Nico held his breath. "Who is s*he*?"

"Doctor, his blood pressure is going off the charts," the nurse reported.

Camilleri moved forward and pushed Nico out of the way. "That's enough, Sinjur Moretti. You need to leave. Now."

After being banished from Mifsud's room, Nico pulled out his mobile phone. What did Mifsud mean? Who was "she"? Could he mean Francesca? And where was Elle? There were still so many questions, and Nico felt like he was no closer to the answers. But there was something he could do.

Nico had become friends with James Padwick, after meeting at a seminar on counterterrorism a few years ago. A former senior police officer within the Metropolitan Police, James had taken early retirement from the force after his wife, a Scotland Yard detective, had been shot and killed on the job. However, unable to settle at home, his path took a different direction, and now he headed up the security team at none other than Heathrow Airport.

"Great to hear from you, mate," James said after they'd chatted a few minutes. "How can I help?"

Nico caught him up and relayed what Mifsud had said about Elle's name not being on the flight to the UK.

"Your inspector there was correct," James said after checking. "There is no Elle Sinclair on the manifest for that flight. Because her reservation was canceled."

"Are you sure?"

"Absolutely. Do you want me to see if she rebooked on another one?"

"Please," Nico said, and listened while James instructed one of his staff to run a search.

While he waited, Nico tried another angle. "What about Francesca Bruno? Is that name on any flights?"

He heard him typing. "No, nothing."

Nico let out a quiet sigh of relief. He still hadn't heard if there had been any sign of her having been at the vineyard. He only knew the police hadn't found her when he and Mifsud were there.

But where was Elle? Surely she would have called to let him know if she'd changed her flight. He'd left her umpteen messages both during and after he'd been in the hospital.

His ears perked up when he heard someone in the background mention the name Sinclair.

"No, sorry, Nico," James said. "It doesn't appear that she's rebooked."

Why would Elle have cancelled her flight without letting him know? Nico's gut churned as a whole new set of alarm bells went off in his head.

Nico thanked him and was about to hang up when James said, "Hang on. That's odd."

"What?"

"Sinclair traveled from Malta to London on the third of May with a child by the name of Massimo Calleja. Wait a minute, wasn't that the surname of the prosecutor who was assassinated?" James asked. "Anyway, accompanying documentation shows she had a consent letter from the parent."

Oh my God! She'd told Nico she hadn't come to Malta until the day after Ariana was killed. And that she didn't know where Max was.

"Then," James continued, "she flew back to Malta on the eighth. Alone."

The day after the Tropea bombing. Elle—not Francesca—had taken Max out of the country prior to the bombing. With Ariana's consent.

A lthough a couple of painkillers helped take the edge off, Nico felt as if he'd run headfirst into a brick wall. After his conversation with James Padwick, he'd called Elle's mobile repeatedly, each time pleading with her to call him back. But he knew it was futile. No matter what kind of spin he tried to put on it, he was out of theories that could explain her lying to him. James had reported what he knew to the police, and now all Nico could do was go back to his hotel and wait.

Unable to summon the energy to go down for dinner, or even to check on Gabriela, he replied to a few emails before collapsing into bed. He'd just turned out the light when his mobile rang. He snatched it off the bedside table.

"Nico, it's James."

"Have you found them?"

"Not that I'm aware of, but once they leave the terminal, it's out of my hands. Listen, I'm not sure I should be telling you this, but after I'd finished with the police, something occurred to me. I'm sure you're aware there are CCTV cameras all over the airport, inside and out."

"Of course." It was a sad commentary that with terrorism being so prevalent in many countries across the world, it was almost impossible to commit a crime without being caught on camera. A colleague in Singapore had told Nico that thanks to CCTV, criminals there have roughly eight minutes to disappear before being nabbed by the police. If only they had that in Calabria . . .

"Well," James said, "I pulled the footage that covers everything coming in and out around the airport. People being picked up or dropped off in private vehicles, buses, hotel vans, taxis—everything. They come into different locations, but we have cameras on them all. It's impossible to enter or leave Heathrow, even on foot, without being seen."

"And?"

"We have confirmation that Elle Sinclair got into a taxi with a child matching Max Calleja's description thirty minutes after her flight had landed on the third of May. He appeared to be going with her willingly."

"You've reported all of this to the police?" Nico said.

"Of course. Obviously, the first place they looked was the address registered on her passport, but there's no sign of her or the boy. I imagine they're canvasing her neighbors as we speak. Presumably, all the police have to do now is find the taxi driver who picked up a tall woman with a small boy and find out where they dropped them off."

"And pray to God she paid the fare by credit card rather than cash," Nico said.

Chapter Nineteen

Despite the late hour, Nico threw on some clothes and headed to the Valletta Police Station. On arrival, he asked to speak with whomever was covering for Inspector Mifsud whilst he was in hospital.

"I'm very sorry, Sinjur Moretti," the officer at the front desk said. "The acting inspector is tied up in another matter. I'm afraid it will be several hours before he can meet with you."

Dismally, Nico looked around for somewhere to sit.

"There's an all-night café across the street. If you like, I can call you when he's available."

Despite his exhaustion, Nico was actually hungry, so he headed across the street and ordered mushroom bourguignon and a salad. While he waited for his food to come, he fired up his laptop and started his search into Elle Sinclair's journalism vitae.

She'd gone to Iraq as a war correspondent for the BBC after 9/11. Living in a war zone might explain skills such as expertly breaking into apartments without detection and driving as if to elude capture. Nico recalled Elle telling him she'd left the BBC because she refused to abide by their personal safety precautions. However, the article indicated they had summoned her back to London and, after a brief desk job assignment, they fired her.

The next reference he could find was when she started freelancing for the UK's *Guardian* newspaper. He scratched his head. Not only would that have been an enormous drop in pay, but there was a six-month period before that where she appeared to be unemployed. That was an awfully long time between jobs for such an accomplished journalist. He searched for any more links that might come up with her name. Nothing. For half a year, it was like Elle Sinclair had dropped off the face of the earth.

Nico read on. She seemed to have surfaced at the *Guardian* as suddenly as she'd disappeared. Judging by the multiple-page spreads devoted to her exposés, she'd made a rapid transition from war correspondent to reporting on white-collar crime. The criminals she'd investigated were like the Bernie Madoffs of the world. Many of whom were in prison serving life sentences, in part, because of her reporting. Pretty impressive stuff.

He clicked on more links to Elle's investigative pieces. One in particular had garnered her an award. That must have put her front and center in people's minds. A lot like Ariana. Before he knew it, he had multiple tabs open on his laptop, each link taking him down a different rabbit hole.

Then he saw it.

He'd clicked onto the *Sun*'s website. He leaned in and rubbed his eyes, sure they were deceiving him. It wasn't possible. But there she was, in living color. He clicked on the video. There was no mistaking the visibly inebriated woman kicking a bouncer who was trying to prevent her from cutting in line outside a popular nightclub in Soho. Nor the man with her, who was attempting to keep her from rendering the poor bouncer a eunuch. The shock on the man's face when Elle turned and struck him with her purse was only eclipsed by his pained expression when the police arrived to break up the melee. The caption that accompanied the video read: *Married Journalist Caught in Tawdry Affair.* The man being bashed about the head? The infamous journalist Nico had yet to meet — Vincenzo Testa.

Nico thought back to the conversation with Elle as they drove back from Mdina after she broke into Anna Braithwaite's apartment. At the same time she told him she'd never heard Ariana speak of Francesca, she said she'd never met Vincenzo Testa. He bit the inside of his lip as he replayed the video again, and vacillated between disbelief, hurt, and rage. How could Ariana have trusted this woman? But then again, why had he?

Much as he hated to do it, time was of the essence, and he needed to find out everything he could about Elle Sinclair. The only way he knew how to do that was to dangle the bait and hope he got a bite.

While he ate his meal, Nico made a couple of calls and had a trace put on Testa's mobile phone. After which he called Vincenzo Testa's wife. It took less than fifteen minutes for the reporter to contact him.

"You son of a bitch," Vincenzo Testa railed when Nico answered. "How dare you call my wife! What do you want?"

"Calm down, Signore Testa. I only want to chat." Nico felt a twinge of guilt that he'd intimated to Testa's wife that he was concerned for her husband's safety, but it had the desired effect.

"You said you'd call me back after you arrived at your destination," Nico said, then waited patiently while Testa blustered on a few more minutes. "Where was it you said you were going?"

"Cut the bullshit, Moretti. I didn't tell you where I was going. Now, before I call the police, not to mention your employer, what is it you want?"

Nico looked at his watch. He'd kept Testa on the line for the mere seconds needed to trace the journalist's where-abouts. "Relax, all I want is to ask you some questions about Elle Sinclair."

"That crazy bitch. What about her?"

"That's funny. She said she'd never met you. But that's not true, is it?"

"You already know the answer to that, or we wouldn't be speaking."

"Your wife said you have a new baby. Congratulations. Girl or boy?" Nico didn't give a rat's ass, but he wanted to keep him on the phone a few seconds longer. He'd asked Sergio to arrange to have the call tapped.

The anger in Testa's voice suggested that, if given the opportunity, he'd reach through the phone and strangle Nico. "You scared my wife half to death. She thought something had happened to me." His tone was steely. "You have thirty seconds to tell me what you want or I swear to God, my next call will be to the authorities."

Sergio's chat message popped up on his computer.

Testa is in Istanbul. Arrived two days after Ariana Calleja's assassination and hasn't left since.

Shit! After seeing the video of Elle and Testa together, he'd thought Testa might somehow have been involved in Elle's deceit and Max's disappearance. Nico ran his hand over the stubble of his two-day-old beard. Where to go from here? Testa was a new father. Maybe that was the angle. He swallowed his pride. "Mr. Testa, I apologize. I think we may have got off on the wrong foot. I need your help."

"You call my wife and frighten her half to death and you want my help? Have you lost your mind?"

"No, but I think I might have lost my perspective." It was now or never, before he hung up again. "Were you aware that Ariana had a son?"

There was a long pause. Nico felt the need to fill it, but as a prosecutor he was an expert at using silence to give defendants just enough rope to hang themselves. Now, however, he was desperate. "You were a friend of Ariana's and you're a new father. Please, Max is missing and I need to know if Elle ever spoke of him or saw him in your presence."

"Oh, my God."

"Excuse me?"

"Please tell me that evil woman hasn't done something to Max."

Chapter Twenty

When the call came in from the police station, Nico let it go to voicemail. He was alarmed Vincenzo Testa thought Elle could have been involved in Max's disappearance. Consent letter or not, she appeared to have gone to great lengths to hide the fact that it was she who had taken him out of Malta.

Additionally, whether it was out of guilt, or genuinely wanting to seek justice for Ariana's murder, Testa offered to share her research files—everything he had—with Nico.

Despite their bumpy start, Nico had the distinct feeling the journalist had waited a long time to unburden himself. He volunteered that his colleague, Ervio De Rosa, was already in Istanbul working on a story when Ariana was killed. They'd considered returning to Italy until things died down, but their security team advised against it. So, Testa had gotten on a plane and joined him. There had already been several threats on both men's lives, but Testa assured Nico they were committed to carrying on Ariana's work under Journalists for Justice.

"I don't need to tell you, Signore Moretti, Ariana was

dealing with some very dangerous people. Be careful. You'll see from my materials that many of them, including members of organized crime groups, have far-reaching tentacles. Heads of state, corporate CEOs, and many others in high places literally have been controlling Malta's economy for decades."

Testa cleared his throat. "I'm very sorry about the lambasting Ervio and I gave you in our exposé after you lost that big corruption case."

"Unnecessary, and please call me Nico."

"Very well, thank you. In all fairness, I think the reason we were so hard on you was that we'd both been in close touch with Ariana. She'd had multiple threats on her life, and as I was one of the few people who knew she had a child, I worried about her and Max's safety."

"I understand. Can you tell me more about how you knew her?"

"Of course. I loved Ariana like a sister," Testa continued. "We met in a journalism course when we were undergraduates. Had it not been for her encouragement and fierce dedication as a prosecutor, I'd never have been able to nail that series I did on the 'Ndrangheta a year or two back."

Nico remembered the piece well. It resulted in a huge takedown of several key players in the 'Ndrangheta—the most dangerous Mafia clan, some would say, in the world. They made the Sicilian mob look like choirboys.

"It was after that, that Ariana asked me to help with some of the exhaustive research she needed for her investigation into Malta's private bank. I don't know if you're aware, but the bank has some highly questionable clients. Ariana was an equal-opportunity crusader. While she never actually named them, in several interviews she made it quite clear who she thought they were."

Nico's ears perked up. Was this what she was about to

announce before she was killed? "Do you know any of their names?"

"No, but I do know that somewhere there is a list, and that her office was planning on making a big announcement last Wednesday, the day after Ariana died."

"Are you aware that Italian police have charged two men with her assassination?" Nico asked. "Wouldn't that tend to suggest the bombing was connected to someone in Italy rather than Malta?" Having said that, he knew that Calabria also had its share of oligarchs and despots. His office was currently working a case that involved Russians who were aggressively buying up real estate including restaurants, hotels, homes—and in some cases, entire villages. Had Ariana identified certain individuals in Malta who were also players in Italy? Is that why she was killed in Tropea? Nico shuddered at that thought.

"Those two men they arrested are nothing but paid thugs," Testa scoffed. "With all due respect, catching them makes the Italian government look good and takes the heat off Malta. While it's possible they carried out the bombing, I guarantee you it was at someone else's behest. Someone who had a lot to gain by killing Ariana."

"Do you have any thoughts on who that would be?"

"Not definitively, no," Testa said. "But as you'll see in the research notes I'm about to send you by encrypted email, there is no shortage of potential candidates."

Eventually, the subject of Elle came up again. Although curious about what Testa had to say about her, Nico hadn't wanted to interrupt him while he was so forthcoming about Ariana.

"Elle and I first met when we were both covering the Iraq war," he said. "The constant tension and danger that we lived under eventually stretched many of us beyond our limits. And we did things we would never have imagined doing back home."

"I can certainly understand that." Nico knew of several men and women who had come back from Iraq suffering terrible PTSD.

"It's not something I'm proud of," Testa said, "but after being under siege for twenty hours following an ambush on our Humvee, Elle and I sought solace in each other's beds. I just chalked it up to the circumstances that we'd had a one-night fling. I was married and didn't plan for it to happen again."

"Did you tell her that? Elle, I mean."

"I did, but it would seem she had other ideas."

A tingle went down Nico's spine—the hairs on his arms stood on end. "What do you mean?"

"I was weak," Testa replied, "but we were living through strange times. Even when I was able to make calls back home to my wife, she didn't fully grasp the horrors I'd witnessed."

Nico didn't imagine anyone did unless you'd lived it. It was almost certain Testa would have suffered emotional issues after he returned home.

"So, for two more months in Iraq, Elle and I had an on-again-off-again affair. We reported for different news organizations, but we were often embedded in the same military vehicles. We were almost ambushed once, and her quick thinking saved my life and that of my cameraman."

Nico could see that. With Elle's quiet, focused demeanor she'd likely stay calm under fire.

"Maybe I felt beholden to her, I don't know, but I let it go on longer than I should have. But eventually it was time for us to return home—her to the UK and me to Italy. I had someone to return to. She didn't. She called me repeatedly, and after I told her several times it was over, someone started calling my home and hanging up. I suspected it was Elle and I lived on eggshells, worrying that my wife would suspect something.

"A few weeks later, I had an assignment in London. It was then that I discovered Elle had been assigned to a desk job at the BBC and subsequently fired."

"Do you know why?" Nico asked.

"No, but a friend who still worked at the BBC told me that they'd forced her into rehab and mental health counseling, neither of which went well."

Jesus, and Ariana had entrusted her son with this woman.

"Anyway, after several days in London, I was out with some colleagues at a popular nightspot in Soho when I ran into her. I was shocked at how much she'd changed. She was rail thin and seemed edgy. Brittle, would be the only way I can put it. Unfortunately, she spotted me and staggered over to our table. She was so drunk, or possibly high, that I was embarrassed to introduce her to my friends. So, I took her aside and tried to talk some sense into her. But she was way past the point of reason."

Judging by the change in Testa's tone, Nico suspected that whatever happened next had gutted him.

"I tried unsuccessfully to steer her out of the club. Eventually security got involved, and they threw her out. Despite my embarrassment in front of my friends, I went outside to make sure she was all right. When I got there, she was trying to crash the line to get back in. When I tried to intervene and hustle her into a waiting taxi, she hauled off and belted me."

That was obviously what Nico had seen on the tabloid video.

"Then, rather than get into a cab," Testa said, "she pulled out her mobile, made a call and put it on speaker. With so much noise outside, I couldn't hear who she was speaking to."

But all too soon, he did. While Testa spared Nico the coarse vernacular Elle had used to inform his wife of their relationship while in Iraq, he wasted no words in telling Nico that she was "pure evil."

"Like something the devil spawned," he said. "Elle would absolutely be capable of talking Ariana into letting her take Max somewhere, and then keep it from everyone."

Nico felt sick. *Who does that?* Who tells the wife of a man you've had an affair with that she's pregnant with his child?

Something the devil spawned.

He wanted to punch something. How could he have been so stupid to allow himself to be duped by this mentally unstable woman? And Ariana, what the hell were you thinking letting her have anything to do with Max?

"I understand how angry and betrayed you must have felt," Nico said. "But Elle doesn't strike me as the maternal type." He thought back to her disinterest in helping him with his hospital meal. "Why would she want to keep Max?"

"Don't be so sure. On the surface, Elle Sinclair may not appear to be maternal, but she is without a doubt, a bitterly sore loser."

"And you say that, why?"

"Because it was the day after we'd found out my wife had miscarried our first pregnancy that Elle shared her good news on the phone outside the club that night."

"I'm sorry, I don't understand."

"She told my wife she was three months pregnant with my child and she'd never felt better." Testa's voice cracked. "But Elle had told me in Iraq she couldn't have children."

. . .

S till having heard nothing from either Padwick or the UK
police, after a quick breakfast, Nico sequestered himself
in the hotel's lounge. The proprietor told him she wouldn't
need the room until cocktail time mid-afternoon. It was with
some degree of optimism that he left the door open a crack,
hoping Gabriela might pad in and greet him with a lick and a
tail wag. In the meantime, he got down to work.

First, he downloaded everything Testa had sent him via
encrypted email. As he drank his coffee, he scanned the
copious volume of material before him. Then, reluctant to
push his luck by taping pieces of butcher paper to the
brocade-covered walls, Nico created a basic mind map on his
computer.

After hours of flipping back and forth between Testa's
notes and his own schematic, he sat back and looked at what
he had. Matching what he already knew against the journalist's detailed research, it didn't take long to figure out that his
own limited knowledge barely skimmed the surface. Testa
and Ariana had been light-years ahead of him in how they'd
connected the dots between Baldisar Bank and high-profile
heads of states and corporations. And, most particularly, their
connection with Heritage Pharmaceuticals.

For at least a decade, it appeared that Baldisar Bank had
been cleaning money for clients who needed to stay off the
grid. There were references to several individuals being on
Europe's terrorist watch list, as well as a couple of Russian
oligarchs and dictators. Whether or not Ariana or Testa knew
who these individuals were, if they'd had even an inkling
they were being investigated… Nico shuddered to think.

In addition, the passports-for-sale scheme Francesca had
told him about—a Russian could buy a Maltese passport for
six hundred and fifty thousand euro—were the commissions

the bank received on their foreign investment transactions. If each of the clients gave the bank the equivalent of ten million dollars, at only a five percent commission, the bank's income per transaction was five hundred thousand. Multiply that by ten highly questionable clients—and from what Nico could see, they had at least that—and you had a hundred million dollars being invested per year. That equated to commissions of ten million a year for the bank. If they'd been doing that for the past five to ten years . . . Well, the amount was astronomical.

Ariana had detailed a complex paper trail in her notes. Baldisar had set up so many offshore accounts and shell companies that it made even Nico's head spin—and he was used to tracking down complex tax-avoidance instruments in the drug and money-laundering cases he prosecuted. What he was looking at reminded him of an ultrasophisticated game of snakes and ladders.

Now to Heritage Pharmaceuticals. As far back as 2016, Ariana had suspected someone inside the drug company was leaking information. Nico could see that had been relatively easy; she'd simply followed the money. Months before news had broken about a promising new cancer drug the company was developing, Heritage's stocks had started to shoot through the roof. By the time the positive results were finally lauded in the medical journals, a lot of investors had become significantly wealthier. Alesandru Baldisar being one of them. However, someone in the Cambridge lab had uncovered evidence that there was a serious issue with one of the control groups in the drug trials. If that were true, it would be a game changer.

Ariana found out who the insider was, and she had managed to interview him. Anonymously— very cloak and dagger. She hadn't even used initials to identify who it was.

In the transcript Testa had sent him, the person was only referred to as "Source."

As Nico scanned the more than fifty pages of painstakingly detailed questions and answers, he gained a whole new respect for Ariana's skills as a lawyer. While characteristically direct, in this case she danced expertly between drilling down when necessary, then backing off to finesse the meat of what she wanted to extract. What struck Nico was the raw emotion the interviewee exhibited in answering some of her questions. Whoever this insider was, there seemed to be some serious vitriol there.

Nico read on, making more notes of his own, but the next few pages were largely scientific jargon, and his attention waned. It was time to get some questions answered. After messaging Testa via the encrypted app he'd instructed Nico to use at all times, he poured himself a coffee and eyed the bottle of limoncello the proprietor had left as a welcome-back token. What the hell—maybe the liqueur would counteract the caffeine, which would surely keep him awake later. He poured himself a glass, savored the taste of fresh citron, and stretched out on the bed to await Testa's call.

When Nico answered, the first thing Testa asked was whether he had switched on the encryption settings on his mobile phone.

"Yes, right after you told me to." Given what he'd seen in Testa's investigative notes, Nico had a whole new appreciation for the reporter's abundance of caution.

"Very good. Now, you said you have some questions for me. Fire away."

"OK. They mainly have to do with the relationship between Baldisar and the Braithwaites," Nico said. "I don't mean to be judgmental but—"

"But they're not as glamorous as the Hollywood set he's typically seen with, I know."

"Well, yes. But I gather they had something more valuable to offer than celebrity."

"So you've got to the end of my notes," Testa said.

"Yes, and they're very impressive. But why would a respected research scientist, on the fast track to a full professorship at a prestigious university, share the inside secrets of the drug she was developing? And why Baldisar? With Heritage Pharma's backing, she didn't need his money." Nico scratched his head. "What am I missing?"

"On the surface, you're correct. She was more than adequately funded by Heritage."

"But?"

"Well, that's a bit of a long answer."

Nico topped up his limoncello. The coffee was as cold as the night threatened to be long.

"I'm listening."

"Alright, first off, I just sent you a few photographs. Have you had a chance to look at them?"

"I'm looking at them now." The first was of Alesandru Baldisar. Nico could see why women would be attracted to the CEO. Of average height, he was impeccably groomed and dressed. For a man in his early sixties, he appeared to be in exemplary shape. The stunning people he was photographed with included everyone from famous movie stars to supermodels.

Next, he scrutinized the one of Anna Braithwaite. While not unattractive, Nico thought she looked quite plain. But apparently, within the scientific community she was reported to be one of the preeminent research scientists to watch.

"Ariana had discovered the Braithwaites had met Baldisar at a charity event of some sort in Malta," Testa said. "I think it had something to do with children and cancer research. The bank, and the Baldisars personally, had made sizeable donations and Anna and her husband Clarence were there to lend their faces to the cause."

"That's a bit odd, don't you think?" Nico said. "I don't know how things are in Malta, but certainly in the UK, it's unusual to see scientists at galas." Typically, they were introverted and preferred to stay in their labs.

"Not sure about that, but according to Ariana's notes, Baldisar was very interested in Anna's research."

"The new cancer cell-inhibiting drug." Nico said.

"Yes. She might not have discovered the cure for cancer, but what she was working on could have been the next best thing."

That matched with what Elle had told Nico in Mdina.

"This is where it gets interesting," Testa continued. "From what I observed in Ariana's notes, Baldisar had a small list of elite but dangerous clients who very few banks in the world would deal with. Based on the Braithwaites' assurance the trials had succeeded, and the drug was poised to hit the market, Baldisar—being the greedy bastard that he was—systematically approached those clients. Through a complex labyrinth of holding companies, he invested significant sums of their money in a legitimate vehicle—Heritage Pharma."

"Well, that must have made them happy," Nico said. "Why would that be a problem?"

"They were," Testa agreed. "Until someone inside the research lab found out some of the data was faulty."

Nico let out a low whistle.

"The potential ramifications were huge," Testa said. "Investing early on in Heritage Pharma would have resulted in millions in commissions for Baldisar. If word got out about the faulty trials, certain clients who were all too happy to jump on a legitimate investment would come gunning for him."

That was an understatement. Baldisar would last only so long, before a poisoned doorknob or an assassin's silenced gun would get him. That brought Nico to his final question. He hadn't seen anywhere in Ariana's notes, the identity of the person inside the lab.

"Vincenzo, do you know the identity of the whistler-blower Ariana interviewed?"

There was such a long pause, Nico wondered if he'd lost the call. "Vincenzo, are you still there?"

"I do, yes." Testa cleared his throat. Nico waited.

"It was Clarence Braithwaite."

Stunned, Nico sat bolt upright on the bed. "Why would he blow the whistle on his own wife?"

"Good question. Clarence was a highly regarded PhD in his own right. He had been head of his own department at University College London until Heritage convinced him to jump ship and join them."

"Wow, it must have been quite an offer to make him give up tenure where he was."

"I would think so. Anna Braithwaite had the full backing of Heritage Pharma, which included her fully funded lab at Cambridge. Basically, she had carte blanche to run her own show. I guess Heritage thought having two highly respected research scientists on the project would be golden. However, it wasn't long before Clarence discovered that he'd essen-tially been reduced to working for his wife. There were rumors that he regretted the move and was looking to get back into UCL."

Having given up tenure—and moving to the competition—Nico knew the chances of Clarence getting his old job back would be next to impossible. That must have smarted.

"Two weeks after Ariana's last interview with Clarence," Testa said, "he was killed in a car bombing in Saint Julian's, Malta."

Holy mother of God! Exactly as Elle, and Italy's special investigator, Roberto Pezzente, had said. Except it wasn't three men involved in a money-laundering scheme who were helping themselves to the profits. It was Anna Braithwaite's husband. And until someone discovered what Ariana knew, no one would have been the wiser.

"You said *certain* clients would come gunning for Baldisar," Nico said. "If Ariana had a list of who those people were —well, that could certainly explain why she was killed."

That could also explain why Francesca had been threatened. As she was known to be close to Ariana, it would be a natural assumption that she might also have known the names of those on the list. And for Testa to be rightfully anxious that he could be next.

"That's why you were already in transit to Istanbul when I contacted you."

"Yes."

"Are you safe there?" Istanbul was certainly colorful, but not a place Nico would have considered a good hiding spot. Especially not in light of the 2018 killing and dismembering of journalist Jamal Khashoggi.

"I don't know that I'm safe anywhere, but now you know why I take such extraordinary protective measures in our communications. I'm blessed to have a wife who's forgiven me and a baby boy who I love dearly."

"I understand. So where do we go from here?" *Was* there anywhere to go? Or had they been going around in circles only to reach a dead-end? A stalemate. Stuck between a corrupt banker who, until recently, Nico had believed could be responsible for Ariana's murder. And a list of the most dangerous oligarchs and dictators who would think nothing of silencing someone who got in their way.

After all this, it seemed he was back at square one. But, if he could get his hands on that list…

"I have a plan," Testa said. "But I won't lie to you, it comes with some risk. The first thing you need to do is check out of where you're staying."

There was a long pause. Nico lay in silence. Tallying: three women murdered, one child missing. Check. Another taken from her apartment where he was attacked. Check. A stint in hospital from which he still ached. Inspector Mifsud in critical condition after being shot. And now Testa wanted him to move from the one place he felt safe.

Then he thought of Ariana. Of the gentle expression that hid her fierceness. The veracity with which she'd implored him to help put a stop to the corruption that was eroding both their countries. Of the last evening they'd spent together, fraught with anger and recrimination. When he learned about the son he didn't know he had. And might never get to meet.

"I'm listening."

Chapter Twenty-One

Nico was still sleeping when he heard a gentle knock on the door. He awakened to find himself looking into a pair of black button eyes surrounded by white fluff. "I hope I was a gentleman," he said to his bedmate. Then he looked past the little dog and saw the time on the bedside table clock. It was after nine.

There was another light knock. "Sinjur Moretti, I'll leave your breakfast tray out here for you. Please let me know if you need anything."

"Thank you," he called back as he climbed out of bed. Then he realized he had nothing to feed Gabriela and she most assuredly needed a walk. He threw on a robe and leaped to open the door.

"Excuse me," he called as the hotel's staff member retreated down the hall. "Would it be possible for someone to take Gabriela for a walk and to feed her?"

She turned and gave him a warm smile. "Of course, sinjur, I'd be happy to." Gabriela had hopped off the bed and was already at the door.

"Come on, little one," the young woman said. "Let's give

you a walkie before breakfast, shall we?"

Nico was fully packed by the time the girl brought Gabriela back to his room. He thanked her and insisted she accept a small tip.

"Anytime, sinjur. You only have to call the front desk. Everyone loves Gabi and would be happy to help."

With some regret, Nico did one last check around before heading downstairs to check out. At the concierge desk, the proprietor looked up from something she was writing. Looking surprised, her gaze shifted to his bags. "Sinjur Moretti, you're not leaving us, I hope?"

"I'm afraid I am, signora, but it is with great reluctance. You and your staff have been so good to me."

"I understand. Is it time for you to return home?"

He remembered Testa's words. *Leave no destination, no forwarding address.*

"Yes, I'm afraid so." He looked at Gabriela, who had followed him down the staircase to the foyer. He felt a twinge of something he couldn't quite name. The proprietor looked at him, an unasked question in her eyes. He swallowed the lump that rose in his throat. "Gabriela seems happy here. Are you and your husband still willing to keep her?"

Her eyes misted up. "Of course we are, but may I make a suggestion?"

Nico nodded, afraid his voice might fail him.

"She's welcome to stay here as long as you'd like. But why don't we foster her for you?" She swiped away a tear. "That way, once you get home and caught up on things, if you'd like her back, we could send her to you."

"You'd . . . you'd do that?"

"Absolutely!"

Nico hesitated.

"You don't have to decide right now." She handed him a business card. "I have your mobile number. Keep in touch." She scooped Gabriela up from the floor. "In the meantime, I promise you we'll take great care of her."

He definitely couldn't have a dog with him with what he was about to do. That would be exactly the kind of "distinguishing factor" Testa had warned him about.

"I know you will, thank you." He put out his hand and petted the little ball of fluff in her arms. "Be a good girl, Gabriela. And don't argue with Groomba." He referred to the automated lawnmower he'd observed from his balcony as it had daily run-ins with the hares on the property. "He'll win every time."

T he first thing Nico did was return his car to the rental company, telling them he'd be leaving Malta to go back to Tropea, and asked for a ride to the airport. At the airport, he made sure the driver saw him enter the departures entrance and turned to see that he'd driven off.

Next, he bought a ticket for the next flight to Calabria. But instead of going through security, he hung about looking in shops and having a coffee at a stand-up bar. All the while, he kept a close eye out for anyone who might show the slightest bit of interest in him. Finally, he looked at his watch, headed down the escalator, and walked out of the airport.

As Testa had promised, a car of the specified make and color awaited him outside. The driver got out and in one fluid movement walked past him, exchanging the key from his hand to Nico's. Before a second warning from the security guard instructing him to move out of the pick-up-only area, Nico pulled away from the curb and drove off.

He'd been on the road for an hour and was satisfied he wasn't being followed. Testa had guaranteed him that the car he was driving had been fully "cleaned," meaning someone had gone over it with a fine-tooth comb, looking for any GPS tracking devices or bugs. Likewise, he'd given Nico explicit instructions on how to ensure his smartphone and other devices couldn't be used to hack, phish, or watch him. He'd even walked Nico through how to set up all his devices so Testa could wipe them remotely if he was detained anywhere. That thought alone gave him the heebie-jeebies. Where he'd once thought of Testa's extreme caution as cloak-and-dagger theatrics, the mounting toll of dead or missing individuals had rapidly changed his mind. Next to tracking down Ariana's killer, Nico's sole focus was to make sure he wasn't the next victim to be checked off anyone's hit list.

He was on schedule to catch the next ferry to Gozo and make the short drive to The Fishing Eagle bar by the agreed-upon time. It turned out that the heavyset man who'd been wiping down the bar when Nico had last been there was Lydia Rapa's brother. While Testa couldn't assure Nico that the man could be of much help, he said he was definitely one of the good guys. If he knew anything about his sister being a whistleblower, maybe he'd be more motivated to cooperate after her murder. One could only hope.

The sun was out, and the temperature had soared unchar-acteristically high, when Nico turned into the gravel parking lot outside the bar. With a *Closed* sign at the entrance, it wasn't surprising there were no other vehicles in the lot. He got out of the car and, upon being assaulted by the heat, shucked off his jacket and left it on the front seat.

As instructed, he went up a flight of wooden steps on the side of the building—the same ones he'd watched Lydia descend and make a hasty retreat the first and last time he'd met her. Since his last visit, a solid iron gate had been added at the top and a large Beware of Dog sign was on prominent display. On the wall to Nico's left was an intercom. He pushed the buzzer, sensing he was being watched on camera. There was a pause. He heard a click, and the gate opened.

He'd no sooner stepped through it than the large man he'd met only briefly a week before appeared. Either his T-shirt was too small, or his trousers too big. Whichever the case, his large hairy belly cut through the middle as a gulf might cleave two distant shores. Instinctively, Nico stepped back when the man's herculean arm shot forward. He exhaled when he realized he was only reaching around him to pull the gate closed.

You must be Brutus, Nico wanted to say. Instead, he put out his hand. "I'm Nico Moretti. You must be Giorgio." Ignoring his hand, the man gave something of a grunt, turned his back and walked along the outside of the building. Nico assumed he should follow.

They came to a hidden entrance that blended seamlessly into the faded wooden siding. When Giorgio pulled open the door, the largest dog Nico had ever seen leaped towards him, snarling at the end of a chain he silently prayed would hold.

"Caesar!" his master shouted. "Go, lie down."

Instantly, Caesar lay down. Meek as a lamb. But as Nico gave him a wide berth, he felt the dog's eyes cut through him like a laser through butter.

He sat across from Giorgio, trying to relax while sipping from a can of beer. It hadn't seemed prudent to ask for a glass of water instead. Giorgio chugged his beer back in short order and reached for another. He raised an eyebrow at Nico, who shook his head. The man's head reminded him of a Chia pet —as follicularly abundant as Nico's was sparse.

"I'm very sorry for your loss," Nico said. "It's good of

you to see me so soon after… well…Vincenzo said you might be able to shed a light on who might have wanted Lydia dead."

"Since my sister's death, the police have browbeaten me," the man replied without acknowledging Nico's condolences.

"How so?"

"They took everything from her home—computers, mobiles, tablets, everything. Then they started hounding me. Did Lydia have a safe-deposit box? They even threatened to get a warrant to search her lawyer's offices."

"Do you know what they were looking for?"

"No, and it wouldn't have done any good to ask them."

"You've installed some extra security since I was last here," Nico commented.

"Had to. Shut down the bar as well. The press was coming around at all hours of the day and night."

"Do you live here?"

"Not normally, but I am right now. I couldn't keep both places secure, so Caesar and I moved in here for a while."

Nico cocked his head and Giorgio explained.

"I've had several break-ins both at my house and here at the bar. Wouldn't be surprised if it was the police. They're too damned lazy to apply for a warrant, even though they threatened to."

Before Nico replied, he considered his options. Whatever Testa had said to Giorgio when he arranged their meeting, the journalist apparently trusted him and he seemed certain Lydia's brother had some valuable information, but regardless, Nico sensed he should tread lightly.

"Giorgio, did Lydia ever talk to you about certain members of her party that she was . . . well, perhaps concerned about?"

He sighed. "Everybody knew Lydia was the leaker of that

report. I told her not to get involved. But when she met that Calleja woman—the one who was assassinated—Lydia said her conscience wouldn't let her stay quiet any longer."

"Did she ever share with you what the report contained or who initiated it?"

Giorgio remained quiet. Without warning, he picked up what looked like a piece of sausage and threw it to Caesar. The dog caught it midair, his jaws snapping shut with an unnerving click. He repeated the performance several times. Whether it was for his guest's benefit or part of the canine's routine, Nico didn't know. He tried not to flinch as he waited out the game between canine and master.

Finally, game time was over. Giorgio rose from his place on the saggy couch and motioned for Nico to follow. "Come with me. Testa said I could trust you."

Yes, but can I trust you*?*

Nico followed him down a dark stone staircase that led to a dank-smelling basement. In the dim light, Nico could make out various pieces of equipment and detritus that would be associated with running a bar. When he thought they'd reached a dead-end, he stood a safe distance behind Giorgio and wondered why the man was standing in front of a cement wall. Then, with a meaty hand, he reached behind a rusted shelving unit. There was a buzz, and the solid wall slid open. Without looking back, Giorgio stepped inside another room. Apprehensive, Nico remained where he was.

"You're not claustrophobic, are you?" his host asked when he noticed Nico hadn't followed.

"No, I'm just not sure that . . ."

"That you can trust me?"

Nico felt his face flush.

"If I were out to do you harm, trust me, I could have

saved myself the trouble and turned you over to Caesar already."

He had a point. All the same, if Giorgio's intent was to lure him into a cement-encased crypt and lock him inside, he'd almost rather be the dog's dinner. At least it would be over quickly.

"As I said, Vincenzo Testa trusts you, and when he called and asked me to meet with you, I figured you're one of the good guys. But hey, if you don't want to—" He shrugged and turned his attention to a safe that was bolted to the floor.

Nico took a deep breath and walked across the threshold.

He watched as the man punched in a code, opened the door to the safe and reached in to remove a thin manila envelope. He handed it to Nico.

"Before you arrived here on the day you met her on the ferry, Lydia gave me this. She said that if anything were to happen to her, not to give it to the police or any of the authorities."

Nico turned the envelope over in his hand. The flap was sealed, but the initials Nico saw written across the seal made his heart stop. It was Ariana's unmistakable scrawl.

"Who . . . Where did this come from?"

"Like I said, Lydia gave it to me before you got here. Before they killed her."

Nico was flummoxed. Why hadn't her brother opened it? "Didn't you want to know what was inside? It might have had something to do with her death."

Giorgio turned off the light to the small anteroom and gestured toward the door. Something vaguely akin to a sad smile crossed his ruggedly lined face. "Let's go upstairs to the bar. You look like you could use a drink."

Sitting at the bar, Giorgio poured them each a stiff rum, mixed with what could only be described as a splash of Coke.

Cognizant that he had to drive, Nico took a gulp and poured the rest of the can of soda into his glass. The envelope sat conspicuously between them, still unopened. He watched as Giorgio wiped down the bar as he'd seen him do when he'd come to meet Lydia. It seemed to be a natural movement for him, like breathing.

"You asked me why I haven't opened it," he said to Nico. "Whatever is in it won't bring my sister back." The bags under his eyes looked like he hadn't had a good night's sleep since Lydia had died. "Any more than it will bring the Calleja woman back." He jabbed the envelope with two fingers. "She gave this to Lydia, and now they're both dead. I want nothing to do with it. The less I know, the better."

But he'd kept his sister's secret, Nico mused. He'd locked it somewhere it would never have been found had he not volunteered it. This great hulk of a man *did* want whatever was in the envelope to be seen; he just didn't want to be the one to shoulder what was clearly going to be a heavy burden.

Giorgio cleared his throat, breaking into Nico's thoughts. "I've got some stuff to do out back. Take all the time you want, but I wouldn't suggest leaving here with that—" he pointed to the envelope "—in your possession. It could be hazardous to your health."

He put down the rag and headed toward the back door. "Oh, and one other thing. Don't go walking out the front door. Caesar will be right outside in case we have unexpected guests."

Chapter Twenty-Two

Alone with his thoughts and his half-finished drink, Nico stared at the envelope that seemed to burn a hole in the bar. Was the answer to who had killed Ariana and Lydia inside? If this was the list of names Ariana had been about to expose, would Nico be the next one to meet a nasty end? He pulled at the neck of his shirt as a trickle of perspiration rolled down his back. His hands shook as he picked up the envelope. For a potentially lethal missive, it weighed next to nothing.

He stuck a thumb under a corner of the flap and worked it open. Again, he paused. Once he'd seen what was inside, he couldn't unsee it. With a slightly steadier hand, he pulled out the contents: a single piece of paper, typewritten. But as hard as he might, he couldn't get his eyes to focus. The print before him seemed to flutter up and down, and his vision was blurred. For God's sake, pull yourself together! He put the paper on the bar, and starting at the top, he scanned the document.

Santa madre de Dios! This was it. In his hands, he held a list of names—twenty or thirty of a select group of Baldisar

Bank's clients and their respective countries. As Ariana had noted, there were a couple of Russian oligarchs, several heads of state of countries the European Parliament had sanctioned and, last but not least, a well-known member of Italy's Mafia — a relative of the defendant in the case Nico had recently lost. At first glance, it would seem that while all the individuals were, at the very least, corrupt, if not downright dangerous, none of them appeared to have anything else in common. Except, opposite each one were the words *Heritage Pharma*, and the amount invested in euros. The numbers made the cases Nico and the Justice Department prosecuted look like chump change. He hadn't even come close to calculating the commissions Baldisar Bank was earning off some of the world's most diabolical individuals.

He would never have thought that having the dog with the snapping jaws outside the door would have brought him comfort but given what he held in his hands, he felt a sense of relief. He contacted Testa on the encrypted messaging app and awaited his callback. When his mobile rang, he snatched it off the bar.

"Send me a photo of the list," Testa instructed when Nico had finished describing what he'd found. "Then give me a minute to look at it. Don't hang up."

Nico did so, then sat quietly with the phone to his ear.

"My God, Nico, you found it!" Testa's voice burst down the phone. "This is the list that Ariana was about to expose."

"I don't get it, though," Nico replied. "If she had the list, why didn't she give it to you?" He looked around the bar. "And why did Lydia Rapa have it?"

"All good questions," Testa agreed. "This is only supposition, and I could be wrong. But over the years Ariana and I worked together, I got to know her patterns and behaviors. Although she used technology, she had a deep distrust of it.

She worried her information and sources could be hacked, even when they were stored in the cloud. Having said that, I think she probably had digital copies of the list and gave the original to Lydia for safekeeping."

That made sense and matched what Nico knew about Ariana. "But wasn't it Lydia who was purported to be the leaker? Even her brother has acknowledged that. In which case, she would have had the original list herself, wouldn't she?"

He heard a sigh at Testa's end. "I know. I can't figure that part out either. Did Lydia say or do anything unusual when you met with her?"

Jesus, define "unusual" these days, Nico thought. Since Ariana's death and all the ensuing things since then, he'd lost all sense of normalcy. Something niggled at the back of his mind, but it hovered frustratingly out of reach. He remembered sitting on a bench in the sunshine with Lydia and little Gabriela. When he'd asked about Ariana's son, Lydia had become tense, asking him how he knew about Max. Once he'd mentioned knowing Francesca, she'd relaxed a bit.

Suddenly, what he was trying to grasp clicked into place. He'd had the sense Lydia was about to tell him what she knew about Ariana's investigation when her phone pinged. She had looked at the screen and immediately jumped up, saying she had to go. It was then that she wrote down Elle Sinclair's name and number and handed it to him before running down the stairs to her car below.

"Do you know who Lydia got a text from?" Testa asked after Nico recounted this to him.

"I haven't a clue. But minutes later, she was run off the road right in front of me."

"Like someone knew exactly where she'd be."

"Yes. Exactly like that."

Testa was silent for a moment before speaking again. "OK, we need to get Lydia Rapa's phone records immediately preceding her death," Testa said. "The local police would have them. It would be one of the first things they would have looked into following her death. Or they should have."

"How am I going to get her phone records? I have no jurisdiction here unless I'm working a joint case." When the Gozo police had interviewed him after the incident, Nico got the distinct feeling they wouldn't be at all forthcoming in providing information to an outsider, albeit an Italian prosecutor.

"What about Giorgio?" Testa asked.

"What about him?"

"He's family. He can get a court order to request Lydia's telephone records. If the police won't provide them, her mobile phone company would have to."

Given Giorgio's distrust of Gozo's authorities, Nico wasn't at all hopeful he would be willing to help. But hearing him coming in the back door, he promised Testa he'd talk to him, and then hung up.

Giorgio pointed a meaty hand to Nico's empty glass. "Another?"

"No, thank you. It's getting late and I should go." Nico looked at the man behind the bar and tried to gauge how best to approach him. "Giorgio, would you have any idea who Lydia might have received a text message from before she ran off . . . ?" Mere minutes before a car intercepted her and ran her off the road to her death.

Was it Nico's imagination or did Giorgio's expression flinch ever so slightly? The big man looked away and, as if by reflex, reached for his trusty rag and wiped down the counter he'd just cleaned. This was his "tell." His nervous tic. "Giorgio?"

Outside, Caesar barked. Furiously. Then he stopped mid-bark, punctuated by a yelp. In one swift movement, Giorgio reached for something under the counter. "Stay here," he ordered as he came around from behind the bar, gun in hand.

"Giorgio, wait! Don't open the door."

But it was too late. Before Nico could stop him, the big man had crossed the floor, unlatched the dead bolt on the door, and pulled up a solid iron bar. They both squinted into the blinding sunlight.

Giorgio saw the blood on the cement step before Nico did.

"Caesar!" he cried. Instinctively, Nico reached out to grab him by the belt, then leaned back with all his weight to keep him from darting out the door.

"My Caesar!"

"Giorgio!" Nico shouted at him. "They must have run away when he was shot, but poor Caesar's injury means someone is after us. If you go outside, they'll pick you off in seconds." He looked around. "Is there another way out of here besides the back door?" The solid iron gate would hold off whoever was outside, but not for long. And their guard dog had run off.

The man's face crumpled. Rooted to the spot, he stood there, staring blankly at Nico.

"Giorgio, do this for Lydia. Please."

In that split second, Giorgio's expression turned from shock to grim determination. Nico held his breath as he watched him close the door, then take one lumbering step toward him. He seemed ready to collapse, and Nico reached out to steady him. As if to remind him of their predicament, he asked again if there was another way out.

In answer, he made for the area behind the bar. Nico followed, propelled by fear and adrenaline. He nearly ran smack into Giorgio when, past the end of the bar, he stopped dead and leaned over. Nico thought he was going to be sick from the shock of his dog being shot, but instead, he reached down and grabbed a metal ring that sat flush with the floor. He tugged on it and up came a trapdoor. He turned and pushed Nico down a set of wooden stairs, then followed him in and heaved the door closed behind him.

The area was so dimly lit that Nico went down each step, feeling his way along the cold stone wall. Any minute, he expected to tumble down the rest of the stairs and split his head wide open.

"You have two more steps to go." Judging from the distance of Giorgio's voice, Nico assumed he was behind him, still at the top of the stairs. Then he heard a rattle of chains and a distinct click of a padlock being locked. "We need to hurry," Giorgio hissed. "The chain will hold forever, but the old wooden floor won't."

"Shit, Lydia's envelope!" Nico had taken a photo on his phone and sent it to Testa. But even so, he didn't want it found by whoever was after them. "I left it on the—"

"I have it. I'll hide it along the way. Now go!"

Nico sighed with relief that the man's instinct for survival had kicked in. "Which way?" He heard the panic in his own voice.

"To your left."

Somewhere between the top of the stairs and the bottom, Giorgio had acquired a flashlight, and he shone it past Nico, illuminating a long passageway that had been bored through solid rock. Above them, they heard a thud and then the sound of something repeatedly hacking through wood.

"Run!" Giorgio shouted. "Watch your head and don't stop till you get to the end."

Then what? Nico wondered as he held on to his aching

side and sped through the tunnel, ducking at overhead rocks that threatened to remove a layer of his scalp. They heard voices, then the sound of feet lumbering down the stairs they'd just descended. Shit! Their pursuers had made it inside.

"In a few meters you'll see daylight. Head toward it," Giorgio called, this time more quietly. Or was it that the big man had lagged farther behind? Nico couldn't tell.

As Giorgio had said, up ahead was an enormous circle of daylight. Nico's lungs felt ready to burst, but he raced toward it. Then into a corrugated metal tube. Still running at full speed, he heard the sounds of gunshot behind him. Jesus, had they gotten Giorgio?

"Can you swim?" he heard a voice coming up behind him.

Why? Nico wondered. When the ground went out from under him, he got his answer. He was high above the small marina he'd noticed when he sat with Lydia and Gabriela on the bench behind the bar. And now he was on his way into the crystalline water below.

He entered the water feetfirst, like a torpedo. The pain from his cracked ribs was agonizing, and he panicked that he was going to black out under water. It seemed forever before he hit bottom, and then he kicked upward with everything he had. He shot out of the water like a champagne cork. Coughing and spluttering, he silently thanked God for all the years he'd disobeyed his mother and gone cliff diving off Capo Vaticano. Otherwise, fear might have caused his heart to stop dead before he had plunged into the sea.

Frantically, he looked around for Giorgio. Given his enormous size, Nico feared the man might have sunk like a stone. He called his name multiple times, hoping that whoever had been chasing them couldn't hear from above.

"Over here," he heard.

Nico swiveled his head as he continued to tread water, but saw nothing.

"Beside the dock," came an urgent whisper.

Nico scanned the long dock to which several boats were tied. His eyes darted back and forth, trying to make out where the voice was coming from.

"Between the blue hull and the white one, near the far end."

Then Nico saw it—a slight movement. Suddenly, several shots hit the water close enough to Nico that he dove back under and made a beeline for where he'd seen Giorgio. Their pursuers must have seen him too. The clear water was both a boon and a curse. He could clearly make out Giorgio's legs treading water. That meant whoever was shooting at them could too.

When he bumped up against Giorgio, Nico surfaced and stared into the big man's face. "We need to dive under this dock," he whispered to Nico. "My boat is on the other side."

They both ducked as another bullet pinged off something metal.

"I'll go first so I can start the engine. Swim to the far side of the boat, facing away from the dock. There's a metal ladder hanging down."

The next shot broke the surface of the water not three meters from them.

"Now!" Giorgio shouted, before disappearing beneath the surface.

As instructed, Nico followed. He hadn't dived deep enough and felt something tear through his shirt and scrape his back as he swam under the dock. When he saw the near side of a hull and Giorgio ahead of him, he swam to the far side and waited until Giorgio had climbed up the ladder.

He was already at the wheel when Nico pulled himself on deck. "Stay low and slip the lines off!" he yelled.

Crawling across the boat, Nico let off the stern line, then the bowline. Giorgio gunned the powerful V-8 twin engines. The boat shot forward as though from a canon. Nico sprawled onto the deck and clung to a cleat for dear life as they crashed through the waves like a buzz saw gone wild.

They rounded the breakwater and were out to sea before Nico felt the boat's speed slow. When Giorgio waved him back to the helm, he pried his hands from the cleat and gingerly made his way aft.

"You OK?" Giorgio asked when Nico jumped into the cockpit.

"Yeah, just," he said, trying to ignore the searing pain in his side. "What the hell do you feed this thing? It feels more like a rocket ship than a cruiser."

Giorgio laughed and looked out to sea.

Nico reached a hand over his shoulder where his shirt had ripped. "Check my back, will you? I scraped it under the dock."

"It's nothing serious. A few scratches. Not deep. You might want to get a tetanus shot though, just in case."

Yeah, I'll be sure to do that, Nico grumbled to himself. *If I live long enough.*

Chapter Twenty-Three

About ten kilometers out, Giorgio expertly piloted the boat to a serene azure cove, after which he cut the engine and they drifted through one of the many protective arches. Nico suspected they were very near the famous Blue Lagoon on the western coast of Comino Island.

He watched Giorgio go up to the bow and throw out an anchor. Large though he was, the agility with which he moved told Nico he was an experienced boatman. He jumped back into the cockpit and opened a locker from which he extracted two cans of beer. After tossing one to Nico, he pulled off the metal tab and, in one long drink, emptied its contents. He reached for another.

"Got this locker refrigerated," he said, winking at Nico.

The cold liquid hit the spot. Nico finished it in a few swallows and accepted another. "Do you have any idea who those people were back there?" Who clearly wanted them dead.

Giorgio put down his beer, as if to say something. There were tears in his eyes.

"I'm sorry about Caesar, Giorgio, but don't give up hope. There wasn't much blood. He probably ran away and hid."

Giorgio picked up his beer. "I know it's crazy, he's just a dog, but he's my buddy."

Nico thought of little Gabriela—Lydia's beloved dog—safe with the owners of the hotel. He couldn't bear the thought of what might have happened if he'd brought her with him. "Not crazy at all."

A ray of warm sunshine penetrated a hole in the top of the stone archway. For a time, they both sat in silence as the boat swung in languid circles. Nico stood and felt his pocket for his cell phone. Miraculously, it was still there, but it would do them little good after its time in the water. The same could be said for his glasses, which were smashed and twisted beyond repair. He watched Giorgio do the same, but after patting all his pockets he came up empty.

"Do you have a VHF radio?" Nico asked.

Giorgio shook his head. "Never saw the need. I grew up on these waters. I could navigate them blind."

Nico knew from the bereaved look on the big man's face that he was thinking of going back to find Caesar. "We need to go to the police. It's not safe for you to go back to the bar."

The big man's answer was to take another draw on his beer.

"Giorgio, why didn't you claim Lydia's dog after she was killed?"

"Gabriela? The police told me she died with Lydia in the crash." He stared at Nico. "She's alive?" He shook his head. "Those bastards."

Nico thought back to the police interrogation following Lydia's murder. Suspicious of the Gozo police even then, he had told them he'd be returning to Tropea immediately. But he had given the animal shelter his contact information in case someone came looking for Gabriela. That was the missing link he couldn't put his finger on when Panetta had asked who else had known where Nico was. Had whoever attacked and nearly killed him in the alley, gone looking for Lydia Rapa's dog and found out where he was staying?

In a heartbeat, Nico nixed the idea of going to the Gozo police with the list. "Fire up the engine, Giorgio. We need a plan."

"And that would be?"

"Well, we definitely can't go back to your bar. Whoever was after us seemed intent on making sure we didn't make it out of there alive."

"So what other suggestions do you have?" Giorgio asked, making no move to turn on the ignition.

Aware they were running out of options and time, Nico ran through the alternatives in his head. If they docked at the busy Mġarr Harbor, it would only be a matter of time before someone spotted them. Either the police or the bad guys— possibly one and the same—would close in on them faster than vultures to a rotting carcass.

"How far is the Blue Lagoon from here?" he asked.

"Not far, but it's full of tourists at this time of year. It would be a nightmare."

"Exactly! We could blend in with the crowds. It would give us some cover for a while."

Giorgio looked skeptical. "Right, and then what? We don't have a working mobile phone between us. Basically, we're screwed."

Don't bail on me now, big man. "Maybe we could get a cheap throwaway phone there," Nico said. "Giorgio, we're sitting ducks out here. We have to do something."

. . .

N ico sat in the cockpit, barely registering the exquisite scenery as they sped toward the lagoon. With Mifsud hanging on by a thread in the hospital, Nico racked his brain for who they could contact once they arrived at their destination. He couldn't contact Panetta the corrupt SOB. As he sat there ruminating on what to do, the boat veered suddenly, nearly throwing Nico across the cockpit. What the hell?

"Giorgio, what are you doing?" Nico's eyes scanned the surrounding sea. Had he spotted someone in pursuit?

"Hang on," Giorgio called over his shoulder as he shoved the throttles forward. "I have an idea." They were going so fast Nico prayed the cruiser wouldn't burst open at the seams.

In the distance, a church spire came into view on top of the cliffs. As they got closer to land, Nico could make out what looked like a small village clustered below it. The boat slowed as they approached a dock on high pilings with a marquee mounted above it. A restaurant. Are you kidding? As hungry as he was, this was hardly the time to think of dining out. He was about to complain when their speed dropped to a few knots. They coasted past the dock, then crawled slowly along the rocky coastline. Rubbing his bruised ribs, Nico joined Giorgio at the helm. He was squinting toward the rocks, apparently searching for something.

"Look for a large rock painted white, with two little red ones beside it. Behind them there's an opening."

Nico's eyes scoured the shoreline, but all the rocks blended together in a solid line of gray. He couldn't see any opening.

"There it is." Giorgio pointed.

Sure enough, as they got closer, Nico saw the three rocks. "Where are we?" His question, mixed with the lapping water, echoed around the cave they'd entered.

"I'm going to bring her in as slow as I can, but there's a bit of a swell so prepare to push off the rocks."

Bring her in where? Nico wondered as he moved to the starboard side. There was nowhere to go but into a solid-rock dead-end. When the bow had almost nosed the wall ahead of them, Giorgio reached out with a boathook in one hand and pushed the boat back while turning the wheel hard with the other.

"OK, prepare to fend off," he instructed Nico.

Sure enough, they were alongside a low platform made of ancient-looking bricks, crudely fashioned into a landing. Nico slid his hands along the slippery arch above it and pushed the boat back as best he could. Giorgio cut the engine and leaped over to Nico's side and handed him the boathook. While Nico held them off against the swell, Giorgio retrieved a couple of bumpers from under one of the boat's seats and expertly dropped them into place. "Good job," he said.

Nico gazed around the cave. "Where are we?"

"In part of an old air-raid shelter. It's slippery, so be care-ful." With a flashlight in one hand, Giorgio held out his other arm and signaled for Nico to jump off the boat. When Nico grasped it, it was like hanging on to a solid iron post.

"Follow me."

"Where?"

For the first time since they'd left the bar, the big man smiled. "First, to get something to eat. Then, hopefully, a way out of here."

After threading their way through arches that in spots were so narrow Nico seriously wondered if Giorgio might get stuck, they duck-waddled through a series of dank passages. Like the bunker he'd raced through beneath the bar, he kept a close eye out for the ragged spikes that hung from the ceiling. Were they stalagmites or stalactites? He tried to remember back to his middle school geography. Whichever they were, they looked capable of puncturing his skull like it was a soft-boiled egg.

Nico was wondering how far underground they were when up ahead he saw lightbulbs surrounded by wire cages. Electricity? It looked like nothing in here had been touched in centuries. Giorgio turned off the flashlight, and it took a few seconds for Nico's eyes to adjust. When they did, he saw they were at the bottom of a set of stone steps, at the top of which was a rough-hewn wooden door recessed into the wall. He stopped at the bottom of the stairs and watched as a hunched-over Giorgio banged one of his meaty fists against the door. Nothing. Again, he rose his fist to the door, but this time it was as if he was hammering out Morse code. In a rhythmic beat, he alternated between his fist and the open heel of his hand.

Breaking through the quiet, they heard the grating sound of metal moving on the other side, and the door swung open. The smell that emanated from the illuminated doorway was enough to make Nico's mouth water. The man on the inside shouted something in a language Nico didn't understand and threw his arms around Giorgio. Even from his position at the bottom of the stairs, he could see, over Giorgio's shoulder, the tears rolling down the stranger's face.

"Sami," Giorgio said. "I need your help."

"Come in, come in!" Their host waved them both in. "Anything, my friend. But first, you have to eat."

. . .

As dish after dish was placed on the table inside the restaurant's kitchen, the two men caught up in their native language, then no doubt noticing Nico's confusion, they would apologize and switch to English. But when Nico went back to mopping up the garlicky tomato sauce on his earthenware plate of *aljotta,* fish stew, they'd forget themselves and revert to the curious blend of Arabic, Italian, and several other languages that make up the Maltese mother tongue.

Finally, when Nico politely declined any more food, Giorgio pushed himself away from the table. "Sami, we need your help. Some people are after us."

"Anything. What do you need?"

"My boat."

Sami clapped his friend on the back. "We can look after it for you. No one will find it down there."

"No, I want you to take it out to sea and set fire to it. Then report it to the Coast Guard."

Sami's eyes widened, but he said nothing.

"We need burner phones and money. Can you arrange that?"

"The money will be easy. I have that in the safe. But you will have to stay overnight for me to get the phones."

Giorgio looked across the table at Nico, who nodded in agreement. Truth was, the food and wine had taken the edge off, and the thought of a good night's sleep in safe surroundings was more than he could have hoped for.

After apologizing that they'd have to share a room in the attic, Sami handed them a pile of sheets and blankets. Nico insisted Giorgio take the bed and he would take the couch.

"You will be safe here. Sleep well," Sami said. "I'll leave

early in the morning and be back with what you need before midday. Someone will bring breakfast up to you."

When Sami had closed the door to the loft, Nico turned to make up the couch. Lumpy though it was, it was the most luxurious bed he could imagine at the moment. When he turned around, Giorgio was sitting on the edge of the bed, elbows on his massive thighs, holding his head in his hands. Was he thinking of his sister? His dog? Given what the poor man had been through in the last few weeks, it was likely all the above.

"Your boat. Are you sure?" Nico asked as he got under the covers.

Giorgio shrugged, his expression long and drawn. "I have nothing left to lose. Having whoever was after us think we died in a boating accident is the easiest way to get off their radar."

Nico pulled the sheet up under his chin. He had seen the names on Ariana's list. Not one of them would be satisfied until they destroyed anyone and everyone who could identify them and their ties to money laundering. The ruse of him and Giorgio dying in a boat fire might work for a short time, but it wasn't a permanent solution. But, Nico mused as he drifted into the welcome oblivion of sleep, he sure as hell wouldn't want to be in Alesandru Baldisar's shoes right now. He would be looking over his shoulder for the rest of his life. However short that might be.

Chapter Twenty-Four

Nico awoke to the sound of Giorgio returning to their room. The scent of soap mixed with fresh coffee and something delicious as he walked past. He took a quick shower before sharing a generous breakfast of eggs, potatoes, and scones—Giorgio having Nico's share of the bacon too— that someone brought from downstairs. They were both getting eager to move on when, true to his word, there was a rap at the door. "It's me, Sami."

Giorgio opened the door and stood aside for their host to enter. Sami put a rucksack on the table and pulled out two mobile phones. He handed one to each of them. "These are burners and can't be traced, but keep them turned off and remove the batteries when you're not using them. Don't give your phone to anyone or leave it unattended. Do you understand?"

Both men nodded.

"And use the factory reset on each of your phones regularly."

As Nico listened, he was wondering how a restaurant owner knew so much about mobile phone security when Sami handed him a shirt. "I think we're about the same size, so this should fit." He tossed an extra-large T-shirt to Giorgio.

Grateful, Nico took off his torn shirt, stiffened by the salt water, and donned the new one. It fit perfectly.

"We'll stop at the safe in my office downstairs on your way out." Sami looked around the room. "Do you have everything?"

"Yes," Giorgio said. "You have no idea how much we appreciate this."

Sami merely nodded. "It's time. You need to go. I have a boat and a driver waiting outside to take you wherever you want. You can trust him."

They followed Sami down the stairs, through the restaurant kitchen and into a small vestibule situated inside where Nico and Giorgio had entered from the subterranean level below. He kneeled, opened the safe, and extracted a white paper bag. He handed it to Giorgio.

Giorgio opened it and gasped. "This is too much," he whispered. "We don't need . . ." He swallowed. "I'll pay you back every penny."

Sami shook his head. "I owe you." He clapped an arm around Giorgio's shoulders, then extended his hand to Nico. "Godspeed. Stay safe, both of you."

N ico and Giorgio sat inside the launch's cabin, any view of them from the outside obscured behind tinted windows. If Giorgio had any misgivings about the impending demise of his own boat, he didn't give any sign as they'd hustled past it to board the vessel that would take them to their destination.

Nico's number one priority was to get in touch with Vincenzo Testa to let him know they were safe. Thank God he had a good head for remembering numbers. He also wanted to find out if the journalist had heard anything regarding Max or Francesca. If the police had tried to contact Nico, they must have been wondering why he hadn't returned their calls. Next, he intended to get to the bottom of who was behind their attack at the bar. With the murder of his sister and possibly his dog likely front of mind, Giorgio was willing to follow Nico's lead.

Leaving Gozo's scenic hills behind, they sped past what was left of the Azure Window— the natural limestone arch had, heartbreakingly, collapsed in 2017 from erosion and over-tourism. As they settled in for the ride, the two men went through their checklist and how they would handle their arrival. Giorgio had already briefed their captain that instead of going into Valletta's Grand Harbour, he should pull into the fishing village of Marsaxlokk on the south side of the mainland. There, he explained to Nico, they would easily blend in with the hordes of locals and tourists who came to buy from the fishermen's markets every day.

Soon, they felt the boat slowing, and the captain rapped on the roof of the cabin. Nico looked out the window. Gradually, the colorful boats known as *luzzus* came into view. As they got closer, Nico spotted Eyes of Horus adorning every bow; the symbol was painted on each to protect the fisherman from harm. Their skipper leaned into the cabin and said something to Giorgio that Nico couldn't understand.

"We're not tying up," Giorgio explained. "He's going to come alongside the stone wharf, so get ready to jump." Grabbing the rucksack, they climbed the steps to the cockpit.

No sooner had they put their feet on solid ground than they were they greeted by a snarling mastiff who appeared to be guarding the nets and ropes piled beyond the boats. Nico stopped dead in his tracks. Giorgio said something to the dog in Maltese and put out his hand. The dog sniffed it, then turned tail as if completely bored.

"What did you say?" Nico asked.

"To be a good dog and go lie down."

Shaking his head, Nico grinned and followed Giorgio as he pushed through the crowds surrounding the fishmongers, grocers, and honey stalls. The farther away from the markets they got, the more the overpowering smells of fish mixed with the sweetness of pastries faded. The cacophony of the crowd lessened, and they found themselves on a quiet back-street. As they walked side by side, Nico marveled at the crayon-box effect of the front doors that faced the street. Regardless of how ancient the buildings were, each door had been freshly painted. They reminded him of brightly colored sentries standing at attention.

At the end of the block, Giorgio took a sharp right. He stopped and looked around as if trying to get his bearings. Then he pointed to a blue door that, unlike all the others, was arched and had a wrought-iron balustrade above it. They crossed the street and stood outside the entrance. While Giorgio ran his finger down the list of names, each with its own buzzer, Nico noticed the camera mounted above the entrance. Halfway down the list, Giorgio found what he was looking for and punched the button. Nico assumed they had passed muster when he heard a click, and Giorgio pulled open the heavy wooden door.

They wound their way up the ancient stone steps, then along a narrow corridor before stopping at a door marked *3A*. As Giorgio raised his hand to knock, the door opened. On the other side stood a woman Nico estimated to be in her mid- to late-seventies. She wiped her hands on her apron and, with tears in her eyes, reached out her arms. Thin and frail-look-ing, she virtually disappeared in Giorgio's embrace.

. . .

After sharing a basic but satisfying meal of seafood pasta, Giorgio encouraged his mother to retire early. After some vehement objections over Nico and her son cleaning up, a tired-looking Mrs. Rapa gave in and went into a small bedroom off the main living area.

Nico looked around the apartment. He wondered if there was a Mr. Rapa Senior and if he'd ever lived here. While the elderly woman was well-dressed—her clothes were simple but of good quality—the surroundings could only be referred to as dingy. The carpets were threadbare; the furniture worn and sagging. Judging by the scuffs and chips on the walls, the apartment's interior hadn't seen a coat of paint in decades.

"Has your mother lived here a long time?" he asked casually as Giorgio washed the pots and he dried. Giorgio began to scrub the pot he was washing a little harder. Finally, when the last dish had been returned to its meagerly stocked cupboard, Giorgio opened the fridge. He pulled out two bottles of Cisk, flicked off their tops, and handed one to Nico. They sat across from each other, Giorgio's beefy arms resting on the plain wooden table. Absently, he reached for the dishcloth Nico had left on the tabletop. There it was again: the nervous tic Nico had observed back on Gozo.

Giorgio put down the cloth and looked Nico square in the eye. "Before they shot Caesar, you asked if I knew who Lydia received a text from right before she left the bar." He fiddled with the rag again, then put it down. "It was from my mother."

Nico sat back in his chair, not knowing what to say.

"Since my father died several years ago, she's lived with us—my sister and me—on Gozo." As if to fortify himself, he took a swig of his beer, half draining the bottle. "As you know, when you met with Lydia right after getting off the ferry the day they killed her, I was at the bar."

Nico waited to exhale.

"I had left my phone at home that day. My mother used it to text Lydia that she wasn't feeling well and needed her to pick up a prescription." He looked toward the closed door of the bedroom. Quietly, he placed his empty beer bottle on the table. "Later, I discovered there was spyware on my phone. I have no doubt there was on Lydia's as well. She had many threats that she suspected came from members of her own party because of her friendship with Ariana Calleja."

Nico finished his beer and set the empty bottle next to Giorgio's. "Does your mother know?"

Giorgio shook his head. "It would kill her to think she was in any way responsible for her daughter's death. I moved her here—this is a friend's place—right after I discovered the tracking app on my phone. She doesn't go out. I've arranged for everything to be delivered to her."

Nico's memory reeled back to the awful fire and explosion after little Gabriela was catapulted from the car. "Was Lydia's phone recovered after the accident?"

"If it was, the police never told me. I've been waiting for them to come after me when they got my sister's mobile phone records." The big man's brow furrowed into a deep rut. "I don't know which is worse, the cops or whoever killed Lydia."

Nico nodded solemnly. They could be one and the same.

While Mrs. Rapa slept, Giorgio settled into a hollow on the couch and flipped through the few TV channels that were available. Nico used the opportunity to reach out to Vincenzo Testa. Unable to use their secure method of

communication, he sent a regular text. Within seconds, Nico's
burner phone rang.

"*Grazie Dio* you are all right," Testa said. "Where have
you been? I've been trying to reach you."

Nico scratched his bristly chin. "Yeah, it's been an interesting forty-eight hours. Have you heard anything about
Francesca Bruno or Max?"

"No, nothing. Giorgio . . . is he—?"

"Yes, I'm looking at him right now. We're safe." For now,
at least. Nico knew better than to divulge his location, burner
phone or not.

"Have you seen the news?" Testa asked.

"No, we only have a few stations here. Why?"

"This might not be the best time to tell him, but someone
torched his bar last night. Burned it to the ground."

Nico tried to keep his expression neutral as he sneaked a
look at Giorgio. "Any idea who?" Ordinarily, a fire in a bar
wouldn't have attracted much attention, but given it had
occurred on the tiny island of Gozo, and everyone knew what
had happened to Lydia, it would have been big news.

"No. If the police know, they're not saying anything
publicly."

Nico didn't dare tell Testa about their underground
escape, lest Giorgio ask about the bar or anything back on
Gozo.

"Were you able to get him to request his sister's mobile
phone records?" Testa asked.

"Ah, no. But I have some more info on that. I'll send it to
you when we get off the phone. Giorgio says hello."

"OK. In the meantime, here's what I suggest you do."

·   ·   ·

"What did Vincenzo have to say?" Giorgio asked as he settled back on the couch after getting himself another beer, which he seemed to drink like water. Nico opted for a soda, wanting to keep a clear head. He felt at any moment that he might himself crash from pain and fatigue. He'd texted Testa and told him why they no longer needed to get Lydia Rapa's mobile phone records. Now he needed to turn his attention to a much more pressing matter.

"He said I need a plan to draw out whoever is after us," Nico replied. "And judging by the names on that list, it better be good."

"My friend who owns this place has a car we can use," Giorgio volunteered. "It's parked in a garage a few blocks from here. I don't know about you, but I want to get back to my bar and raise holy hell with the cops in Gozo. You're welcome to stay with me there. If they come after us again, we'll be prepared."

Nico paused, as if considering the thought. "I don't think it's a good idea to go back there so soon."

"Why not? Don't you want to find out who tried to kill us?" That hollow look returned. "And maybe killed Caesar."

Poor Caesar. For the first time, Nico was glad they didn't have access to local news. Hopefully, the dog had run off somewhere to lick its wounds. Otherwise, he was sure to have been cremated in the bar fire. It would only be a matter of time before Giorgio found out, and then Nico didn't know what the man was likely to do.

The only way to carry out his plan successfully was to split up. As Testa had emphasized, traveling on his own would attract less attention. Second, if Nico could convince their attackers it was him who possessed the information they were after, it would take the focus off Giorgio.

"Your mother looks frail. Don't you think it would be a good idea for you to stay here with her for a while? Until you can both safely return to Gozo."

"And what will you do?"

Nico hesitated while, in his head, he put the finishing touches to his plan. The truth was, he intended to surface as publicly as possible, using himself as bait. And he didn't want Giorgio or his mother to be a part of that. Whoever had been after them had sent a clear warning when they'd set fire to the bar in Gozo. He thanked God Giorgio had hidden the original list somewhere underground, where hopefully, even fire couldn't have got to it.

Chapter Twenty-Five

Mrs. Rapa was still asleep when, before the early light of dawn, Giorgio led Nico to a garage a few blocks from the apartment. After handing him the keys to the Fiat, he gave him a rough clap on the back.

"Be safe, my friend." He reached into his jacket and handed Nico a paper bag. "Half the money that Sami gave us."

Nico was loath to take it, but he couldn't risk using his credit cards until he was ready to be found. And he only had a few euros in his water-stained wallet. "I will pay him back," he assured Giorgio. "Your share, too. This is my fault. I'm so sorry I got you involved."

Giorgio shook his head. "They involved me when they murdered my sister. Even before that, when members of her own party threatened her." He looked down at the rough stone floor of the garage, his foot fussing with a loose pebble.

"I've never told you how sorry I am about your friend. I blamed Ariana for getting Lydia involved." He finally looked up and into Nico's eyes. "But they were both courageous women. Find out who killed them. That will be payment enough for me and Sami."

Nico cocked his head.

"Sami is our brother. My parents adopted him as a teenager, to keep him from going to jail. He and Lydia were very close."

That explained the blood-like bond Nico had witnessed between the two men.

Giorgio opened the driver's side door for Nico. "But take care of my friend's car. Come back safely and I'll tell you the entire story."

A ll the way along the drive from Marsaxlokk to Valletta, Nico berated himself for being a coward and not telling Giorgio about the demise of his bar. But he dare not risk Giorgio throwing a wrench into his plan out of grief or anger. Hopefully, keeping his elderly mother safe would be at the forefront of his mind when he eventually found out. Which Nico was sure he would, one way or another, very soon.

Nico's gut tightened when the signs for Valletta came into view. The hotel he had in mind would be expensive, but thanks to Sami, he had the cash and he didn't plan to stay for long. Just long enough to be noticed.

Upon check-in, he was offered a glass of champagne and given a tour of the iconic five-star hotel that had hosted the likes of Queen Elizabeth II. If the elegant concierge was alarmed by the state of Nico's dress and that he had no luggage, she covered it well. Once escorted to his deluxe harbor-view suite, his first priority was to take a shower. He'd had one at the restaurant and again at Mrs. Rapa's, but except for the shirt Sami had given him, he'd had to get back into the same clothes he'd been wearing since their escape from Gozo. He'd swear his trousers could stand up on their own.

After wrapping himself in a thick terry robe and ordering room service, Nico phoned the concierge and asked if someone might be available to purchase some clothes for him at the luxury men's store he'd noticed off the hotel lobby. After giving his sizes, and this time his credit card number to an enthusiastic young man, he settled in to wait for his meal to be delivered. He tipped heavily, both the room service porter and, later, the concierge who delivered his new wardrobe. After changing into one ensemble, he headed up to the rooftop club lounge, where he ordered a bottle of the most expensive wine on the menu. He took a long sip from the heavy crystal glass as he looked beyond Grand Harbour to the sparkling lights of Valletta.

Here I am, you bastards. Now come and get me.

Chapter Twenty-Six

It took two days and an obscene amount of cash and credit card chits, but they finally took the bait.

"Excuse me, Sinjur Moretti," the concierge said when Nico answered the door to his suite. "This came for you, marked urgent, so I thought I'd bring it right up."

Nico handed her a tip and took the envelope, careful to only touch one edge with his thumb and index finger. After casually questioning her about the person who'd delivered the envelope to the hotel—it was a courier they regularly used— he thanked her and closed the door.

Holding the envelope with a pair of tweezers helpfully provided in the hotel's complimentary toiletry kit, Nico carefully slit it open and extracted a folded sheet of paper.

Tonight. 9 p.m. Albert Town wharf.
  We each have something the other wants. Come alone.

His pulse thrumming, Nico placed the paper on the marble counter. Then he sent a text.

Game on!

It was dark when the cabdriver dropped Nico off at the vast stretch of concrete dock in the Albert Town. In the absence of streetlamps, Nico caught sight of an enormous heap of rusted heavy-gauge chains in the glow of the taxi's lights as it pulled away into the night. He stood by a metal-link fence that ran parallel to the deserted stretch of road. Looking toward the water, he could see the moorage lights of commercial fishing boats, and what appeared to be a private yacht. It stood out amongst the others, its pristine condition a stark contrast to the rust buckets floating beside it. Was that the vessel that would come for him?

It was said that Malta had a church for every day of the year. Although he wasn't a praying man, looking along the coastline, Nico took some solace in seeing a lit spire punctuate the night sky. A sign he chose to view as a comforting omen.

Alone on the dock, Nico felt like a singular pulsing beacon. He was vulnerable from every direction; they could take him out in a heartbeat. But then, that wouldn't serve any purpose for whoever he was yet to meet. They had something they wanted from him. And he sure as hell knew what he wanted from them.

Nico had lost count of how many lengths of the wharf he'd paced when he heard a car's tires crunching over gravel. The vehicle slowly edging toward him must have been dark in color. All he could see in the blackness of the night were two pinholes of light from the car's parking lights. He slowed his pace as every muscle in his body tensed. So much for the yacht.

His eyes strained to penetrate the opaque darkness. He heard a car door open.

"Nicoló Moretti?"

"Who's asking?"

"I don't have time for games."

Like car lights flashed on high, and like a deer caught in the headlights, Nico froze.

"Remove your jacket. Hold it, and your other hand, at your sides and walk toward me."

They were going to check him for a weapon and probably a wire. He took a deep breath, shrugged off his jacket, and took several paces forward. The man standing beside the car was a good six inches shorter than him, but built like a tank. He stepped directly in front of Nico, then bent down and patted one of his legs from hip to toe. He repeated the same thing on his other side.

"Open your shirt."

Nico did as he was instructed.

"Get in the back." The man slid in next to him, then tapped the driver on the shoulder. "Let's go."

"Where are we going?" Nico asked, buttoning his shirt.

The man shook his head. "I'm just the deliveryman."

Great. Where and to whom am I being delivered?

Using himself as bait was seeming less and less like a stellar idea.

The sickly sweet scent of his escort's aftershave wafted over him as they sat side by side in silence. Nico felt each jarring bump and pothole as they sped along the road that led from the wharf. Their driver glanced rather too often in both his rearview and side mirrors. By the time they reached the main highway, he seemed confident no one was following them.

Nico estimated they'd gone about twenty kilometers when the car crossed two lanes before exiting to the left. Again, he noticed the driver checking his mirrors, ensuring no one had followed them off the highway. From the dim lights dotted along the road, they appeared to be in an old warehouse district.

The car slowed, then turned off the road. The driver pulled up in front of a gate topped with enormous curls of razor wire. He rolled down his window and looked up at the camera mounted above. Within seconds, the gate slid open and they drove into what looked like a disused mini storage facility. Several expansive buildings ran parallel to each other; each had a straight lane of cracked and faded asphalt between them. The driver took the last lane to the far right and drove about halfway down before stopping behind a black Jaguar XJ sedan that was parked outside a rusty metal door. Nico fought to slow his racing heart. The sound of his own pulse was deafening, and his mouth was as dry as dust.

"Get out," Mr. Cheap Cologne said.

Nico slid from the back seat, hoping his trembling legs would hold him.

His escort rapped on the door before opening it. "Inside," he ordered.

Coming in from relative darkness, the lights inside the warehouse assaulted Nico's eyes. When his vision cleared, he half expected to see the clichéd single wooden chair sitting in the middle of this cavernous room. Instead, a man of average height strode out from a darkened corner as if he was an actor entering stage right. Wearing sharply creased navy trousers and a pale blue linen jacket, his well-shined brogues tapped across the concrete floor as he walked toward them. Recognizing him from his photographs, Nico knew he was looking at none other than Alesandru Baldisar.

"Sinjur Moretti, thank you for coming. I believe we have something to discuss that is of mutual interest."

A wave of nausea hit Nico. Was Francesca here? Being held somewhere in the background, bound and gagged?

"Get to the point, Baldisar."

"Ah, I see you're not a man for small talk. Very well." He tilted his head and nodded at his man, who was still standing inside the door. He turned and slipped back outside.

His hands clasped behind his back, Baldisar paced in tight circles. "Are you a gambling man, Sinjur Moretti?" he asked with a smile, though it came nowhere near to reaching his eyes.

Nico was trying to decide how to play things when the door opened. But instead of seeing Baldisar's man, he saw a tall individual with a black sack over his head stumble in ahead of him. His hands were cuffed in front of him and on his left wrist he wore a large Oyster Rolex. He was shoved to a halt in front of Baldisar.

"Take off the bag," Baldisar ordered.

His goon had to stretch on his tiptoes to pull it off.

"Turn around."

Slowly, the captive turned.

Nico looked into the eyes of Special Investigator Roberto Pezzente.

His face was swollen and bruised, his eyes barely visible in the puffy folds of flesh. His bloody nose sat at a sickening angle, flat against one cheek. There were angry red ligature marks around his neck.

"I believe you two know each other." This time, Baldisar's smarmy grin illuminated his face like a twisted jack-o'-lantern.

In that moment, Nico raged with emotions. This man, one of his own countrymen. He'd suffered, yes. Hit rock bottom, yes, but to work for this disgusting man. It was all he could do but to spit at—

Pezzente's eyes flicked side to side.

Nico opened his mouth to speak. Pezzente still faced him, his back toward Baldisar.

Pezzente's swollen and red eyes moved again. Then again, this time more urgently. What was he playing at?

Nico scowled and moved aside. "Is this what you brought me here for? You told me you have something of mutual interest." He looked back at Pezzente. "What is this bullshit?"

Baldisar looked momentarily caught off guard. "Admittedly, my people were a little rough on him, Sinjur Moretti, but are you telling me you don't recognize a fellow citizen of *Italia*?"

Nico stepped right into Baldisar's face, causing him to take a step back. "I don't know who the fuck this is, and I'm not interested in whatever game you're playing. Either you have something to trade or you don't. Which is it, old man?"

Mr. Deliveryman stepped forward, but Baldisar cut him off. "Wait outside!" he snapped. It appeared Baldisar didn't like to be shown up in front of his people.

"Well, what's it going to be?" Nico asked more aggressively than he felt. *Shit!* Why the hell would Baldisar have Pezzente and was he about to suffer the same fate when he discovered Nico didn't have what he'd come for? Ariana's list.

Nico's heart raced. He was grateful for the jacket he'd

been allowed to put back on after they had searched him. It hid the fact that his shirt was stuck to his back, soaked in sweat. Out of his peripheral vision, he saw Pezzente raise his cuffed hands to wipe his forehead.

He tried to piece together how the investigator had come to be there. He'd clearly turned rogue, but why would Baldisar's people have beaten him to a bloody pulp? He'd be on their side, right? But Pezzente had definitely signaled not to acknowledge him.

Jolting him from his thoughts, the door to the warehouse suddenly flew open and in burst Cheap Aftershave. Baldisar's expression darkened. "I told you to wait—"

"Boss, we need to get out of here, now!" He crossed the floor, pushed Nico out of the way, and hissed something in his superior's ear.

The color drained from Baldisar's face. "How long ago?" he asked.

"Ten minutes. Sir, we need to go now!"

Baldisar looked at Nico, then at Pezzente. "Bring him."

Nico's pulse raced. Did he mean him, Pezzente, or both of them?

The man threw the sack over Pezzente's head and within seconds, the three of them bolted for the door. Nico ran, lunging at it before it slammed closed with a bang. He knew before he tried the handle that it had been locked. Turning, he scanned the empty expanse of the warehouse. Along the back wall, from where Baldisar had first emerged, were a couple of closed doors and a row of internal windows that had been papered over. They must have been offices at one time. A trickle of sweat rolled down his back as he crossed the cement floor. With a sense of foreboding, he reached for the handle of the first door. Locked. He rattled the second, and then the third, but they were all locked. Baldisar had brought him here for a reason. Had he meant to obtain the list in exchange for Francesca?

"Hello, hello, is anyone in there?" he called out.

Nothing.

He was about to call again when he thought he heard a muffled bump. He stopped dead, straining to hear. There it was again! The doors were made of metal, but he was sure he'd heard repeated bumps coming from inside.

Frantically, he scanned the warehouse for something he could use to smash through a window. Nothing. Then he saw it: a red fire extinguisher haphazardly hanging in a corner. He ran and snatched it off the wall, then raced back to the nearest of the three offices. Holding the extinguisher with both hands above his head, he heaved it against the window. He leaped back as paper and splinters of glass flew everywhere. Then he shrugged off his jacket and wrapping it around his fist, he knocked off the jagged pieces around the perimeter of the window. As he prepared to climb through, he halted.

There was nothing in the tiny room but four walls. Not a stick of furniture, nothing. Now what? The only tool he had was on the inside, so he hitched himself up, feeling a piece of glass cut through his jacket and into the soft palm of his hand. Ignoring the pain and his aching side—this is not what Dr. Camilleri would describe as 'moderate' activity—he jumped through the opening and landed clumsily on the other side. He grabbed the fire extinguisher from the floor and was about to turn and jump back through when he heard a thunderous bang. He looked over at the warehouse entrance literally before the steel door exploded into the room. A blaze of black-clothed men in helmets charged in like locusts, assault rifles collectively pointed at Nico.

"Don't move!"

Still standing on the inside of the office, Nico dropped the extinguisher and winced as he shot his hands in the air. As he thought he was about to lose control of his bodily functions, he read the bold letters on the front of their bulletproof vests. *Pulizija.* Thank you, God.

"Please," he shouted. "Someone's in there."

Chapter Twenty-Seven

Still pointing their assault rifles at Nico, the sea of black uniforms separated. An officer, wearing a vest and helmet but considerably less weaponry, emerged from the gap and strode toward him. Quickly, efficiently. "Sinjur Moretti?"

"Yes," Nico said, his trembling hands still in the air.

"I'm Inspector Farrugia. Are you all right?"

Nico lowered his arms. "Yes . . . yes, I think so."

The inspector turned and gave his men an affirmative nod, and they lowered their weapons.

"The two men." Nico asked. "Baldisar and Pezzente?"

"Someone must have tipped them off, and they'd gone by the time we got here," Farrugia said. "We have a team out looking for them."

Looking for him? The bastard had escaped!

"Right now, we need to clear this place and get you out of here." When Nico hesitated, Farrugia said, "If there's anyone in there, my men will find them. Follow me."

Nico reluctantly followed Farrugia out of the building and along the cracked asphalt lane to an open area inside the barbed-wire fence. Empty when they'd driven in, there was now a cluster of black SUVs and vehicles in what looked to be a makeshift operations center. The inspector motioned toward the steps that led up into a customized van. "I have to get back to my team, but there's someone inside who's eager to see you."

"But what about—" Nico began to ask, but the inspector had already turned on his heels and left.

Nico climbed up the stairs into the van, which was tall enough to stand up in. To his right, at the dash of the vehicle, two uniformed officers worked at computers. Nico looked to his left and saw someone grasp the back of one of the seats and, with a grunt, pull themselves to a standing position. Leaning on a cane with one hand, a tired-looking Inspector Mifsud extended the other.

"Good to see you, my friend," he said.

The paramedics gave Nico a once-over and bandaged his hand before he and Mifsud resumed their briefing. Someone had brought in hot coffee and food. After wolfing down a couple of sandwiches—he didn't even ask what was in them—and refilling his coffee twice, Nico joined the inspector at the back of the command center, away from the hustle of the team members who were coming and going.

"How did you find me?" Nico asked. Once Mifsud had confirmed that he'd received the text that the plan was about to go down, Nico had no choice but to give it over to him and to God. There had been nowhere the police could have hidden a surveillance car at the pier, and he recalled that once on the highway, the driver had checked his mirrors repeatedly. They couldn't possibly have been followed to the warehouse.

"Ever heard of a GPS dart system?" Mifsud asked.

Nico shook his head. There was no way whoever had

picked him up and taken him to the warehouse wouldn't have swept the car for attached tracking devices. But obviously something had worked, or he wouldn't be sitting here, shaken but miraculously alive.

"I know what you're thinking," Mifsud said. "And you're right. In a way." He tilted the coffeepot toward Nico, who shook his head. The fatigue and adrenaline had mixed to form a weird buzz in his ears. The last thing he needed was more caffeine.

"Fairly recently, US highway patrol units began using a system that uses compressed air to launch a tracking device from the bumper of a police car. The tracker sticks to the vehicle they're following, then the police can back off from a potentially dangerous high-speed chase without losing the subject."

Nico had never heard of it, but he still couldn't fathom how any car could have gotten close enough to them to shoot the GPS without being noticed. There had definitely been no vehicle following them when they exited the highway onto the road that ran along the warehouse district.

"Police don't even have to stay in proximity to the target's vehicle. They can track it remotely from kilometers away. Even in the next city or town," Mifsud said, taking a sip of his coffee. "I never thought I'd say this, but America's technology is something to behold. We were fortunate to get a few units before several other European countries. Anyway, once our guys shot the dart at the car you were in, our technicians monitored it from right here in this van."

Nico ran his fingers over his head. They came away gritty. "The technology makes sense, but where along the route were they able to shoot the dart?" He was virtually certain there hadn't been another close vehicle in sight.

A grin lit up Mifsud's gaunt face. "We had a camouflaged

vehicle hidden in the woods as you came out of the pier's car park. Fortunately, that gravel road was bumpy, full of potholes, because sometimes, you can detect the GPS dart hitting the car. In this case, there must have been enough noise and movement to distract the driver. I won't lie to you, it was still a bit of a risk."

One Nico was inordinately grateful they'd taken. "And the men who escaped?" he asked.

"That was unfortunate," Mifsud admitted. "But we have helicopters with infrared cameras in the air and tracking units out everywhere. They can't have gotten far. We'll find them."

"Inspector?" A woman came from the front of the command center. "It's affirmative. They're waiting for you."

"Thank you," Mifsud said. He leaned heavily on the cane as he slowly pushed himself up.

"Have they found them?" Nico gingerly got up to follow him.

"Stay here. I'll be back as soon as I can." The two police officers left the van, shutting the door behind them.

Nico looked around the van for a window. There were none. Then he tried to handle of a rear door. It was locked. Dammit! All he could do, yet again, was sit here helplessly, wondering where Mifsud had gone.

H is head had lolled back against the leather chair when he woke up with a start. Someone was gently shaking his shoulder. "Sinjur Moretti, the inspector is ready for you. Please come with me."

Embarrassed, Nico wiped the drool from the corner of his mouth. As he tried to stand up, one leg collapsed, having fallen asleep. He smiled sheepishly at the woman, whose demeanor remained professional. "Take your time, sir," she said as she handed him his jacket.

Nico followed her to the front of the van. But the inspector wasn't there. "He's waiting for you outside. Just go down those steps," she said. That made sense, given the pain Nico suspected Mifsud was still in, he'd probably want to minimize the number of stairs he had to tackle. Given the state he'd been in when Nico last saw him, it was a marvel he was out of the hospital at all.

Sure enough, there was Mifsud, outside the van and leaning on his cane.

"Have they found them?" Nico asked.

Mifsud shook his head. "Not yet."

Nico's hopes faded.

"But they did find someone. Would you like to see her?"

Would you like to see her? Why hadn't Mifsud said who it was they'd found in the warehouse? Nico's gut tightened. If it *was* Francesca who'd been in one of the abandoned offices, he wondered how he'd react when he finally saw her. Had she, as Elle had intimated in Mdina, had something to do with Max's disappearance? Or, as James Paddington had reported, was it Elle who'd absconded with him? Even once Sami had provided Nico and Giorgio with burner phones, he hadn't dared contact London police for an update.

He and Mifsud picked their way across the vast warehouse yard that was now congested with police and other emergency vehicles. Up ahead, there was a row of ambulances parked a safe distance away from the scene. Nico had observed them earlier, waiting on the other side of the barbed-wire fence. Along with what he knew to be the forensics coroner's vans.

As they reached the ambulances, Mifsud, who had been walking alongside Nico, hobbled ahead of him, taking the lead. "Would you mind waiting here for a minute?"

Nico watched him disappear behind an ambulance. Minutes later, he reappeared and waved Nico toward him. "You can see her now."

He took a deep breath, and he could feel his heart racing as he forced himself to take the few steps forward. As he rounded the corner, he saw her. A blanket around her shoulders, she sat on the bumper of the ambulance, her bare legs hanging over the edge. Her hair was matted, her face smudged with dirt. Her bottle-green eyes shone with tears. The blanket drifted onto the ground as she held out her arms.

"Nico," Francesca whispered. Tears ran in rivulets down her grimy face. "Thank God you're all right!"

A fter being thoroughly checked out at the hospital, the police took Francesca Bruno into protective custody, where officers would debrief her. As relieved as Nico was that she was alive, he felt a hollow spot in his gut. Part of him had wanted it to be Elle. He'd desperately wanted to believe that the woman Vincenzo Testa referred to as "the devil's spawn" hadn't been behind Max's disappearance.

There was so much he wanted to ask Francesca. But for now, he sat with her in the back of the ambulance, holding her hand. He could hear the dispatcher announcing their ETA and some medical statics. She had closed her eyes and Nico scanned every inch of her face and head, looking for any tangible signs of the trauma she'd narrowly escaped. A female officer had been assigned to debrief Francesca, and he prayed that in addition to what she'd obviously endured, she hadn't been sexually assaulted by one of Baldisar's men.

Mifsud had explained that Baldisar had brought her to the warehouse as his trading currency. Francesca had been in one of the remaining two offices, bound and gagged. If the police hadn't broken through the main door of the warehouse, Nico would have found her himself.

"What was Baldisar going to trade her for?" Nico had asked Mifsud before getting into the ambulance. "Ariana's list?"

Mifsud shook his head. "Possibly, but it was you he was after."

"Me?"

"Baldisar was going to let Francesca walk free in exchange for you killing Pezzente. He'd found out that he was your prime minister's special investigator. Having infiltrated Baldisar's inner circle, he knew too much and needed to be disposed of."

"Why wouldn't Baldisar just have one of his thugs kill him? It looked like they'd already done a good job beating him to a pulp."

Mifsud shrugged. "Why would he do that when you would go to prison for the rest of your life for the murder of a top government official? Someone had already eliminated Malta's toughest prosecutor on organized crime. Now, Baldisar could put her Italian counterpart away for life. Especially one that could identify him and some of his shadier investors."

And he almost got away with it, Nico thought. And could have killed Francesca in the process.

As the ambulance pulled into the emergency bay, he saw a cluster of staff in white coats standing outside the hospital doors. He gave Francesca's hand a squeeze as he stood up.

"Put on your best smile, you have a welcoming committee," he said as the doors opened. "I'll be right outside."

As he stood on the pavement waiting for Francesca to be brought out, another ambulance pulled up to the emergency entrance, sirens blasting. The cluster of white coats moved as one unit to the back of the incoming vehicle.

Two paramedics jumped out and removed the stretcher from inside. "Gunshot wound," one of them said. In the seconds it took them to whiz by on the way to the trauma center, Nico caught sight of the occupant on the stretcher. Face as pale as the sheet that partially covered him, lay Roberto Pezzente.

I t was after midnight when Nico said his goodbyes to Francesca at the hospital. She was wan and still shaken, but despite everything she'd been through, she appeared to be holding up remarkably well. Nico had met the police officer who would be guarding her door, and he was confident Francesca was in sensitive and capable hands.

He was about to call it a night when he ran into Inspector Mifsud in the hallway. The man looked exhausted.

"Inspector, what are you still doing here? I thought you'd gone home."

Mifsud nodded. "I just got the report from the police who found Roberto Pezzente. They found him in an abandoned car by the side of the road, not far from the warehouse."

"Was it one of Baldisar's men who shot him?"

"Yes. Apparently, they had ditched the car and run into the woods, an area that covers several hectares. Pezzente had tried to disarm Baldisar's driver and in the scuffle, he was shot. It looks like they left him there rather than letting him slow them down."

Miserable shits. "Have they located them?"

Mifsud shook his head. "Police helicopters stayed in the air with heat-sensing equipment, but as yet nothing. They'll resume the search again at first light.

"The doctors said the bullet only grazed Pezzente's leg rather than penetrating it." Mifsud yawned. "If he has a good night, they'll release him in the morning."

"Go home, Inspector, you're not long out of hospital yourself."

After making sure Mifsud did indeed, go home, Nico looked in on Pezzente, but the guard who was posted outside his room said he was sleeping. That the PM's special investigator had got so close to Baldisar was remarkable, but even Mifsud had admitted to Nico they had a long way to go in order to ascertain in what capacity he was working. Much as he desperately wanted to question him himself, he'd resigned himself to the fact that it was a matter for the police. He'd also come to the conclusion that he may never know who was behind Ariana's murder. Now he needed to focus on something he could do something about.

As Nico left the sounds and smells of the hospital behind and inhaled the fresh night air, he thought of Max alone somewhere without his mother. He must be terrified.

Mifsud could handle Pezzente. It was time for Nico to go to London.

Chapter Twenty-Eight

Having managed to catch five hours of sleep, Nico awoke with more questions than he had answers. Despite Mifsud's assurance the search for Baldisar and his men would have resumed at first light, it did little to assuage his conflicted feelings as he walked to the police station for his meeting with the inspector. The minute it was over, he'd contact his office and let them know he was taking an indefinite leave. And then he'd book his ticket to London.

While Nico still felt drained from the previous day's events, Mifsud seemed to have found his second wind as he related what they'd garnered from Francesca's debriefing. Although he had no obligation to share the details with Nico, it seemed that Mifsud now considered him his equal. After they'd both got themselves a coffee, they settled into a quiet office and the inspector shut the door.

"Does she know who her captors were?" Nico asked.

"No. However, we're certain the man we killed at the vineyard was a hired thug. He had a long list of priors. Miss Bruno confirmed he was the one who abducted her from her apartment, but she said anytime she heard him on the phone, he appeared to just be obeying orders. And that he wasn't too bright."

"Baldisar's orders, do you think?"

"Tough to say. She said she never actually saw him until the incident at the warehouse. She was taken directly there from the abandoned property."

"Was she able to tell you anything more about Max?" For the life of him, Nico couldn't figure out what one could have to do with the other, but Elle's remarks that day in Mdina still niggled at him.

The inspector cleared his throat. "She did, actually."

Nico waited. *Please don't tell me he's—*

"Nico, why didn't you tell me Max is your son?"

The question caught him off guard, and he felt the hot sting of tears that welled up out of nowhere. "I . . . I was going to before you were shot," he said truthfully. His cheeks burned, and he looked away, embarrassed.

Mifsud reached into his trousers pocket and passed a freshly pressed handkerchief across his desk. "I know it was you who arranged to rush my wife and daughters to the hospital when I was in critical condition. I understand both the joy and the pain of being a parent. I wish you'd told me."

The ache in Nico's throat prevented him from speaking. He'd certainly experienced the pain, but would he ever get to experience the joy?

The inspector came out from behind his desk. "Thanks to you, I got to see my family again. That would have been enough for me even if I hadn't made it." He clasped Nico around the shoulder. "You mustn't give up hope, my friend. Believe me when I tell you that the UK police won't stop until they find him."

. . .

With the inspector's optimism in mind, Nico made an effort to distract himself by returning to the hotel and dealing with some work-related emails Gina had forwarded on to him. A number of them were marked as urgent, and while he was grateful Sergio was doing his best to handle them, not one of them held any importance for him. He scrolled through the case summaries that had been his life just a couple of weeks ago and scanned their contents dispassionately. Regardless of whether they found Baldisar—or Max for that matter—he wasn't sure he could face going back to the sheer drudgery of countless hours of investigation that, at best, would result in a temporary halt in serious crime. Did their efforts even do that, he wondered, or were the criminals just laying low until the dust settled and they'd start up again? It was like bailing a leaky boat; the water just rushed in again, until eventually it sank.

Except for that one case he'd lost, his unblemished record could have easily put him in line to be a future magistrate—as he'd hoped Ariana would have become rather than take on the role she had. While it might sound attractive to the lay person—that he would have the ultimate responsibility of making a harsh and final judgment against the criminals that were parasites in his region—there were other challenges. Significant ones. While the Americans led the world in gun violence, Nico's jurisdiction in Italy had chosen bombs as their weapons of choice. Why? Because they were easy to make and difficult, if not impossible, to identify who was behind them. But most of all, death by explosives was a powerful statement. A warning to those who might be considering crossing the line.

Calabrians could fool outsiders—if not themselves—that they lived in one of the most beautiful regions of the world.

While there was still more poverty there than any other part of Italy—save parts of Sicily—tourists still romanticized the region. When something happened, like the bombing that killed Ariana and others at Cannone Square, citizens said it was the exception, that there was no longer a large presence of organized crime in their country. That was the stuff of television shows and movies. Tell that to the mothers and wives and sisters. The sons and daughters who would never see their family member grow old. Tell that to him, Nicoló Moretti, a career prosecutor sworn to uphold and enforce justice in a region that had taken so much from him.

As he powered down his laptop, his mobile rang. Mifsud. With a sigh, he picked it up.

"How soon can you meet me at the hospital?" he asked. "Pezzente has something I think you're going to want to hear."

Chapter Twenty-Nine

When Nico and Mifsud entered the hospital room, Roberto Pezzente was perched on the edge of a chair, fully dressed. The bruises on his face had turned into an interesting collage of brownish-yellow blotches. Steri-Strips covered several lacerations on his cheek and forehead. Nico's eyes traveled to a spot on his scalp that exposed a zippered line of stitches. He was a pathetic sight, but Nico had a hard time feeling sorry for him.

Pezzente struggled to rise from his seat and extended a hand, which Nico ignored. He was there solely out of respect for Inspector Mifsud's urgent request, but had little interest in anything the PM's supposed "special investigator" had to say.

"Look, I'm sorry," Pezzente said. "I think things will make more sense when I've explained everything."

"Really?" Nico said. "Which part would you like to explain? The part about you taking money from Alesandru Baldisar, or the part about you lying to me about the circumstances in which three men were blown up outside the hotel in Saint Julian's?"

Mifsud attempted to cut through the tension in the room.

"Based on some things I've been able to confirm," he said, looking at Nico, "I think we need to hear Investigator Pezzente out."

It infuriated Nico that Mifsud would even refer to Pezzente as an investigator. While he did have empathy for the man who had endured the horrific loss of his family, he had no patience for someone who appeared to have turned against his own country. Or was possibly working both ends against the middle. It might have been better for everyone if Baldisar's man had done a better job when he'd shot him.

Pezzente looked contrite as he acknowledged the inspector's comment. At Mifsud's suggestion, Nico sat down.

"I've been working a complex money-laundering case for over two years. Initially, it was a joint investigation between Italy and Malta, but it turned out to involve more countries and jurisdictions than we'd first suspected. We were getting incredibly close when Ariana Calleja was assassinated. I had managed to get close to Baldisar, and while I felt an obligation to keep you posted, Nico, I simply couldn't risk everything we'd worked so hard on when I didn't know which side you were on."

As if Nico wasn't angry enough, at Pezzente's last comment, he saw red. "I thought we were on the same goddamned side. In case you've forgotten, I'm responsible for prosecuting those cases." His voice rose an octave. "You didn't see fit to fill me in?"

Pezzente looked chastened, but at the same time, he was firm. "We couldn't be sure, given your relationship with Ms. Calleja and the fact that you lost that recent case—what with your flawless record, we couldn't know whether you'd thrown it on purpose."

"This is *bullshit*. I don't know what game you're playing,

Pezzente." Nico turned to leave. "I'm sorry, Inspector, but I'm not going to listen to any more of this."

"Please," Mifsud replied. "I'm confident you're going to want to hear this. It concerns Miss Calleja's assassination."

At that instant, Nico feared his heart had stopped dead in his chest.

Over the next hour, Mifsud and Nico listened as Roberto Pezzente unraveled the moving parts of the sting he'd been working on since Italy's former prime minister was ousted.

"As you know," he said, "I was kept on by the new anti-corruption PM. My team was all but ready to expose the identities of the oligarchs and dictators who were on several European countries' watch lists. Baldisar, who had been just another link in Malta's chain of corporate corruption, inadvertently ended up playing a much more significant role than perhaps he'd planned."

"How so?" Mifsud asked.

"Well, like so many men who come from monied families, Baldisar's ego caused him to think he was more important than he really was. He'd never been as successful or as respected in certain circles as his father and grandfather, so he compensated by playing the big man.

"Vanity and greed caused him to throw his lot in with people much more diabolical than he was accustomed to dealing with. Crimes that would have landed him in prison for insider trading and money laundering, ended up throwing him into the deep end of an international shark tank notorious for devouring its own."

Nico was getting impatient. Right now, he wanted some quick answers. Otherwise, he'd sooner be making plans to travel to London. "What does this have to do with Ariana's assassination?" he asked.

"Baldisar had met Dr. Anna Braithwaite," Pezzente continued. "Initially, it looked like they were having an affair —it was well known she and her husband had been having problems—but Baldisar knew he'd hit it big, and based on her stellar reputation for cutting-edge cancer research, he invested heavily in the pharmaceutical company that funded her."

"Heritage Pharma," Nico said. So far, Pezzente hadn't told them anything they didn't know already. "Get to the point."

"Yes. But when news was about to get out that her medical trials were flawed regarding the miracle drug Baldisar had touted to some of the world's most dangerous people, his world turned upside down. It wasn't that the autocrats and warlords who'd invested with his bank feared the potential monetary losses—for many of them it was mere pocket change—it was the harbinger of international exposure that they took personally.

"We had all of Baldisar's communication devices tapped. He started receiving so many death threats we couldn't keep up. He fired most members of his inner circle and pulled the few that remained closer." Pezzente paused, as if considering his next words. "That's where I came in."

Mifsud had been patiently listening without saying a word, but now he interjected. "With all due respect, Investigator, why would the new prime minister have kept you on when you had been part of the former PM's administration? The corruption in his predecessor's inner circle was well known. Wouldn't he have wanted to wipe the slate clean?"

While Pezzente acknowledged the inspector's comment with a single nod of his head, his expression was one of defiance. His eyes were the color of carbon, and the relaxed smile he'd tried in vain to engage Nico with was a thin, straight line.

"My employer was never our prime minister. Neither the former, nor the current one."

Nico and Mifsud stared at him.

"I am, and have been for some years, employed by a joint task force between the Guardia di Finanza and the Direzione Distrettuale Antimafia."

Nico let out a low whistle. Mifsud's mouth hung open.

"Neither prime minister that I served was aware that while they might have signed my paychecks, I wasn't in their employ."

With that one revelation, all the doubts and questions Nico had about Italy's special investigator had finally been answered. Well, all but one, but he held his tongue for now.

"But for the record," Pezzente said, "I believe our new prime minister is who he claims to be: someone determined to wipe out Italy's decades-long history of corruption."

"You said you have a lead on Ariana's assassination?" Nico said. If that was true, it begged the obvious question: why wouldn't Pezzente have reported it immediately? His suspicions came crawling back. This man was used to being duplicitous. Of playing both ends against the middle.

Pezzente nodded. "Yes, we have the one person who knows who killed Clarence Braithwaite." He paused. "And may have ordered Signorina Calleja's murder."

Mifsud was limping badly and looked about ready to drop from sheer exhaustion as the three men left the hospital. On the way to the safe house where this so-called witness was being kept, he'd told Nico privately he thought it prudent that, for now, they wait before advising any other authorities. Nico knew the police inspector was livid at not being kept in the loop in his own jurisdiction, but if what Pezzente had told them was true, his witness was potentially in enough danger to warrant the highest level of security. For now, the fewer people who knew of their existence, the better.

Upon arrival, Nico observed at least four men in plain-clothes who were clearly guards. And that was just around the perimeter of the nondescript safe house. Two more were posted outside the front door. Under their civilian clothing, Nico detected the bulkiness of bulletproof vests. He'd observed the same scenario many times when witnesses had turned state's evidence and were awaiting trial. For those guarding them, it could be a hazardous line of work. In less than a heartbeat, a drive-by shooter or hidden sniper could take them before they even realized what was happening. Nico had seen more than one such soul never make it home to their families. Judging by the security, it would seem this witness was of critical value.

Inspector Mifsud acknowledged each of the guards as they stepped aside to let them enter. Once inside, they were asked to put their weapons on a tray. As Nico didn't have one, only the inspector's gun was collected. After abject apolo-gies, they were both body-searched and after one of the agents gave the OK, they stood in silence and awaited the appearance of Pezzente's witness. Nico tingled with anticipa-tion, but at the same time a sense of dread descended over him. Would he finally know who was responsible for Ariana's murder?

They heard approaching footsteps and some muffled conversation. Nico and Mifsud looked at each other question-ingly, the atmosphere in the room heavy with tension. Pezzente nodded to the agent who stood in the dining room that had been set up as a command center. From out of the shadows stepped a diminutive figure, maybe five-two or five-three. Wearing an oversized gray hoodie and baggy sweat-pants, the person looked like the whisper of a breeze could lift them off their feet. As they stepped forward, a small hand reached out and pushed the hood back from their face.

"Allow me to introduce you to Dr. Anna Braithwaite."

You could have heard a pin drop as Nico and Mifsud stood in stunned silence.

She pushed a stray lank of reddish-blond hair from her face.

"Dr. Braithwaite," Pezzente said, "this is the special pros-ecutor from Tropea, Nico—"

"Mr. Moretti," she said. "I'm so sorry for your loss. I understand you knew Ariana Calleja personally."

Rather than acknowledge her remark, Nico just stared. This was Pezzente's witness? The woman who had covered up her faulty research and tried to pin it on her husband? And whom, by all accounts, had been complicit in his murder. Nico clenched his hands by his side, trying to tamp down the rage that boiled within him.

"Please sit down," Mifsud said, as if sensing what was about to happen. "Why don't we all sit down, and perhaps Dr. Braithwaite can start at the beginning?"

Anna looked to Pezzente, who nodded. "Please call me Anna," she said, barely above a whisper.

"I was the one who told Ali . . . Alesandru about the drug trials. We'd started a . . . personal relationship—my marriage wasn't going well, and he'd invested heavily in—"

"Dr. Braithwaite," Nico snapped, "I'm really not inter-ested in your love life, nor what role you might have played in insider trading. That will be for the authorities to deal with—"

Mifsud put a hand on his arm.

Anna nodded. "Alesandru was being blackmailed. He didn't know by whom." She clasped her hands in her lap so tightly Nico could see the whites of her knuckles. "He eventually told me that he was behind the car bombing that killed my husband. He said he'd done everything to keep *us*," she made air quotes, "from being exposed."

Everything he'd done. Nico's heart skipped a beat. Did that include ordering the assassination of… ? But he couldn't get the words out. In the background, he could hear someone speaking, but it was garbled as if he was underwater. Mifsud tightened his grasp on his forearm, jolting him from his revelry.

"Everything points to Baldisar being responsible for the bombing that killed Miss Calleja," Pezzente said. "We just don't have proof."

Anna's eyes glistened with tears. "I'm sorry, Mr. Moretti. I tried, but I just couldn't get him to admit to it. When I told Alesandru I was going to tell the police everything"—she took a ragged breath, "he gave Mr. Pezzente here the order to kill me."

Nico sat back in his chair. Stunned. "You were Baldisar's fixer."

D ays before the fateful day that Anna had met up with Baldisar at his palatial island home, Roberto Pezzente, knowing Anna was being investigated by the securities authorities in both the UK and Malta, contacted her and made a deal she literally couldn't refuse. If she did, she could potentially go to prison for the rest of her life. Initially, she'd said no. That all she was guilty of was insider trading and she'd take her chances of receiving a lesser prison term.

However, when Pezzente spelled out to her that they believed Baldisar, or someone he knew, had ordered Ariana's assassination, and she could be charged as an accessory, she capitulated and agreed to wear a wire. The blackmail call was made, and then they waited.

Like a hound to the scent of blood, Baldisar did exactly what they'd hoped for. He reached out to the only person he could confide in. Anna Braithwaite.

Pezzente had replaced Baldisar's helicopter pilot with one of his own people. Anna wore the wire as planned, and the rest fell into place exactly as planned. Pezzente made the arrangements for her to be taken off the island by helicopter, after which he placed her into protective custody. Then Pezzente reported back to his "boss" that the job had been done.

"It was after that," he said, "that Baldisar found out who I was and . . . Well, you know the rest."

"Why did you go back?" Nico asked. "You were free, you could have just put an end to it."

The investigator absently touched the stitched gash on his scalp. "Number one, I needed absolute proof that he'd ordered Ariana… Miss Calleja's assassination."

"And number two?"

"I needed one more piece of the puzzle—the identities of the foreign players Baldisar was in bed with. He was in way over his head. Some of the individuals his bank was laundering money for would make him look like a saint."

Nico had to agree. Even though he now considered Baldisar as a low-life piece of slime, he'd seen the names on Ariana's list. They included some of the most tyrannical despots on the planet. "And by staying on the inside you thought you'd have enough to take him down."

Pezzente nodded. "It was a risk. But it was something I had to do."

Nico looked at the investigator's bruised and swollen face and thought of his twin daughters and his wife who'd been murdered in cold blood. What more did the man possibly have to lose?

Chapter Thirty

Following Anna Braithwaite turning state's witness, every police force in Malta joined in the manhunt for Baldisar. On an island twenty-seven kilometers long and fourteen wide, Nico would have thought it wouldn't be that difficult to locate a fugitive. Knowing he could virtually be anywhere, on land or off, police orchestrated simultaneous raids on both his country and island homes, as well as his private yacht. The latter resulted in them taking Baldisar's captain and crew into custody, but they provided nothing on their boss's whereabouts. If they knew anything, they certainly weren't divulging it to police, and without charges to hold them, they were released. With Baldisar still at large, they might have been safer being arrested and held in jail.

"Is there anywhere else he could be?" Pezzente implored Anna Braithwaite. "The police have searched everywhere they can think of. I suspect his wife would give him up in two seconds, she's pretty pissed off at being under house arrest in Valletta. But we have questioned her and she says she has no idea."

Anna shook her head. "The only place we ever met was on the yacht or the island."

Where does a rat go when he is out of places to hide? Nico wondered. "Roberto, would there be any point in going back to the area around the warehouse? It's odd that even with infrared, the police haven't found them yet. I'm wondering if he could have gone underground. Literally, the way we've seen certain Mafia leaders do."

Pezzente shrugged. "We've tried everything else. What have we got to lose?"

"A warehouse!" Anna jumped from her chair so quickly both men were startled. "Was it near water?"

"No," Nico said. "It was about twenty kilometers from the Albert Town dock. Inland, why?"

"Ali had a storage unit on the water somewhere out of town. He took me there once when we had to pick up something before going out for a weekend cruise."

Pezzente seized on the information. "Do you know the address or how you got there?"

"No, we pulled in by boat. His captain offered to go, but Alesandru insisted on going himself."

"So you tied up at a marina?" Nico asked.

Anna paced the sitting room in tight circles, twisting a lock of her hair around her index finger. "We took the launch from the yacht and . . . Oh, God, why can't I remember?"

Nico took her gently by the shoulders and led her back to the chair. "Anna. I want you to sit down and close your eyes."

She looked at him as if he were mad.

"Please, just trust me. Close your eyes." She sat and did as she was told. "All right, now visualize coming into the harbor. What time of day was it?"

She brought a shaky hand to her chest, then both hands to her temples. "It was late afternoon, the sky was turning dusky and the wind was getting up—that's why Ali didn't want the yacht to go in too close." She squeezed her eyes tighter. "A high-rise. There was a tall building in the background, then a row of low-rise—maybe blocks of flats—in the foreground."

Nico looked at Pezzente, who shook his head.

"OK, a tall building and some low ones. Can you remember anything distinctive? Maybe a statue or—"

"No! It wasn't a marina or flats." Her eyelids were fluttering and Nico worried she was becoming hysterical. He needed to keep her focused. "It was a nightclub. On the beach! All along the beach were these huge cubes of blue."

"Cubes of blue? Like cement blocks? Buildings painted blue? Anna, what?"

"No, they were enormous blocks, all topsy-turvy." Her eyes flew open. "They were blue lights. I remember hearing the music pounding as we got in near the shore. The lights were pulsating to the beat of the music."

Pezzente was already on his phone. Nico could hear him questioning whoever he was talking to about a nightclub on the beach with huge blue-light squares out front.

"We've got it! The Blue Dragon, about thirty kilometers from here. Let's go!"

"Hang on, wait," Nico said. "Anna, you said there was a warehouse there. Was it part of the beach club?"

"I don't know, he made me wait at the bar while he went inside. I don't know where he went from there. But I heard the captain tell him whatever he was picking up was in the warehouse."

F ortunately, their driver knew exactly where to take them. "How long?" Pezzente asked from the back seat of the unmarked police car.

"In this traffic? An hour or more." Nico's hopes plummeted. "But for you, *sinjur*, thirty minutes."

Nico fastened his seat belt while Pezzente worked the phone, calling Mifsud and requesting backup.

"They'll meet us there," he said, buckling his own seat belt as they went the wrong way down a one-way alley.

Nico wouldn't have been remotely able to explain how they got to their destination. They'd woven in and out of so many streets and flown through alleys that if it not for the digital compass readout on the rearview mirror, he'd have had no idea in what direction they'd been traveling. Tires screeching, their driver suddenly swerved off the road and hurtled down a long driveway toward the sea. As they got to a long, low-rise building, he looked for a place to pull over. But a solid line of enormous luxury coaches parked end to end, took up the entire length of the curb.

People were emerging from the coaches, all decked out in formal wear, each wearing a name badge around their neck. *Minchia!* This was not the place for a police showdown.

"Let us out here!" Pezzente said. "And stick around—we might need you."

They leaped from the car and raced past the incoming guests, trying to avoid colliding with anyone. The doorman tried to stop Pezzente, but even after his injuries, he flew past him like a heat-seeking missile. Nico attempted to keep up with him but his side was throbbing. By the time they made it to the front desk, however, there were six uniformed security guards standing shoulder to shoulder, forming a human shield. Pezzente flashed his ID. One guy looked at it and nodded, but while they moved aside to provide an opening, they abruptly closed it when Nico tried to follow.

"Roberto!" Nico yelled.

Pezzente looked back over his shoulder. "He's with me,

let him through. Nobody else gets in or out unless they're police."

The inside of the club was all but empty except for wait staff dressed in black and white, putting the finishing touches to the tables. The room looked large enough to hold several hundred people. On a raised stage at the far end, the band was doing a sound check. The entire back wall was made of accordioned glass and was open to the outside. Beyond, on the beach, there were the huge blue-light cubes Anna had described. They were spread out all along the sand between a long line of outdoor tables and the edge of the water. On the horizon, three police boats raced toward them.

"You stay here to direct them," Pezzente said. "I'm going to find out the lay of the land."

The second the flat-bottomed police boats came right up onshore, officers wearing Kevlar helmets, ballistic vests and night-vision goggles around their necks, bailed out and rushed the beach. Nico was wondering if any of them had been part of the team that rescued him and Francesca at the warehouse, when he spotted Inspector Farrugia in the lead. He hoped this time, they'd have better luck finding their target.

One of the last off the boats was Inspector Mifsud, easily distinguishable by his limp. An officer had hung back and was trying to offer assistance. Except the inspector was having none of it and broke away, caning his way up from the water.

Nico looked around and hoped that with all this fire power, Anna hadn't given them the wrong location. He didn't doubt she'd been here, but could she have been mistaken about there being a warehouse? He looked up toward the club to see Pezzente speaking with Farrugia, who was nodding his

head. As he turned and huddled with his team, Pezzente
broke off and walked back to where Nico stood.

"If he's here, they'll find him," he said. "One of the security guards said there are still some old boathouses and
storage lockers in back of here—part of the original structure
before they converted it into a nightclub."

"Do they have any reason to believe Baldisar is in there?"
Nico asked.

"Not him specifically, but the guard reported seeing lights
in there recently. He just assumed it was one of the owners
working on their boat in dry dock."

By then, a slightly out of breath Mifsud had joined them.

"Inspector, there are, what"—Pezzente looked at Nico for
confirmation—"at least six coaches of conventioneers out
front. We need to get them out of here as soon as possible."

Mifsud's face brightened. "*That* is something I can do.
Take me to them."

He and Nico stood out the front of the nightclub,
watching as disappointed guests grumbled and complained as
they were escorted back onto the buses. "This is seriously
cutting into my cocktail hour," Nico heard one man say, to
which his fellow revelers roared with laughter. *Ignorance is
bliss*, Nico thought. Just a couple more people to board and
they could get everyone out of here safely without them ever
knowing there was a police incident unfolding.

"What the hell?" Nico muttered under his breath. He
turned to Mifsud. "Did you see that?"

Without waiting for an answer, he bolted to where
Farrugia stood.

The coaches had started their engines in preparation for
leaving. It was a slow process, as each bus had to execute at
least a three-point maneuver to leave the narrow parking area.

The second bus was just making its final turn, while the one ahead of it was slowly climbing the steep driveway.

"He's on one of the buses!" Nico urgently said to Farrugia.

"How do you know?"

"I just saw a guest without a name tag, looking completely disheveled. His wife was upset—fussing over him and trying to fix his glasses."

Farrugia looked at him skeptically. "Do you know which bus they got on?"

"No." Nico pointed ahead. "They just walked between those two buses."

To Farrugia's credit, he turned his head and spoke into his headset. "Stop that bus!"

Officers with rifles swarmed the driveway. Two ran around to the front of the first bus, blocking its exit.

"Our target is on one of these buses," Farrugia spoke again into his headset. "Find him."

Nico's eyes swept the four coaches that remained at the curb. People were staring out the windows, their expressions confused and anxious. An older man in a tuxedo was trying to comfort his wife as she frantically pointed outside.

The maximum capacity on the side of the luxury coach closest to Nico said fifty-six passengers. He did the math. If every one was full, that amounted to three hundred-plus living, breathing souls. On any given coach, fifty-six people plus the driver could be taken hostage in a heartbeat. Either by trained officers who knew how to minimize loss of life. Or by Alesandru Baldisar, a man who wouldn't hesitate to sacrifice as many lives as necessary in order to save his own. Either way, Nico thought, this would not end well. God, what if he was wrong?

Then he spotted him. The only passenger standing up was

wearing a T-shirt with a name tag on a lanyard around his neck. For a split second, their eyes met. Alesandru Baldisar. *You son of a bitch.*

"There he is! He's on bus three." Nico hissed to Farrugia.

"Are you sure?"

"One hundred percent."

"Stay here," Farrugia said. Nico could see him speaking into his mic as he made his way down the curb and stopped outside bus three. In a slow, strategic manner, armed officers were making their way over.

"Open the door," Farrugia commanded the bus driver. Eyes bulging with fear, he shook his head.

"Open the door. Now!"

Nico heard the hiss of air as the hydraulic doors opened. People sitting near the emergency exits tried to open them. Several scrambled over each other. He wasn't sure if they were helping or wanted to be the first to escape.

Farrugia waved the driver toward him. "Stay low," he said quietly, "and come to me."

The driver slid from his seat and bolted down the stairs before collapsing into the arms of an officer who led him inside the nightclub.

Outside, movement at the rear of the bus caught Nico's eye. A sniper holding an AK-47 out in front of him, had his back glued to the coach and was sliding along underneath the high back window. Crouched low, another officer slid a portable black metal staircase under the bus. Nico looked away quickly so as not to draw anyone else's attention to them.

A member of the tactical team had entered the bus and stood at the front, near where the driver would sit. Nico could hear him speaking to the people inside, but not what he was saying. Suddenly, a woman screamed. "He has a gun!"

The sharpshooter had climbed onto the metal step ladder, a question in his eyes. His teammate shook his head, and he ducked back down. Nico's chest tightened, afraid he was about to witness a massacre.

The sound of a single gunshot pierced the air. Women were screaming, men were putting their arms over their wives' heads. Pandemonium had officially broken out on the bus. *Oh, dear God, please don't let this be a bloodbath,* Nico prayed. When he looked back, Baldisar had disappeared from view.

Sharpshooters rushed the bus until Farrugia put up his hand. "Stand down!" he commanded. "Stand down!" They held back.

A woman put both palms and her forehead on the window, her mouth open in a silent scream as everyone held their breath, waiting for the next shot. But there was nothing more than an eerie silence. Whether it was mere seconds or minutes, Nico didn't know, but the officer who'd entered the bus came into view.

"We need an ambulance. Stat!"

R ather than taking one of the police boats back to Valletta, Inspector Mifsud elected to ride with Nico and Pezzente in the same unmarked car that had brought them to the scene. Though several bus passengers had to be treated for shock—the bus driver among them—only one ambulance was required to transport the solitary shooting victim to hospital. All three men watched as paramedics loaded Alesandru Baldisar in and took off, sirens blaring.

Thankfully for the three hundred-plus party-goers, the man had proven to be a coward. Others might have seen it differently; that he chose not to take anyone with him when he had ample opportunity. It was one thing for someone to commit suicide while under extraordinary stress or mental illness. Nico's heart went out to those individuals. But in Baldisar's case, he was a coward. Plain and simple. Rather than be captured and face the consequences, he had put the gun to his own head and pulled the trigger. And he'd even screwed that up. While clinging to life by the thinnest of threads, he was fortunate not to be in a coroner's wagon. But then again, it was still early.

Nico and Pezzente rode in the back seat, while Mifsud sat up front. "How did the police know he was trying to escape on one of the buses?" Roberto asked.

Inspector Mifsud turned to answer. His cheeks were pink and his eyes sparkled. "Nico noticed a man without his lanyard," he said.

"Out of some three hundred or more people?"

Nico thought of the tens, if not hundreds of thousands of tourists he'd witnessed getting off tour buses at the Vatican. Someone always forgot their name tag and would try to bargain their way through the admissions area. Women often didn't wear them because they clashed with their jewelry.

"I'd seen this one man just minutes before, and he had his on." Nico said. "The next time I saw him, he wasn't wearing it."

"For God's sake, he could have just lost it." Pezzente chuckled and shook his head. "How did you know?"

"His hair and the collar of his suit jacket were sticking up as if he'd just pulled a sweater over his head. They were the last ones back to the buses and his wife was straightening out his glasses, which were twisted, and the lenses broken. I figured Baldisar had grabbed it off him and then headed to the buses."

Mifsud smiled and turned back in his seat.

"But," Nico continued. "It wasn't until I saw a man dressed in a dirty T-shirt and a lanyard around his neck, that I knew which bus he was on."

Pezzente elbowed Nico's side—fortunately his uninjured one. "Pretty good detective work, Moretti. If the prosecutor thing ever doesn't work out, we could use you in special investigations."

Chapter Thirty-One

The police car had no sooner dropped Nico off at Valletta's main square on the way to his old hotel, than his phone rang. It was Mifsud.

"Long time no see," he answered. "Shouldn't you be going home?"

"Nico, they've found Elle Sinclair."

He stopped dead in the middle of the deserted street. Nico's breath left his body. "Is she alive?" He could barely get the words out.

"Very much so."

Oh, thank God. Regardless of how it looked, there *had* to be an explanation. She must have known something Nico didn't. That's why she hadn't told him it was she who Ariana had entrusted with Max. After all, he'd thought the worst of Pezzente and in a way, he'd turned out to be a hero. He'd saved Anna Braithwaite's life and had at least brought some closure to Ariana's death.

"Security at Malta International Airport apprehended her trying to board a flight with fake ID, using the name of Eleanor Wilcox," Mifsud said.

Nico was stunned. She'd been in Malta all this time?

"We've got her, Nico. Now we just have to find out where she took your boy."

My boy. "Max isn't with her? Can I talk to her?"

"They're bringing her in now. I have a couple of phone calls to make. Get something to eat and I'll meet you back here in an hour."

Too keyed up to eat, Nico walked straight to Valletta Police Station. He was given a visitor's pass and taken to Mifsud. Given the events of the past forty-eight hours, he couldn't imagine how the inspector was still standing.

"Have I missed anything?" Nico asked.

"That was quick! Take it you skipped on that snack? Anyway, no, but from what I can see, she's not going to give up much. She's repeating word for word what she told airport security. Come with me."

Nico followed him down a long hall, through a bullpen area with desks and through another door. As the door closed behind them, the cacophony of phone conversations faded, and they entered a quiet area. Mifsud tapped twice on what Nico knew was one-way glass and pushed the button for sound.

His initial impression as he watched Elle sitting rigidly on a metal chair was how old she suddenly appeared. In the harsh fluorescent lights, her face had taken on a sickly hue, aging her in its flickering glow. He heard the brittleness in her voice when she asked for a glass of water.

While it wasn't the clichéd good-cop-bad-cop routine, it was clear the male agent was the one responsible for taking the softer approach in an attempt to put her at ease.

"Interpol?" Nico asked. Mifsud nodded.

"We know you didn't mean to do anything wrong, Miss Sinclair," the agent said. "You had parental consent to take the boy out of the country. But now we need to know where he is."

Elle stared at the agent, her bland expression giving nothing away.

The female agent jumped in. "Harboring a child who is now the subject of an Amber Alert, is serious. You need to tell us, Elle, or things will get very bad for you very fast."

That was obviously the wrong button to have pushed. Elle drew herself up in the chair and looked the woman up and down like she was something the cat had coughed up.

Good Cop jumped back in. "What my colleague meant to say, Miss Sinclair, is that we know you want the best for the little boy, right?"

Still, Elle said nothing. With a steady hand, she reached for the glass of water and took a long drink.

"Why were you attempting to travel to the UK under an alias?" Bad Cop asked.

Slowly and deliberately, Elle put down her glass. "My maiden name is Wilcox. I simply reverted to using an old ID. Is that a crime?"

Mifsud turned to Nico. "Has she ever been married, do you know?"

"Not that I'm aware of."

Mifsud tapped on the window.

"My colleague and I need to step out for a moment, Miss Sinclair," one of the agents said. "Can we get you anything?"

Elle gave an indignant sigh and looked at her watch. "I'll have a cup of tea— strong, no sugar."

"That's one tough cookie," the male agent said after

exiting the interview room and Mifsud had flipped off the microphone. "No offense," he said to his partner, "but I think I'll get further with her on my own."

"None taken. Whatever will get us what we need on the boy. Time is not on our side."

After getting themselves a coffee, Nico, Mifsud and the female Interpol agent resumed their position behind the glass. Before the other agent returned to the interview room, Mifsud handed him a collection of mug shots. Nico recognized one of them as the man police had shot at the vineyard.

The agent tossed his empty cup into the trash and went back in. He took a seat opposite Elle and turned on the recording device. "How's the tea, Miss Sinclair? Can I get you anything else?"

She didn't respond, but Nico couldn't help but notice she'd wrapped her hands around the steaming cup as if clinging to a tree trunk in a windstorm. "How much longer are you planning on holding me before you provide me with a lawyer?"

"You can call a lawyer anytime you like. But I can't help you once you do."

Elle raised an eyebrow.

The agent turned the mug shots to face Elle and pushed them across the table. "Do you recognize any of these men?"

As Elle looked down, Nico's eyes were riveted on her, looking for any sign, however subtle, that she might know one of them.

"There is a little boy's life at stake here, Miss Sinclair. He's already lost his mother and he must be terrified. If you know and don't tell us where he is, you will be charged with child endangerment. Possibly kidnapping. And if we don't find him alive—"

The veneer finally cracked. "That's absurd! I loved Max."

Loved? Why past tense? Nico felt like he was going to be sick.

Elle took a deep breath, appearing to steel herself for what she was about to say. "I haven't seen Max since Ariana asked me to take him to his father in Kent. If he's done something with him, that has nothing whatsoever to do with me." Nico's blood ran cold as he listened to her bald-faced lie.

"She told me she didn't know who Max's father was," Nico hissed. "That he wasn't a part of his and Ariana's life."

Mifsud rapped on the window and waited for the agent to come out. "We're done here. I'll have one of my officers put her in a holding cell where she can cool her heels until her lawyer arrives."

He looked as weary and frustrated as Nico felt.

"What do we do now?" Nico asked.

Mifsud shrugged. "Nothing we *can* do. Legally, we can only hold her for forty-eight hours without charging her. Let's hope her lawyer talks some sense into her." He looked at Nico with tired eyes. "Go home and get some sleep. And pray that she'll give up the location of the boy."

The next morning

The icy confidence in Elle Sinclair's eyes was gone. Nico sat across from her in the small holding space— no longer an "interview room." Her face was still devoid of color, her radiance faded like the last ray of sun on an icy lake as nightfall descends.

"How did you know?" she asked him.

"The police had my DNA from a water glass I drank from when I reported Francesca missing," he replied. "They suspected I might have been involved in her disappearance and they used it to compare prints and DNA left at Francesca's apartment."

"And?"

"And unfortunately for you, they also found two other sets of prints. One from the felon who kidnapped Francesca." Nico paused while Elle squirmed and looked away. "And the other were prints the police matched to the ones taken when you were arrested outside that nightclub in Soho. You know, when you were there with Vincenzo Testa, the journalist you said you'd never met."

She scowled, her impenetrable persona cracking, and all at once, Elle Sinclair's true persona was laid bare.

Nico stared at her. And to think she had almost convinced him that Francesca was involved in Lydia's death and Max's disappearance.

"Why?" he said. "What possible reason could you have had to break into her apartment?"

Elle looked away and shrugged. "I couldn't have children. I loved Max and I knew Ariana had named Francesca as his guardian if anything should happen to her. But Ariana had entrusted him to me—when she died, he should have been mine, not Francesca's."

"But that's not what Ariana intended. You knew that." Nico shook his head. "And you hoped to find the guardian-ship papers in Francesca's apartment after she'd been abducted."

The door opened, and a policewoman entered. "It's time," she said. "Miss Sinclair will be remanded until she either pleads or goes to trial."

Nico put up his hand. "Please, just five more minutes." The window was closing and he had to get Elle to confess to where she'd taken Max.

"Five minutes, that's all." The officer backed out of the room and closed the door behind her.

"You told me Max always called Ariana 'Mummy.'" Nico pulled the tattered red fragment of paper from his pocket and put it on the table between them. "He didn't call her either of these things. He called her *Omm,* the Maltese name for mother. His eyes bored into hers. "How did this come to be in Ariana's apartment?"

Elle's shoulders collapsed. Her eyes filled with tears.

"You broke into Ariana's apartment before you took Max out of the country. Just like you did Anna Braithwaite's and Francesca's. That seems to be your specialty."

She shook her head and took a ragged breath. "I didn't know Max had left anything there."

Nico exhaled. Elle Sinclair had just confessed. Had she forgotten the recording device was on? Or had she just given up?

"You know where he is," Nico said quietly. "You didn't take him to his father in Kent."

She sat stock-still, barely appearing to breathe.

"You're going to prison for a long time, Elle. If you love Max as you say you do, you need to tell me."

There was a rap at the door, and it opened. "Sorry, time's up."

She sat facing him, hands shackled to the table.

"Elle, please."

The wall of ice was back up. Impenetrable. Nico felt as if he were lunging for the elevator doors before they snapped closed.

The policewoman detached the handcuffs from the table. Elle drew herself up to her full height and faced Nico. "If I can't have him, nobody will."

Chapter Thirty-Two

Nico moved as though wading through quicksand. Desolate, he'd heeded Mifsud's advice and came back to the hotel to catch a few hours of sleep. Elle would appear before a judge in the morning and unless she had a change of heart overnight, Nico might never know where Max was. All he could do was hope that once she was taken back to the UK and put in prison there, she might confess. Unlikely, but if she had any love at all for Max, surely she'd want him to be safe.

Nico was brushing his teeth when his mobile rang. It was a UK number but no other caller ID.

"Nicoló Moretti?" a man's voice asked.

"Yes, who is this?"

"It's Detective Superintendent William Sondhelm. With the London Metropolitan Police."

Nico tried to swallow the nausea that churned in his gut and rose in his throat. But his mouth was suddenly dry of saliva. His knuckles were white as he grasped the back of the chair by the bed. As he steeled himself for the news, he bargained with God. *I will do anything you ask of me, he pleaded. Please just let him be alive.*

"Mr. Moretti, we have found your son."

"Is he . . .?" His strangled voice came out like a squeak.

"He's alive and well, sir."

Still holding the chair, Nico lowered himself onto the bed.

"Where . . . How?" The words caught in his throat.

"We located him two hours ago at a children's camp just out of Southampton. I'm sorry for the delay but we had to be sure it was him.

"There's too much to give you all the details over the phone, but I wanted to call immediately to let you know. He's safe and in the care of a child protection officer here in London. I'm about to address the media, but obviously I wanted to advise you first."

Pressing his palms to his eyes, Nico bowed his head and listened to the scant details of how they'd found Max. Once again, Nico thanked God for CCTV cameras. After a woman in a South London neighborhood had heard a child screaming hysterically outside her window, she'd looked out to see someone "suspicious-looking," as she'd put it, forcing a child into a van. Although she got a license plate number, which she called in to the police, it turned out to be stolen. However, with London having just under a fifth of all the surveillance cameras in the UK, the vehicle was picked up at several locations before being traced to a children's camp in Maybush, Southampton.

"What twigged the camp's education officer something wasn't quite right," Sondhelm said, "was that the woman who took Max there had packed a bag for him with several days' clothing."

A woman? What other woman would have taken Max to a summer camp?

Nico was just about to ask when the detective sergeant continued. "From what we can gather, the woman was hired by Elle Sinclair to look after the child until she returned from Malta. When she hadn't heard back from Sinclair in nearly two weeks and she saw there was an Amber Alert out for him, she panicked. She has a record, so instead of turning him in to the police, she took Max to a children's camp that she thought had a live-in program. When told it was a day facility, she just left your boy there and ran."

Oh my God, Elle was proving to be diabolical. He couldn't decide who was worse, her or Baldisar. They would have made a good pair.

He was afraid to ask Sondhelm the next question. "What did the woman have a record for?" Please tell me it wasn't for anything to do with children.

"That's the thing. It wasn't even for that serious a crime. She'd been caught shoplifting at Harrods. She told us she'd met Sinclair at a therapy group."

As Nico recalled what Testa had told him about BBC sending Elle to counselling, he prayed it wasn't at a group for addicts. God bless them, but he didn't want someone with serious mental health problems looking after his son.

"How soon can I see him?" Nico asked. "I can be on the next plane to Heathrow."

"I understand how anxious you must be, I'm a father myself, but hold off booking anything for now. You have my word we'll contact you the minute he's clear to go."

All Nico could think about was that they'd need to put Max through a battery of tests, to insure he was both physically and mentally OK. But he was alive. That's what mattered.

"In the next few hours, we should also know more from social services. Don't worry," Sondhelm assured him, "I'm assured Max is doing very well, but we have to take it one step at a time. I'm sure you understand."

Fighting back tears, Nico expressed his gratitude to Superintendent Sondhelm and hung up. He was still sitting on the bed when he heard a quiet rap at the door. "I don't need anything, thank you," he called, his voice breaking.

"Nico, it's Mikel. Please open the door."

He wiped his eyes and cleared his throat as he walked to the door and opened it. "I came as soon as I heard, I thought you might want some company."

Nico could only nod as he stood aside to let him in. As the door closed behind him, the dam burst. It was as if his entire being was folding inward and all the tears he'd held in since Ariana's death erupted. He sat on the bed, his head in his hands and wept.

Mifsud sat down beside him. "Now comes the joyful part, my friend," Mifsud said, clasping Nico's shoulder. "But in order to recognize that, first you had to make it through the pain."

Three days later

The Maltese press would have had a field day if a commercial aircraft had brought Max home. The thought of it gave Nico the terrors. But while every newspaper and TV station had camped out at Malta's airport, awaiting Max's arrival, Mikel Mifsud had used his considerable influence to have him flown to Malta on a private jet that arrived at a small hangar on the island of Gozo. Nico would have given anything to be the first person his son saw when he got off the plane. But Max wouldn't even have known who he was, and it was decided that Francesca should be there to meet him. After everything the boy had been through, what he needed now was to be with someone he knew and loved.

One of the reasons the UK police had kept him longer than Nico would have liked, was that a child psychologist had broken it to the little boy about his mother's death. Social workers had wanted to monitor him to be sure he was coping. Nico knew his son would be safe in Francesca's hands and security would be provided at Ariana's home until the police could untangle Baldisar's tangled web of corruption.

Max's face was all smiles on the front page of every paper and newscast in the UK and Malta. But it was a very different little boy reflected in the photographs the police had shared with Nico privately. He'd never actually seen his son. In the photographs taken immediately following Max's rescue, he had dark, intense eyes— Ariana's—but the dyed blond hair cut close to his head looked incongruent against his olive skin. Nico's blood boiled at the lengths Elle had gone to in order to avoid him being recognized.

She had said she loved Max.

Testa had said she was the devil's spawn.

Chapter Thirty-Three

As Nico waited at the main square for his ride, he wondered if the plane transporting Elle back to the UK had crossed paths with the one carrying Max. How would she feel knowing they had found him despite her steadfast refusal to cooperate? He wondered if she'd been told that he was Max's father. She'd dodged a murder charge, but she would remain in a UK prison for a very long time. There was even talk she might have to be put into segregation, as she'd already come out on the losing end of an altercation with another inmate while in Maltese custody. If Elle thought she would be treated differently than any other prisoner once back in her own country, she was sorely mistaken. Many incarcerated women were also mothers. Mothers who didn't take kindly to those who stole other women's children.

Mifsud had told Nico to be ready at 8 a.m. for one of his officers to pick him up and transport him to the ferry that went to Gozo. Within minutes, a dark SUV pulled up at the curb. The window was rolled down and behind the wheel sat Inspector Mifsud.

"Get in," he said to Nico. "All my people were busy, so you're stuck with me."

On the drive to the ferry, Mifsud caught him up on his news. He would now be known as Superintendent Mifsud and would be transferred to headquarters. While obviously proud of his promotion, he told Nico the thing he was most elated about was that he'd be home for dinner with his wife and three little girls most evenings.

"Congratulations, Mikel. You deserve it."

"Thank you. And you, what will you do once you've seen Francesca and your son?"

There was a deep hollowness in Nico's stomach as he considered Mikel's question. "Return to Tropea, I guess. And get back to prosecuting the kinds of cases Ariana was so passionate about." And somehow figure out how to be a single parent to a little boy he'd never met.

"Thanks to Pezzente, Anna Braithwaite has formally entered the witness protection program."

Nico nodded. Even though Baldisar was no longer a threat to her, there was no telling, in his absence, which of his foreign investors might try to retaliate against her. It might be a long time, if ever, before she'd be a truly free woman.

"But what will happen to Roberto?" Mifsud asked.

Nico shrugged. "That's above my pay grade. I was never privy to what he and his team did before all this. I don't imagine that will change now." Although Pezzente had certainly gone up in his estimation.

"Wouldn't it be more efficient if you all worked together in your country?"

It struck Nico as a naïve question coming from a man of the superintendent's status. "One would think so, Mikel. But while Italy is a beautiful country, sadly, it is full of gross inefficiencies."

Both men remained quiet as they came upon the signs indicating the turnoff for the ferry. The inspector flashed his badge as they pulled up outside the ticket booth and came around to Nico's side as he retrieved his bags. "Don't be a stranger, my friend. Keep in touch when you get back to Italy. If there's anything you need, I'm only a phone call away."

"Your people weren't all too busy to drive me, were they?" Nico asked. Mifsud winked.

"Thank you, Mikel." Nico held the inspector's hand in his. "For everything."

O nce on the ferry, Nico eschewed the coffee shop and passenger lounge in favor of the view from the upper sundeck. On his way, he passed a news kiosk. The marquee boasted *Today's London Newspapers on Sale Here Early Every Morning*. Max's face was plastered across the front pages of them all, some alongside Ariana. He swallowed hard as he hustled past. On deck, he pulled up the collar of his jacket against the early-morning wind that whipped the waves into a choppy gray soup. The sky was a montage of fat white clouds gradually giving way to the sun as it tried its best to break through.

So much had happened since the last time Nico had made the crossing from Ċirkewwa to Mġarr. Lydia Rapa was dead, her brother's bar had been reduced to ashes, and Elle was in a British prison. Baldisar had at last been exposed for what he was, but to what end? In his vegetative state of mind, he would likely receive more sympathy than justice. But Francesca and Max were alive, thanks in large part to Roberto Pezzente. Nico had so many questions he wanted to ask him, but he suspected the next time they'd meet would be in their official capacities, with both men playing their respective cards close to their vests. Things in his native land changed slowly. Or not at all.

The ferry crossing went quickly, and they were soon approaching the burnt-brown rolling hills of Gozo. The boat slowed as it passed the tip of the breakwater where several small pleasure craft bobbed up and down. A child waved from one of the boat's cockpits as they glided into Mġarr Harbour, then alongside the cement pier. Heeding the announcement, foot passengers rose from their seats and shuffled down the stairs, where they would disembark. Nico's stomach was in such knots he was tempted to stay on board and make the crossing over and back again, but as the last of the passengers trailed down the stairs, he joined them.

By the time all the passengers were off, there was already a long line at the taxi stand. As Nico waited his turn, he watched with envy the holidaymakers boarding the hop-on-hop-off buses for a day of sightseeing. What was wrong with him that he'd sooner be on a crowded bus of tourists than on his way to meet his son?

The taxi made the journey through the narrow streets of Mġarr and then out onto the highway. Nico strained to pinpoint the exact location where he had witnessed Lydia being run off the road to her death. Really, he didn't want to relive those moments. As they whizzed by kilometers of low stone dike walls and majestic palms swaying gently in the breeze, he thought of Giorgio. And the secret he'd likely keep from his mother until her dying day. Then he thought of Ariana. The Maltese were good at keeping secrets.

The twenty-minute route to the northwestern tip of the island where Ariana had her home essentially bisected the island. The taxi driver was friendly and pointed out various sites along the route, including the historic Basilica of The Blessed Virgin of Ta' Pinu, rumored to be where Pope Paul II celebrated Mass in 1990. Nico wished he could have been more engaged, but his thoughts and emotions churned more intensely the closer they got to their destination.

What would it feel like to step into the intimacy of Ariana's home? Unlike her apartment, which seemed more designed for efficiency than comfort, he would finally get a glimpse into what the real Ariana was like. She'd been a past lover, a friend and confidante, and now, the mother of a five-year-old boy. But what did he really know about her life other than her ardent quest for justice? Had she ever been tempted to tell him about their son as they'd dallied over long dinners and too much wine? He could no longer remember the open and relaxed woman he'd been so attracted to in university. In the months before she died, their discussions had turned into heated debates. The anger and disappointment Nico had seen mirrored on her face still haunted him. Her accusations of living in his ivory tower, unwilling to do what it took to put both their countries' criminals in jail had cut him to the quick. And yet, he knew in his heart she was right.

As they drove higher and higher up into the hills, Nico swallowed to relieve the pressure in his ears. Even on this idyllic historic island, Ariana had chosen to live as far away from the main villages of San Lawrenz and Għar as possible. Or had that choice been dictated by her need for safety? He imagined her coming home late, perhaps after a night in one of the many trattorias and restaurants in town. But would she have been seen in such public places, or would she have had to remain cloistered, choosing her friends and acquaintances wisely? Perhaps Lydia was one of the few she could be open with when she took Max there to play with Gabriela. Or did they meet to discuss the sensitive topic of government corruption within the confines of Ariana's remote property? There was so much he wanted to know, but no one to ask.

His driver exited the highway and turned onto a gravel road. There was no signage or indication of what the street address might be, but he obviously knew where he was going. After showing their identification to the police officer at the entrance to the road, they were cleared to go ahead. Nico estimated they'd gone at least a kilometer before a small farmhouse came into view.

The taxi pulled up outside a set of open rusted gates. Nico paid the driver, giving him a good tip, and retrieved his bags. He was debating if he should ask him to wait when Francesca came into view.

"Nico, it's so good to see you!" She kissed him on both cheeks before waving to the officer that sat in an unmarked car across the road. Inspector Mifsud had indeed seen to it that Francesca and Max had twenty-four-hour security.

"Come in. Your timing is perfect—we were about to have lemonade in the garden."

At the mention of "we," Nico's stomach clenched.

"You must be hot," Francesca said as he followed her across a paved courtyard that led to the house. "Let me show you the guest room where you can freshen up."

The house had cheerful glossy red shutters that lay open against a rough limestone facade. While it had the look of a farmhouse or cottage, Nico observed the iron bars across the windows and the solid iron front door. Inside, a refreshingly cool entrance hall opened to a spacious and well-equipped kitchen. Copper pots and cooking utensils hung from a wrought-iron rack above a large butcher block. He remembered how much Ariana loved to cook. One long windowsill was chock-a-block full of various plants and herbs. A rustic wooden table sat in a sunny alcove that looked out onto the garden. He wondered if Max was out there.

Standing there, face-to-face, a certain awkwardness hung

between them. Despite the cool temperature inside the house, Nico's mouth felt dry and sticky.

"Would you like to put your things upstairs before we go outside?" Francesca asked.

Nico nodded and followed her out of the kitchen to a wooden staircase. Tucked into an alcove at the base of the stairs was a comfy-looking daybed covered with white linen and a proliferation of colorful throw cushions. Against the wall, a small bookcase held various children's books and videos. Beside it, a red chest brimmed with toys. Several framed photographs sat on a shelf. One was of Ariana's late parents with their very young daughter. Sadly, they hadn't lived to see her become a successful prosecutor, or to meet their grandson. But, Nico thought, what a blessing not to have had to endure the pain of outliving their only child.

He followed Francesca up the wide and gently curving stairs to the next floor. She led him past a bedroom on the right side of the hallway with the door open, then stopped outside another room on the opposite side.

"You can put your bags in here. There's a bathroom across the hall. Feel free to use anything that you need."

"Thank you, I won't be long."

"Take your time and when you're ready, we'll be out in the garden."

Nico waited until Francesca had gone before quietly closing the door. He put his bags on the bed and walked over to the window that looked out over the front courtyard where he had entered. He felt like a voyeur being in Ariana's home without her. But at the same time, unlike in her apartment in Valletta, he sensed her essence. There was a vibration he'd felt when he'd followed Francesca in the front door. Her larger-than-life spirit filled the rooms and breathed vivacity throughout the house. He wished he could wander from room to room, alone, absorbing everything that was hers. What other photographs and mementos had she kept of her life? Did any of them include him?

Sighing, he turned from the window and retrieved his toiletries and opened the door. Across the hall in the bathroom Francesca had pointed out, he splashed some water on his face and brushed his teeth. Through the open window, squeals of laughter drifted up from the garden below, but he didn't go and look out. He couldn't put this off any longer. Walking back to the guest room, he deposited his toiletries on the bed and headed for the stairs.

As he passed the open doorway of the bedroom across the hall, he couldn't help but look in. In the middle of the room was a four-poster bed draped in some kind of white fabric, it obviously belonged to a woman—whether Ariana or Francesca, he didn't know. At the foot of the bed was an antique trunk. On the bedside table was a framed photograph.

As if in a trance, he felt himself being drawn into the room. He reached out his hand to pick up the photo, then pulled it back. His face warm, he blinked hard and inhaled a ragged breath. He remembered the exact moment it had been taken. They'd been at a party following their graduation from law school in Milan. It had become oppressively hot and people were getting louder and drunker by the minute. He'd looked at Ariana from across the room and tilted his head toward the exit, a question in his eyes. She got it immediately and after meeting up outside, they'd made their way to their favorite trattoria close to the university.

They had been sitting across a candlelit table from each other when Nico had asked the waiter to take a picture of them. He'd been hopelessly in love with her since they'd met, and even though they were dating, he hadn't summoned the nerve to tell her. That night, as he held her hand across the table, he was plucking up his courage to reveal his feelings when she received the call that her parents had been involved in some kind of accident. At the time, they had both assumed it was a car accident. It wasn't until they had fled the restaurant and he'd put Ariana on a plane home to Malta that he discovered the awful truth. Her father had killed her mother and then shot himself. And Nico wasn't there to comfort her in her grief. By the time she came back to university to pack up her things, she was a different person. The open, unguarded expression had turned to an impervious slate of unreadable thoughts and emotions.

"Nico?"

He jumped at the sound of Francesca's voice and turned his head toward the door. Horrified, he realized he was sitting on the side of Ariana's bed, clutching the photograph in both hands. His face burning, he jumped up. "I'm . . . I'm so sorry. I don't know what I was thinking—"

Francesca smiled. "I was worried you might have gotten lost, that's all."

Self-consciously, he put the photograph back on the bedside table. "No, I—"

"She loved you, you know," was all she said.

F rancesca's words played on an endless loop as Nico followed her through the kitchen and out into the garden. The screen door slammed behind them, reminding him of the carefree sounds of summer. But again, he observed the same steel bars as were on all the windows, as well as the outer door folded back against the house. To a casual visitor, the property gave the outward appearance of being the perfect setting for the endless languid days of hot Gozo summers, while in reality it was a veritable fortress.

But even with such rigorous security measures, Elle Sinclair had managed to take advantage of her friend. This, Nico thought sadly, had been Ariana's life—betrayed by friends and enemies alike.

He put the tray of lemonade and glasses he'd carried out for Francesca on a table that sat in the shade of an enormous fig tree. Everywhere he looked was evidence of what he suspected was Francesca's extraordinary green thumb. Huge terracotta planters lined the stone terrace. A profusion of flowers framed a circular area of lawn that somehow had retained its lush green color despite the unrelenting heat of the sun. Beyond that, silhouetted against where the sea kissed the horizon, was a child sitting in a plastic cooling-off pool.

"Max, I've got lemonade," Francesca called to him. "And we have a visitor, someone I'd like you to meet." She turned to Nico. "I told him you were coming."

The boy turned around and put his hand to his eyes, squinting against the sun. Francesca sat on an iron chair and held a beach towel wide. "Come on, then."

Max jumped out of the water and ran toward them. As he came into the shade and Nico could see his face more clearly, his heart nearly leaped from his chest. It was like looking at a mini-version of Ariana. His hair had been dyed back to its natural color and his curls were springing into being. Max grinned at Francesca as he ran into her arms, and she wound him up in the towel and spun him several times. "Round and round and round we go. Where we stop nobody knows!"

With round penny eyes, he looked shyly at Nico.

"Max, this is Sinjur Moretti, who I told you about. He was a very good friend of Omm's."

"Hello, Max, my name is Nico." His voice cracked when the little boy held out his tiny hand and placed it in his. "*Piacere*. It's a pleasure to meet you."

Chapter Thirty-Four

N ico had patiently waited while Francesca tucked an exhausted Max into bed early and read him a short bedtime story. If nothing else good ever happened in her life, this moment of contentment would keep her going forever. She kissed Max good night, leaving the door open, and tiptoed out of his room and down the stairs.

"Tell me about her," Nico said as they ambled side by side through the lush garden.

"What do you mean? You knew her better than anyone."

"Really?" His voice had an edge of bitterness. "I didn't even know she had a child."

Francesca glanced over and saw the glisten of tears in Nico's eyes. She felt something clutch at her heart as she watched this quiet, but determined man suddenly look so vulnerable. "Well, as you know, she was fierce."

Nico's face flushed as he blinked away the tears.

"She was unrelenting. She took no prisoners. Her sense of right and wrong was polemic—it overrode everything."

"What kind of mother was she?"

The grip on Francesca's heart tightened, and she felt her

insides tense. How should she answer that question? "Ariana was a complex woman. She—"

"Why couldn't she have trusted me?" Nico blurted out.

For a moment, Francesca thought he looked like a petulant little boy. She had seen that exact expression on Max's face many times. When he did that, Ariana's face would go blank. As if she had absolutely no idea how to deal with the complicated little creature she had produced.

"In answer to your first question, Ariana adored Max, but she didn't always know how best to deal with him as a mother. As you know, she was an only child. Even our friendship in boarding school . . . She was the strong, independent one. I grew up with brothers and sisters, but I looked to Ariana to lead the way and protect me. And she always did."

"Did she want Max?"

"Oh, yes. Absolutely."

"But she didn't want me—his father—involved in their life?"

Oh, Lord, where did she go from here? This was the moment she hoped would never come. She led Nico to the iron bench where she and Ariana had often sat in her circle garden with a cool drink at the end of the day. There, surrounded by the beauty she'd tried to create as an oasis for the three of them, against the backdrop of a perfect cerulean sky, they'd gaze out over the sea. It was in that very spot when Max was still in his baby carriage that Francesca heard the words she would remember forever. And hoped she would never have to act upon.

She uncrossed her legs and imagined her feet rooted firmly into the earth. She took a deep breath in at the same time, saying a silent prayer. *Please God, give me the fortitude to deliver this man from his pain. And give him the strength not to take this child from me. Even though he can.*

As she opened her mouth to speak, Nico's mobile rang, startling them both.

"I'm sorry, I need to take this call." He stood and walked to the cliff's edge. *"Pronto,"* she heard him say.

She gazed at his handsome silhouette against the setting sun as he stood, phone in hand, listening. Even though his back was toward her, she could see his shoulders rise as if he'd just taken an enormous breath. Then they settled down his back and he began to pace. Back and forth, back and forth. Not speaking, just listening.

Suddenly, he wheeled around, taking her by surprise, catching her staring at him. His complexion had turned pale and his dark eyes bored into hers. *"Grazie,"* he said quietly, then returned the mobile to his pocket. Francesca watched him walk toward her, and she gulped for air. As her insides turned to water, she knew her life was about to change forever.

The sun had long since dipped into the sea following the call from Inspector Mifsud, confirming that Nico was indeed Max's father. While he'd known without a doubt as soon as he'd seen Max, he'd had to be sure. Somehow, it would bring closure to yet another mystery about Ariana. He'd felt guilty, even doubting her, and he told Francesca so.

Hours later, they sat talking in the encroaching darkness. Eventually, he'd noticed she was chilled and suggested they move inside. She'd insisted on making them something light to eat, and he sat across the table from her, tucking into a simple omelet and a glass of red wine.

"Why didn't she tell me? I would have supported her one hundred percent."

Francesca hadn't touched her food, and she put down her

glass. "She knew that, but she'd already received threats because of the cases she was working on, and she didn't want to put you or Max in danger."

Nico felt his eyes burn, and he looked away. That's what Ariana had told him the night before she died, but he wasn't sure he'd believed her.

"I pleaded with her, Nico. I really did. Especially when Max became old enough to ask questions."

"I can't believe I didn't know." As he'd done before, he tried to work out the math in his head. How long were the intervals when they'd gone without seeing each other? Obviously long enough to conceal a pregnancy.

"Unfortunately, it was during that time that she met Elle Sinclair," Francesca said. "Ariana's pregnancy didn't really show until she was about five months along. She told everyone she needed some time off because of the stress of her job, and she went to London. Being who she was, Ariana couldn't help but poke around for sources even while she was on a leave of absence. She'd stayed in touch with several journalists who had been investigating the same alleged criminals she'd been trying to bring to justice."

"And one of them was Elle," Nico said.

"Yes. I always had a bad feeling about her. Ariana knew that, but at the time, Elle served her purpose. Don't get me wrong, I loved Ariana like a sister, but she was always laser-focused on getting what she wanted."

At any cost, Nico thought.

After he'd helped clear the dishes, Nico stood in the open doorway of Max's room, watching him sleep. Francesca's bedroom was next to Max's, and she'd asked Nico to wait while she went and got something. The room he'd wandered into earlier had been Ariana's. She'd slept in the bed he'd sat on. He imagined her sitting at the antique makeup table, brushing her thick, dark hair.

"She wanted you to have this if anything ever happened to her." Francesca eyes filled with tears. "I still can't believe it has."

Nico nodded, swallowing the ache in his throat.

She held out a small box inlaid with ivory and mother-of-pearl. "Try not to think harshly of her, Nico. She did the best with what she had."

But I didn't get to see my little boy grow up. To hold him in my arms as a baby or chase him around the house as a toddler. As Francesca had said, Ariana always got what she wanted. On the day he'd just met his own flesh and blood, he'd never felt more alone.

He took the box from Francesca's hands.

"Sleep well, Nico." She walked into her bedroom and closed the door softly behind her.

Back in the guest room, he put the box on the bed. A huge question mark hung over it. What did Ariana want him to have? He touched the delicate workmanship, but drew himself away. How long could he delay opening what he sensed would reveal more untold secrets? Not yet.

He went to the bathroom and brushed his teeth. He walked past Max's room again, marveling that this little boy was his. How would he accept the news? Who would tell him, Nico or Francesca? So many conflicting thoughts swirled around his head.

He couldn't put it off any longer. After he crossed the hall to his room and closed the door, he picked up the box from the bed. With trembling hands, he lifted the hinged lid. Inside was a silver filigree locket in the shape of a Maltese cross, and a folded piece of paper underneath. With his thumbnail, he opened the locket. On one side was a photograph of a tiny, dark-haired infant. On the other, Nico stared at the picture of himself. He unfolded the note and through blurry eyes he read Ariana's distinctive script.

Max will be ready when you tell him. I've never told him who you are, just that his papa is a good and kind man. That he loves unconditionally, is loyal to a fault, and will always do the right thing. ~ A

Valletta, Malta

True to his word, Nico had brought Giorgio's friend's car back safe and sound, as well as the money Sami had lent them. After seeing the news about Baldisar's capture, Giorgio contacted Nico to say he and his mother were on their way back to Gozo. Unbeknownst to him, Sami had not scuttled Giorgio's boat as requested. Instead, he'd kept it safe and returned it to Giorgio, who brought it to Valletta when he and Nico met for lunch.

Giorgio had learned shortly after Nico left Marsaxlokk that his bar had been burned to the ground.

"What will you do back on Gozo?" Nico asked.

"I will rebuild, of course. What else would I do?"

"What about the authorities hounding you?" Nico was particularly worried about the police telling Mrs. Rapa that it was her text that had tipped off Baldisar's goons before they ran her daughter off the road.

"After your notoriety at the warehouse, they seem to have backed off," Giorgio said. "They even found Caesar and took him to the vet until I could get back there."

Nico wasn't sure which he was more excited about: that Giorgio's beloved dog had survived, or that its master was determined to rebuild the bar.

"Speaking of dogs," Nico said. "I'm wondering if I can make arrangements to have Gabriela sent over to you. She was Lydia's, and therefore yours."

"What, you don't like her?" Giorgio asked.

"Well, I . . . um . . . of course I do, but—"

"You know, my friend, God has given you a second chance. You shouldn't waste it."

Nico had no earthly idea what he meant. "Sorry?"

"You lost Ariana, but you have the son you both created."

"What does that have to do with Gabriela?"

"Open your eyes, my friend! What do you think every little boy dreams of having?"

Nico scratched his head. "A dog? But she was your sister's. You should have her."

"Be a hero to your little boy, Nico. Keep the dog. Lydia would have wanted it."

"How do you know that?"

"Because she loved little Max." Giorgio winked and let out a hearty laugh. "And she knew Caesar would cheerfully eat Gabriela for breakfast."

Before Nico left Malta, he had one more thing to do. All too often, when prosecuting organized crime, he had convinced himself that the end justified the means. Many times, he'd let one slightly less evil monster go in the hopes they would lead the authorities to the bigger rathole from which they came. Trouble was, even when the strategy worked and they flushed the vermin from their hiding places, Nico found himself pleading a case before a judge who was on the Mafia's payroll. It had become a zero-sum game.

Now, in this final act before he left Malta, he faced an excruciating decision. Baldisar, for all intents and purposes, was a vegetable. Nico could say the word, and he'd be sentenced to life in a federal prison's rehab facility for whatever time he might have left. Or they could release him to his family—if they would have him after all he'd subjected them to—who would have to feed him and change his diapers, perhaps for years to come. He would never walk again, or even wipe the drool from his own mouth. Now an empty shell, he was incapable of grasping what he had done. He was responsible for Ariana's and Lydia Rapa's murder, Francesca's abduction, and Esme Agius's death, after it was determined that one of his henchmen had killed her over fears she could identify him.

Elle would remain in a UK prison for years to come for her role in Max's disappearance. By refusing to tell authorities where he was, she'd earned herself a longer sentence. Though still shattered by her true colors, Nico couldn't help but be glad about that.

On the other side of the ledger, Max had been born out of a night of romance with Ariana almost six years ago. While they'd occasionally been intimate after that, he'd long since come to terms with the impossibility of ever having a permanent relationship. They'd remained close whenever she came to Tropea, but he couldn't let himself fall for her all over again. While he'd accused her of having frozen him out, he realized he'd done the same by keeping her at arm's length emotionally. Even she had said he should get out and date other women. He'd tried a few times, but as a friend once pointedly said, how could any woman compete with the torch he carried for Ariana?

Max was safe. He adored Francesca, and he was young enough to eventually move past his mother's death—even if Nico wondered if he, himself, ever could. Nothing would bring Ariana back, but he'd always have a part of her. If indeed he'd lost his soul, as she'd accused him of the night before she died, he'd been handed it back when he learned he was Max's father. He now had that lifelong commitment he'd so desperately wanted. With his and Ariana's son.

And so, when called by the nurse, he rose from his seat in the hospital waiting room. With sweating hands, he smoothed the creases of his trousers. For most of the previous night and this morning, he'd been asking himself what if? What if the tables were turned and Alesandru Baldisar had to decide Nico's fate? What decision would he make? But he knew in his heart that the old Baldisar would have believed in that zero-sum game. Everything he did, every relationship, had proven to be transactional—quid pro quo. There would have been no other choice for him. He didn't know any other way.

As Nico followed the nurse down the hall and past the guard posted outside Baldisar's room, he wondered, what would Ariana have wanted him to do? How would she have responded if she had been the one to hold the fate of this evil man in her hands? He remembered Francesca's comment about Ariana, word for word: "*She was unrelenting. She took no prisoners. Her sense of right and wrong was polemic; it overrode everything.*"

That left him very little wiggle room. He took a deep breath as the nurse pushed open the door to Baldisar's room. What struck Nico first, before he even focused on the figure in the bed that was attached to tubes and monitors, was the austerity of the room. Although Baldisar had been there for a week, there were no flowers. No cards lined the windowsill. No hand-drawn pictures, like the ones Max made for Nico, were taped to the wall. Where had all the people gone that had constantly surrounded this formerly prestigious banker?

"Is he conscious?" Nico asked the nurse as she turned to leave.

"Do you mean, can he hear you?" She shook her head. "He is in what we call a persistent vegetative state." She stood in the doorway. "Unless you need anything else, I have rounds to make. Let the nursing station know if you need assistance."

A ventilator breathed for Baldisar and a massive gauze bandage was wrapped around his head. Nico had been told that the surgeons didn't try to remove the bullet; digging around in his brain to get to it would cause further harm. Instead, they had tried to reduce as much of the damage as possible. They'd temporarily removed a portion of Baldisar's skull to accommodate the swelling. Nico couldn't help but think of the sequel to *The Silence of the Lambs*, where Hannibal Lecter felt he had to eat Will's brain in order to forgive him.

Was there anything that would allow Nico to forgive Baldisar for what he'd done? Even without absolute proof that he'd been responsible for Ariana's murder—as well as the other four victims that had died that day—he'd taken Mrs. Cilia's granddaughter, Esme, from her. He'd ended Lydia Rapa's life and taken her from her mother and brother as surely as if he'd driven her off the road himself. Being the coward that he was, he'd failed miserably at taking his own life in order to escape the consequences of his malevolence. And now, here he lay.

The hospital's neurosurgeon had told Nico that Baldisar would likely remain like that for six months before succumbing to his injuries. Alternatively, it was possible he could live as long as two to five years before an infection would cause severe organ damage leading to death. In the meantime, he would have no quality of life. He'd lost his family. All the horrific things he'd done to others would go unpunished. Their loved ones would never be able to mete out the retribution they so richly deserved.

But weren't the consequences Baldisar was now facing the ultimate retribution? Who among us would not choose life in prison over existing like this, possibly for years? Some would say he'd gotten off scot-free. Others would say he'd paid the ultimate price.

What would you do, Ariana?

A tiny bird landed on the sill outside the window. It was turquoise, pearlescent. As it hopped closer to the glass, Nico noticed it only had one leg. The bird cocked its head and seemed to look directly at him.

You are a good and kind man. You love unconditionally and are loyal to a fault. You will always do the right thing.

Chapter Thirty-Five

The guard posted outside Baldisar's room bid Italy's special prosecutor Nico Moretti good night and watched him sign out. Moretti walked purposefully to the elevator and stabbed the button once, then again, as if for good measure. There seemed to be a different air about him than when he went in.

The guard watched the elevator doors close behind him, all the while scanning both ends of the corridor. He'd memorized the shift changes that were as predictable as a fine-tuned Swiss clock.

In exactly two-and-a-half minutes, the pretty nurse would arrive to give Baldisar his last medication for the night.

On schedule, she appeared in the hallway and walked toward him. She had parked her meds cart outside the door before she looked up with a note of surprise in her eyes. "Oh, hello. You're not Matthias . . ." Her cheeks grew pink. "I mean, Officer Vella."

"Good evening," the guard replied. "No, he called in sick." That wasn't strictly true, but the fact that the officer lay dead at the bottom of a nearby dumpster qualified him as being a little under the weather. "I'm his replacement."

She shook her head. "I hope he hasn't caught the flu. It's a nasty one this year." She put a hand on Baldisar's door, ready to push it open.

"The man that was just here visiting," he said, holding up a leather wallet. "This must have dropped from his pocket as he got on the elevator."

"Oh, dear. Do you think you might still catch him?"

"I'm not allowed to leave my post." He smiled at her warmly. "Would you mind? He's probably still in the lobby."

She hesitated a moment and looked at her watch. "Well, it's not like our patient's going anywhere, is he?" With a giggle, she took the wallet from him.

After watching the elevator doors slide closed behind her, he pulled a syringe from his breast pocket and swapped it for the identical one she'd left on the cart. Then he poured himself a steaming cup of coffee from his thermos and sat down to wait.

There was a ding as the elevator doors opened. "He said to thank you, but it isn't his," the nurse said, handing him the wallet. "Would you mind taking it to the nurses' station when you change shifts?" She lifted the med tray off the cart and pushed open the door. "I'd better get in there and give our patient his meds."

The medication wouldn't even need to snake its way through Baldisar's veins. The pinprick it took to break the skin would be more than adequate. Thirty seconds later, his useless, disgusting body would convulse uncontrollably, and he would die from cardiac arrest. Or perhaps he would suffocate, drowning in his own fluids as they filled his lungs. Either way, the job would be done.

He felt bad, though. He would have liked to have seen the nurse again.

Chapter Thirty-Six

Tropea, Italy

Nico leaned on the fence and watched Max playing on the lawn of their new home in the hills above Tropea. Max's high-pitched squeals and Francesca's easy laughter lightened the heavy afternoon sky. While still on Gozo, Francesca had offered to sign over guardianship to Nico before he'd even broached the subject. The day, she later told him, she knew he would take Max from her.

"I love Max as if he were my own," she had said with tears in her eyes, "but you are his rightful father. He belongs with you. And it's what Ariana would have wanted."

Inspector Mifsud hadn't known the results of the paternity test Nico had requested when he'd driven him to the ferry. He'd told Nico later that even if by some slim chance Max wasn't his, he'd wanted Nico to discover his feelings for the little boy for himself.

"One doesn't have to be a biological parent to love a child," he'd said, before telling Nico all three of his girls were adopted. "I couldn't possibly love them any more than if I were their biological father."

After closing up Ariana's house for the summer, Nico had prepared to head back to Tropea with Max, and Francesca had been packing her things to return to her apartment in Valletta. But, he would never forget her expression when he'd suggested she come with them to look after Max and pursue her dream of writing children's books. He would need to look for a proper house, rather than the apartment he'd been renting since taking the job as Tropea's special prosecutor. Not wanting to pressure her, he'd suggested they look for something with separate quarters for her, but on the same property. Soon, Max would start school and she would have much of the day to herself.

"You mean nanny's quarters," she'd said with some hesitancy.

"A writer's studio," Nico had replied. "A place of your own, but where you can be with Max whenever you want to."

So, together, they'd found a recently restored farmhouse, not unlike Ariana's, in the hills above Tropea. It was close enough for Nico to easily commute to work and close to where Max would go to school. The guesthouse where Francesca lived, and had begun to write, was on the other side of a small cement swimming pool where they would often share their meals alfresco. Gabriela had decided that Nico was old news and now followed Max everywhere.

It was the smoothest transition Nico could have hoped for. While Max had his moments of tears and asked about his mother and where her soul had gone, he was remarkably well-adjusted. Nico gave Francesca 100 percent of the credit for that. Together, they'd made a pact that they would always be honest with Max, even if it just meant one of them holding him close and telling him they didn't know all the answers.

Nico had arranged for a small private service for Ariana in the church she attended when she was in Tropea. Afterward, they all came back to the house for lunch. Having returned from Istanbul, Vincenzo Testa was there with his wife and new baby. Giorgio had come all the way from Gozo, which touched Nico deeply. Caesar had survived being shot at, and while he had lost part of his hip to the infection that went untreated until someone found him, Giorgio beamed when he'd shown Nico a picture of him. Mrs. Rapa had been invited, as had Mikel Mifsud. She was frail and sent her regrets. Mikel had to pass as well, but he sent along a huge package of toys for "Maximillion," as he called him. He thought Massimo sounded too serious for a little boy. Nico didn't tell him Ariana had named him that as a nod to their son's half-Italian heritage.

Sergio had been at the Lamezia Terme Airport to pick up the three of them and Gabriela on the day they flew home. After Nico got over his shock of his assistant prosecutor coming on his time off to welcome them home, he met, for the first time, his little girl. The one who Nico hadn't even known how old she was. It turned out his daughter was exactly the same age as Max and they would be in the same school together. His wife, Martina, was lovely and taught German in the village.

Roberto Pezzente was the enigma. As Nico had told Mifsud on the way to the ferry, he assumed the next time he crossed paths with the investigator would be in a legal capacity. But unknown to Nico, he'd been sitting at the back of the church during the service. It wasn't until the small group of guests had filed out that Nico noticed a lone figure partially obscured in the darkness.

"Roberto?" Nico asked, uncertain if it was even him.

"I'm sorry, I didn't mean to intrude," Pezzente said

awkwardly. "I... I just wanted to pay my respects. I knew Ariana. Personally."

Nico swallowed, unsure he wanted to hear more.

"When my wife and daughters died, she came here to their service."

Ariana had known Pezzente's family? She would have been in Milan at university then.

"Her uncle—her father's brother—was in the 'Ndrangheta," Pezzente said. "He ordered the murder of my family."

The floor threatened to give way under Nico's feet. After believing Ariana's parents had died in an accident, Ariana had eventually told him that her father had killed her mother and then turned the gun on himself. She was devastated. It was after that, that he understood the change he saw in her when she returned briefly to Milan. But if her uncle had been involved with the Mafia... poor Ariana. She'd carried that burden all by herself.

Pezzente cleared his throat, bringing Nico out of his revelry. "Without Ariana's knowledge, I always assigned a member of my team to surveil her whenever she came to Tropea. For her safety."

Nico had always worried more than usual about Ariana whenever she worked any case that involved the 'Ndrangheta. But had he known this, he would have outright stopped her. Not that she would have listened.

"On her last visit, none of my people were available. I was across the street that day when the bomb went off."

The tall individual Nico had seen getting into a car outside the restaurant.

In shock, he sat down heavily beside Pezzente.

"At the cemetery, after the service, she came up to me and apologized for her family. She swore to me that one day she would see that her uncle and his cohorts would be brought to justice.

"She made good on her promise," Pezzente said. "Through you."

Nico shook his head, not understanding. "Me?"

"Yes, you successfully prosecuted him, but he never did a day in prison. He was killed in a drive-by shooting while out on bail made possible by a corrupt judge."

Oh my God! Nico remembered the case. But he'd never put two and two together. That's why Ariana was so angry with him when he didn't try to get his most recent case retried by an honest judge.

Pezzente rose to leave. "It was a beautiful service you had for her. Quiet, intimate, with no fanfare. That's how Ariana would have wanted it. I'm sorry to have intruded."

Nico saw Francesca peering into the entrance of the church, looking for him, as Pezzente turned to walk out.

"Roberto," he called after him. "We're having a few people up to the house for lunch. I'd be honored if you'd come."

N ico had brought out some cold beer for their guests who had come back to the house for lunch. As they stood side by side watching Max play and Francesca and Testa's wife bring out the food, Roberto looked at Nico. "He looks like you."

Nico didn't see it. All he saw was Ariana in Max's deeply soulful eyes and radiant smile. He saw the brightness and natural curiosity he'd first admired in her at university. The open, unguarded expression that, in the early days, drew people to her like a moth to a flame. The way she was before her dogged determination and fierceness made her the target of the multitude of threats that led up to her death.

"Ariana was an extraordinary woman," Roberto said. "And she loved you, yes?"

Nico swallowed the ache in his throat. So much had gone unsaid between him and Ariana. And, as a consequence, he'd missed seeing his little boy grow up. He'd wondered if he could ever forgive her for that, even though Francesca had told him that she'd kept Max from him out of love.

"She was so afraid something would happen to you," Francesca had said. "And Max would have no living blood-relative."

Nico saw an Ariana-style grin light up his son's face. "Yes, I believe she did," he answered Roberto. He cleared his throat. "Now, what about *you?* What will you do now?"

"After a little time off, I'll go back to my position with the Guardia di Finanza. There is still so much to do. I know you're unsure of our new prime minister, but he's a good man. I believe he wants the same thing we all do: to take back our beautiful country. I think that's all Ariana wanted."

A worthy goal, Nico thought, but he had doubts that it would happen in his lifetime. "Do you ever think about giving up, Roberto?"

"In my head? *Si,* a thousand times." He thumped his chest. "But in my heart? Never."

"I admire you. With everything you've been through. Losing your family . . ." It didn't seem fair that Nico had his son, and Roberto had no one.

"Ah, that is precisely why we must continue our important work, my friend." He pointed toward Sergio's little girl, who had shyly approached Max and asked to play with him. They watched as Max not only nodded but hugged her and gave her some of his toys. Nico felt the sting of tears as he bit his lip.

"If we give up," Roberto said, "what does that mean for the extraordinary women in our lives? We must not allow them to have died in vain." He turned to look at Nico. "You're a good prosecutor, Nico. You—me—we can do this."

Nico touched the neck of his bottle to Roberto's. "*Ad maiora semper, amico mio*. Towards greater things."

———

If you loved the book and have a moment to spare, I would really appreciate a short review on the page where you bought the book. Or alternatively, here is my direct link on

BookBub: https://www.bookbub.com/authors/karen-dodd
Goodreads: https://www.goodreads.com/author/show/7468898.Karen_Dodd

Your help in spreading the word is gratefully appreciated and reviews make a huge difference in helping new readers find the series.

Thank you!

Your FREE book is waiting for you NOW.
THE ST. JULIAN'S KILLINGS

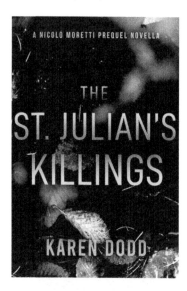

St. Julian's, Malta 2018. A shocking car bombing. Three widows in three countries. What did their husbands have in common?

Get your free prequel to the Nicoló Moretti Crime Thriller series
at
www.karendodd.com
and join my VIP Readers Club.

THE ST. JULIAN'S KILLINGS

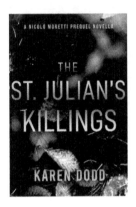

St. Julian's, Malta 2018. A shocking car bombing. Three widows in three countries. What did their husbands have in common?

Get your free prequel to the Nicoló Moretti Crime Thriller series
at
www.karendodd.com
and join my VIP Readers Club.

Acknowledgments

In the spring of 2016, I had the good fortune of visiting the archipelago of Malta. I was enchanted with the entire area, but most particularly, the tiny historic island known to the locals as Għawdex. The people were warm and welcoming; the beauty of its geography nothing short of spectacular. It remains one of the most beautiful places I've been to and fervently hope to go there again.

Within six months of returning to Canada, I was shocked and saddened to hear of investigative journalist Daphne Caruana Galizia's assassination near her home in Malta. As of the writing of this book, her family still has not received justice. I desperately wanted to write her story, but out of respect for her family—and because writers so much more qualified than I have done an exceptional job—I decided to write an altogether different story, but one built on many of the same premises.

The places in the book I take you to are real, except for the names of businesses which have been changed for obvious reasons. While I strived to bring verisimilitude to the settings, I have taken great liberties with the story. So, while I was thrilled to have a former Maltese citizen as a beta (early) reader, any remaining errors are mine. Or they just came from somewhere in my vast imagination.

For all my books, I'm blessed to have a dedicated team of beta readers, as well as those who read the final copy before it goes to print—and who invariably catch embarrassing errors before the release date. These loyal fans read my work purely out of the goodness of their hearts and without them—well, I just can't imagine!

I would especially like to thank Anna Axerio, Peter Axerio-Cilies, Rod Baker, Briar Ballou, Amber Cowie, Ian Grant, Eric Lidemark, John Busswood, Diana Stevan, Ena Fevurly, Lucy Traini, Francine Legault, Lyn Smith and Rachel Wetton (my Maltese connection) and Linda LeQuesne, my beta-reader and proofreader extraordinaire.

I offer a very special thanks to Sergeant J.G. (Gord) Reid of the RCMP. He was always willing to peruse bits and pieces of my writing on a moment's notice (hopefully no criminals went free as a result) and verify its authenticity. Thank you, Gord, for being an invaluable resource. Any errors regarding police procedures are solely mine.

Everybody Knows has, without a doubt, been the most difficult book I have written. It took two-and-a-half years and for reasons I won't bore you with, went through several itera-tions. I would especially like to thank my early editor, fellow Canadian Christine Lagone. She did an amazing job and without saying so, helped me see that the manuscript still needed more work.

Through a successful, multi-published author, I was fortu-nate enough to find my UK developmental and copy editor, Rebecca Millar. Part coach, part weaver of magic, she bran-dished her editor's pen firmly but kindly—without taking my voice. Thank you, Rebecca, for seeing the potential in this story and helping me make it infinitely better. Any remaining lack of "zing" lies with me.

And finally, to the members of my Author Mastermind, I offer my profound thanks. For nearly two years now, each of these five successful authors in multi-genres has gelled and together we have become one powerful mastermind. We've supported each other by reading each other's work, overcoming mind-bending writing obstacles, and some difficult personal situations. We've celebrated each other's wins and helped soften the blow of seemingly unsurmountable challenges. I simply cannot imagine being on this journey without you. Amber Cowie, Sonia Garrett, Rae Knightly, Diana Stevan and Mahtab Narsimhan—thank you from the bottom of my heart. You are my idols and I'm so honored to be in this circle.

Every writer hopes her next book will be better than the last. That's why we toil in a lonely room, often for hours or days at a time. Whether or not the muse visits, we think of you, dear reader, as we try to create the best story we're capable of. I hope you enjoy Everybody Knows and look forward to the next one.

~ Karen Dodd
June 2021

ABOUT THE AUTHOR

Karen Dodd is the author of the Stone Suspense novels. The second book in the series, Scare Away the Dark, won the 2018 Chanticleer CLUE award. *Everybody Knows,* is the first book in her new Nicoló Moretti Crime Thriller series. Karen lives in a small village on Canada's West Coast.

Visit her at www.karendodd.com

Author photo by Studio Two Photography
Jacket design by JD&J Book Cover Designs

Printed in Great Britain
by Amazon